"No one e.... before," David confided.

Megan's strangled "What?" indicated that he'd taken the right approach. "I didn't try to seduce you!" she gasped.

"It's okay. I was flattered. A little surprised that someone of your refined demeanor would be so overtly aggressive," he went on blandly, "but I really was quite flattered. You show excellent taste."

"You've got to be the most immodest man I've ever known!"

"Nonsense. I kept all my clothes on. If I'd known you'd wanted them off—"

"Dave, come on. I'm serious."

"Me, too," he said definitively.

Dear Reader,

If you're looking for an extra-special reading experience—something rich and memorable, something deeply emotional, something totally romantic—your search is over! For in your hands you hold one of Silhouette's extremely **Special Editions**.

Dedicated to the proposition that *not* all romances are created equal, Silhouette **Special Edition** aims to deliver the best and the brightest in women's fiction—six books each month by such stellar authors as Nora Roberts, Lynda Trent, Tracy Sinclair and Ginna Gray, along with some dazzling new writers destined to become tomorrow's romance stars.

Pick and choose among titles if you must—we hope you'll soon equate all Silhouette **Special Editions** with consistently gratifying romance reading.

And don't forget the two Silhouette *Classics* at your bookseller's each month—reissues of the most beloved Silhouette **Special Editions** and Silhouette *Intimate Moments* of yesteryear.

Today's bestsellers, tomorrow's *Classics*—that's Silhouette **Special Edition**. We hope you'll stay with us in the months to come, because month after month, we intend to become more special than ever.

From all the authors and editors of Silhouette **Special Edition**,
Warmest wishes,

Leslie Kazanjian
Senior Editor

CHRISTINE FLYNN
Silence the Shadows

Silhouette Special Edition

Published by Silhouette Books New York

America's Publisher of Contemporary Romance

SILHOUETTE BOOKS
300 East 42nd St., New York, N.Y. 10017

ISBN: 0-373-09465-5

First Silhouette Books printing July 1988

Printed in the U.S.A.

Books by Christine Flynn

Silhouette Romance

Stolen Promise #435

Silhouette Special Edition

Remember the Dreams #254
Silence the Shadows #465

Silhouette Desire

When Snow Meets Fire #254
The Myth and the Magic #296
A Place to Belong #352
Meet Me at Midnight #377

CHRISTINE FLYNN

is formerly from Oregon and currently resides in the
Southwest with her husband, teenage daughter and
two very spoiled dogs.

Megan's Peanut Butter Cookies

Cream until fluffy:

> ½ cup margarine
> ½ cup peanut butter
> ½ cup white sugar
> ½ cup brown sugar
> 1 egg
> ½ tsp. vanilla extract

Mix separately:

> 1 ¼ cup flour
> ¾ tsp. baking soda
> ¼ tsp. salt

Stir dry ingredients into creamed mixture until blended. Form into walnut-size balls and place 2 inches apart on ungreased baking sheet. Dip fork into white sugar and flatten balls with tines in a criss-cross pattern. Bake 10-12 minutes at 350 degrees.

Makes approx. 3 dozen.

Prologue

Dave sat staring at the telephone long after Megan Reese had said goodbye. He hadn't expected her call, or her reluctant invitation. True, she'd only asked him to come by and pick up what was his, but he'd sensed a brief hesitation just before she'd hung up—a pause that had seemed to indicate there had been something more she'd wanted to say.

He reached for a cigarette, dismissing his last thought as highly improbable. Meg had tolerated his presence in her life because he'd been a friend of her husband. Graciously tolerated it, granted, since Meg wasn't the kind of woman who would deliberately make a person uncomfortable. But he knew she wanted as little to do with him as possible.

Squinting through the smoke, Dave swiveled around and leaned back in his chair. On the paneled wall behind his desk, among the diplomas, certificates and civic awards that proclaimed him a learned, licensed financier and an upstanding member of the community, were three pictures.

The largest captured the starboard side of his fifty-foot sailing sloop as it crested a wave in the San Juans. The second, a small portrait his sister had given him, was of her three kids, a gentle reminder that she wasn't the only one expected to present progeny to their parents. Below that hung an even smaller photograph.

A wry smile touched Dave's mouth as he considered the duo in the snapshot. He was the unshaven one on the left side of an upended marlin. Ted Reese, whose dark beard hadn't been a recent acquisition, occupied its other flank. Both were wearing grimy shorts, grins and sunburns. And both, he recalled, had smelled worse than the fish. They'd been out for six days straight before nailing that trophy.

His smile widened. It had been over four years, but he still remembered the horror in Meg's beautiful face when he and Ted had shown up that afternoon. She'd met them at the door and, after one whiff, promptly slammed it shut. Before Ted could find his keys, she'd reappeared again to present them with a bucket and a bar of soap. She'd then pointed to the garden hose.

That memory was wrested to the back of his mind as he studied the detail in the snapshot. The sailboat in the background was Ted's; the one he'd bought within weeks of learning that Dave was having one built. It was also the same one that had capsized and sunk in a storm three months ago. An entire day had passed before Ted and the banker he'd been courting with the hope of closing yet another land deal had been found. Miraculously, the banker had survived. Ted had drowned.

After taking a quick pull on his cigarette, Dave crushed it out. Ted's obsession with his 'deals' had cost him dearly. But before he'd paid that particular price, he'd strained his friendship with Dave to the limit. There were more important things in life than acquiring every available piece of vacant property in Southern California and sticking a mall or an apartment building on it. Unfortunately, Ted had seemed to have forgotten that. He'd also seemed to have forgotten that he had a wife.

Dave's glance strayed back to the telephone. He was glad Meg had called. He'd been worried about her.

Chapter One

Megan Reese pushed aside a packing box and leaned against the storage cabinet in her garage, wondering why widowhood seemed to automatically qualify a woman for unsolicited advice. Nearly everyone she knew in Laguna Beach seemed compelled to counsel her on everything from diet and exercise to possible 'vacation' sites. Not that she was ungrateful for the concern. Not at all. It was just that the advice she needed wasn't what she was getting.

At the moment it was Annie Thompson, Meg's outspoken friend and the director of the women's charity where she volunteered her time, who was offering her rather biased guidance. "Well?" Annie prodded, seeking confirmation of the conclusion she'd just drawn.

Meg pushed aside the ebony curls brushing her own shoulders. Her eyes, a shade of green her father insisted she'd inherited from the leprechauns, held the same droll calm as her voice. "I'm not being impulsive," she said, arching her back to relieve the ache there. "I'm being practical."

"You're being unrealistic," the lanky, sloe-eyed blonde corrected from where she stood by the garage's open double doors. "That's not like you, either. Making a decision like that right out of the blue is not practical or logical or any of those other things you need to be right now. You lost your husband, Meg. Not your common sense." Turning, she stuffed another sack of old clothes into the back seat of her car. The trunk was already full of things Meg was donating to her cause. "Don't you know how dangerous emotional decisions are?" she asked when she'd extracted herself again.

"Oh, I don't know," Meg drawled. "You seemed awfully emotional to me when you were trying to decide whether or not to accept Larry's proposal. Do you think that's dangerous? I mean, if you do you might want to reconsider."

Annie frowned at Meg's teasing. She did not appear to appreciate Meg's rationale or her attempt to change the subject. "That's not what I mean, and you know it. I'm talking about doing something that up until three weeks ago you'd never even considered. One day it wasn't even an issue, and the next, bingo, the thing's on the market."

Meg turned to the open window over the workbench, her glance skimming past her potter's wheel. The honeysuckle had grown so much that it blocked the view of the ocean. But Meg, though she loved looking out at the sea, hadn't cut it down. The leafy orange-blossomed encroachment filled the salty air with its scent, allowing the welcomed breeze to carry it inside. It took and it gave. Meg appreciated the trade-off.

"It wasn't an emotional decision," she said, wondering again at the apathy that had become so familiar to her lately. "I just came to the conclusion that it's something I need to do." It was actually something she had to do, but her pride wouldn't let her admit that. "It was very simple, really."

"But I know how much this place *means* to you," Annie protested.

Meg shrugged, her innate sense of privacy not allowing her to correct Annie's assumption. There were certain things people simply didn't need to know, even close friends like Annie. That was why she didn't tell her that as far as she was concerned the place in question—her home—could slide down its specially reinforced embankment and straight into the Pacific Ocean. The house didn't matter, because what it represented didn't exist anymore. If she were to be honest with herself, she'd have to admit that it hadn't existed for a very long time. She'd just pretended it had.

That wasn't why she was selling it, though. She'd put the rambling Spanish-mission-style hacienda with its beige stucco walls and red tile roof and the terra-cotta fountain in the circular drive up for sale simply because she had no choice. According to what she'd learned three weeks ago, her husband had been rather shortsighted. She was, it seemed, broke. That wasn't the part she had trouble dealing with, however. It was nice to have money and the things it could buy, but possessions hadn't meant as much to her as they had to Ted. Now, though, thanks to the drive that had changed the sweet and caring man she'd married into a man obsessed with success, she was in the middle of a financial mess she had no idea how to untangle.

Taking silence as her cue to continue, Annie forged ahead. Meg, not knowing how to stop her, didn't bother to try.

"Just look at this place," Annie insisted, disregarding the fact that they were in the garage. "You've spent years turning it into what you wanted. It took you forever to find the right wallpaper for your bedroom, and just about as long to find someone to hang your stained-glass work in the bathroom skylights. It's only this year that you finally got the roses to grow up the chimney so you can see them from the second-floor balcony out back."

On a roll now, she planted her hands on the hips of her pink rompers. Meg wasn't sure, but she thought she recognized the outfit as one of those Lucy Bevins had modeled at the country-club fashion show last spring. Meg had been evening gowns. "And speaking of the second floor, what about your studio? What about your view? It was the view and that strip of beach down there that sold you on this place to begin with."

"I know that."

"Then how, pray tell, can you walk away without giving it more thought?"

With deliberate understatement, Meg said, "I have thought about it." She omitted any reference to the number of nights she'd lain awake doing just that. Heaven only knew how many natural sleep remedies she'd hear about if she did.

Growing more than a little exasperated with Meg's unusually inflexible approach, Annie threw up her hands. The gesture was quite theatrical, and very much Annie. "I give up," she announced to the ceiling.

"I doubt it," Meg muttered good-naturedly. "But thanks anyway."

"For what?"

"For being the royal pain that you are."

A grin stole over Annie's face. "Anytime. You're a lot nicer about being nagged than Larry is. Do you want to knock off for a while and go get a hamburger with us? I'm supposed to meet him at one."

"What time is it now?"

"Quarter till."

Meg wasn't allowed to feel relieved that Annie had finally backed off about the house. She hadn't been terribly aware of the time, and discovering that her nemesis would arrive any minute was enough to prevent relaxation in any form. It had been a little over three months since she'd seen Dave Elliott—the longest period of time in the last seven years that she'd managed that particular feat. "Really?" she squeaked, hoping her anxiety only looked like disbelief.

"Actually," Annie said, rechecking her watch, "it's 12:47. No. 12:48. The digit just changed. Do you want that hamburger?"

"I don't think so."

"You need to eat, Meg. Do you want help up?"

Meg answered Annie's last question with a shake of her head. "Thanks, but I'm going to pass on lunch. As long as I'm down here, I think I'll pack up the stuff under the workbench." Drawing herself to her knees, she peered at the shelf holding her pottery glazes. If she kept herself busy, maybe she wouldn't get nervous about seeing Dave. She was very good at keeping herself occupied. After all, she'd had years of practice.

Annie completely misunderstood Meg's refusal to dine with her and her intended. Beneath the pixieish cut of her bangs she frowned. "You and food still aren't getting along, huh? Shouldn't your morning sickness be letting up a little? You're five months now."

"Five and a half," Meg said, quite aware of how far along she was in her pregnancy. There might be times when she couldn't quite believe she was actually going to have the child she'd wanted so badly, but she was definitely conscious of the fact that she was pregnant—even if she didn't look it that moment.

Since she was kneeling, the small swell of Meg's stomach wasn't visible. An old paint-and-clay-splattered art smock completed the concealment, its loose, off-white folds covering even the edge of her navy maternity shorts. "I feel fine today, Annie," she continued, directing a scowl at the collection of crusty cans an arm's length away. "That's why I want to get some of this done."

"Don't be like that. This will all be here when you get back. You could use a break."

"From what? This is the first productive thing I've done all week."

"Well . . . come on anyway."

Meg felt her resolve waver. When she wanted to be persuaded, she could be talked into just about anything. She desperately wanted to be persuaded now. If she ran into town with Annie, the lunch of crow she'd have to eat when Dave got here could be postponed. She'd never been terribly fond of poultry. "I really shouldn't," she heard herself say.

"Why not?"

"Because I'm expecting someone."

"Who?"

"Dave."

"Dave Elliott?" At Meg's nod, Annie frowned. "Why's he coming over?"

"I asked him to."

"Why?"

Meg reached for a bundle of old paintbrushes. "To pick up his scuba gear," she said, giving her nosy friend the same reason she'd given Dave on the phone yesterday. She hadn't quite found the nerve to mention the other matter prompting the call. But she'd have to find that nerve soon. Dave was the only one who could give her the information she needed without asking a lot of prying questions. It wasn't going to be easy asking for his help, though—especially after what she'd said to him the last time she'd seen him. "He left it here the last time he and Ted went diving."

Keys jangled as Annie extracted them from her purse. Acknowledging Meg's explanation with a flat "Oh," she then disappeared behind a pair of huge sunglasses and picked up her floppy straw hat from where she'd left it on the fender of Meg's white Mercedes convertible. "You know, I never have understood why you don't like that guy. Every time I've been around him he's seemed pretty nice. That's saying a lot for a man who happens to have tons of money *and* a body to die for." She gave an exaggerated sigh. "He's also got the most gorgeous...well, second most gorgeous—" she hastily corrected, remembering Larry "—blue eyes I've ever seen."

Meg chose to ignore all but that last statement. "That's an opinion shared by many of our gender, my dear."

"I'd say that makes us a pretty astute bunch."

Meg smiled. "Observant, anyway." Swatting at a particularly persistent fly, she leaned back on her heels. The temptation to avoid facing Dave—to put off the apology she knew she had to make—was the strongest thing she'd felt in weeks. But her sense of fairness was equally strong. She owed him that apology. "You don't want to keep Larry waiting," she said, silently adding masochism to her list of personal faults. "You know how impatient he gets."

Annie's muttered "Do I ever" was joined by the refined purr of the car pulling into the palm-lined driveway. Both women glanced toward the sound. Meg's hand flattened at the base of her throat.

"Do you want me to stay?"

"No," Meg said quietly. "It's all right."

It was easy to see from the pinch of Annie's brow that she wasn't terribly convinced by the assurance. Maybe it had something to do with the way Meg's face had paled or with the smile she offered—a smile that was far too tense to be reassuring.

"Meg—" Annie began.

"It's okay," she repeated, appreciating her friend's protectiveness but not needing it. "Honest."

"Have you seen him since Ted's funeral?"

Meg shook her head, the motion causing a vague sense of vertigo. Attributing the odd sensation to the effect of the gathering heat, she added, "I've had no reason to," and took a deep breath. Within seconds the slight dizziness passed, leaving her with an entirely different kind of discomfort. It was only a moment out of hours, hours that were nothing more than little fragments of memory, but Annie's question had elicited the clearest recollection Meg had of the day she'd buried her husband.

People. There had been so many people. And tuna casseroles. They'd rivaled the potato salads for space on the table her mother, her sisters and Annie had set in the dining room. Dave had been one of the pallbearers, of course, and he'd come up to her after everyone else had left her alone. "Is there anything I can do?" he'd asked, really seeming to mean the phrase she'd heard so often that day.

Instead of offering her thanks with a polite and sincere "I don't think so," as she had to everyone else, her words had come from somewhere beyond her grasp. Like the cold, unforgiving wind that had blown that day, she couldn't seem to catch them to alter their sting or change their course. "Don't you think you've done enough?" she'd returned, and backed away before his grief could become hers.

In the last few months she'd had time to realize how terribly unfair she'd been to him. Not just then, but for the past couple of years.

The engine of the maroon sedan was cut off. Meg looked up to see Dave unfold his six-foot-two-inch frame from the expensive vehicle, and jumped a little when the sharp report of its door closing pierced the momentary silence. Maybe, she thought, this wasn't such a good idea.

The warm breeze ruffled Dave's sandy hair as he approached the open doors. His long strides were confident, as always, and his stance when he stopped just inside the garage was no less assured. Meg had once thought his lazy smile just a touch too arrogant, possibly even smug. Annie seemed to find it charming.

"Ladies," he said, acknowledging them both. Since Annie had stuck out her hand, he turned his smile on her.

Annie beamed. "It's good to see you again, Dave. How've you been?"

From her kneeling position by the workbench several feet away, Meg watched Dave while he exchanged the usual pleasantries of casual acquaintances. At thirty-four, he was a big man; tall, broad shouldered and powerfully built, and handsome in the way of men whose blond-beach-boy good looks have matured rather elegantly. His was the masculine perfection portrayed in the art and anatomy classes she'd taken.

She remembered teasing him about sitting for one of those classes. But that had been a long time ago, back when she and Ted had first been married. During the intervening seven years, Ted and Dave had remained as close as brothers, but she and Dave had grown as far apart as two people could get and still be speaking to each other. She wasn't the only one to blame for that rift. Long before she'd begun to resent the influence he'd had over Ted, Dave had suddenly chosen to avoid her whenever possible. Why he'd done that remained a mystery to her.

She could only hope that, whatever his reasons, he'd be willing to overlook them for a while.

"I was just leaving," she heard Annie announce. "So I'll say goodbye and get out of here. Nice seeing you, Dave." Opening her car door, she tossed her purse inside. "Thanks for all the stuff, Meg. I'll see you Thursday."

"Thursday?" Meg echoed.

"You said you'd help with our fund-raiser, remember?"

"What I said," Meg corrected, thinking it was just like Annie to hit her with something like this when she had other things on her mind, "was that I'd think about it."

Directly contradicting the lecture she'd delivered not five minutes earlier, Annie dismissed Meg's statement with a flick of her wrist. "There's no need to spend any time doing that. I know you don't feel up to going back on the crisis line yet, but there's no reason to let all that organizational ability of yours go to waste. Besides, you know all the denizens at the country club, and with your connections in the art circles around here we can pack the ballroom without spending a fortune on publicity. Thursday noon. Lunch at the Station in Capistrano." With the promise that she'd call Meg later, she hit the ignition.

Meg's slightly exasperated glare followed Annie's car out of the drive. She wasn't really opposed to working on the benefit for the South Coast Women's Shelter. She just didn't know if she was going to have the time. Her life-style was undergoing some rather drastic changes, and it was entirely possible that Annie's charity was going to have to start giving to her instead of the other way around.

"Sounds like you've been roped again," she heard Dave say, and glanced up to find him watching her with his arms folded across his chest. His eyes, nearly the same cobalt blue as the stripes in his polo shirt, remained fixed on her face.

With a smile that didn't quite alleviate the strain shadowing her features, she reluctantly agreed. "It kind of looks that way. I keep thinking that one of these days she'll take no for an answer."

"Maybe you don't sound like you mean it when you say it."

"Could be" was her quiet reply, and her smile faded when she saw that he was serious. "I appreciate your coming over," she hurried on, allowing the cloak of cautious civility that usually surrounded conversations with Dave to slip into place. "I'd have let you know your gear was here sooner, but I just found it when I started cleaning out this mess a few days ago."

"No problem. I haven't had time to miss it."

"Your work keeping you busy?"

"Busier than I'd like."

Having run out of things to say, Meg could acknowledge his reply with nothing more than a nod. Dave was always busy, but that was because his services were always in demand. To say that Dave was a capable financier was equivalent to labeling a Cordon Bleu chef a cook. When it came to wheeling and dealing, the man was, according to what she'd heard, the absolute best.

Brilliant was the word her husband had used. But then, Ted had always used superlatives when describing his best friend.

Dave moved closer, shoving his hands deep into the pockets of his white cotton slacks as he critically scanned her kneeling form. She was wearing one of the smocks she usually wore when she worked with her paints or pottery. The thing was big and shapeless, but she still looked smaller than he remembered. Smaller and thinner. The hollows of her cheeks seemed more pronounced, adding fragility to features already haunting in their delicacy.

He scowled at the shadows beneath her lowered lashes. Those faint bruises betrayed a multitude of sleepless nights and made her once-vibrant complexion look terribly pale. The heat, he concluded, probably caused the bright flush in her cheeks, the color almost as pronounced as the vivid green of her eyes.

She looks like hell, he thought to himself, and immediately glanced away. Over the years he'd developed a remarkable talent for blocking out reactions where Meg was concerned. "I saw the For Sale sign out front." The observation was directed toward the pile of boxes, tools and sporting equipment strewn over the concrete floor. "Are you going back to Springfield?"

It was a logical question. Springfield, Illinois, had been home for the first twenty of her twenty-seven years. Her parents still lived there, as did two of her three brothers and both of her sisters.

"No," she replied, relieved to see that he was no longer looking at her. The way he'd regarded her moments ago, with that critical frown of his, did more than the humid air to make her uncomfortable. "I'm staying here."

Meg saw Dave's eyebrows arch over the surprise in his eyes and could only wonder at that strangely typical reaction. Everyone except Annie expected her to be going home to her family, her family included. Yet moving to Springfield wouldn't accomplish anything. In some ways such a move would be a step backward, and she needed very much to feel that she wasn't losing more than she had already. She didn't need to have decisions made for her, which was what her parents would try to do. The Flahertys could be a very opinionated lot, and though she loved them all, she simply didn't have the energy to convince them that she could handle things by herself.

The surprise Dave had registered lasted only for a moment. At least he had the decency to assume she knew what she was doing. "Have you bought another place?"

"Not yet. I'd like to have a work space, and I need someplace for my kiln. Most of the apartments here don't have separate garages."

"An apartment?" If she wanted to move, he wondered, why didn't she buy another house or a condo? Or move into one of the complexes Ted had bragged about buying last year? In her financial bracket—which had to be fairly comfortable, considering Ted's holdings—it didn't make any sense for her to rent someone else's property. "You don't want to buy?"

Meg glanced down at her hands. Knowing that if she didn't take the opening he'd just given her she'd probably put it off forever, she got straight to the point. "That's sort of got something to do with the other reason I asked you to come over," she told him. "But there's something I need to do before I get to that." Still looking down, she twisted the thick gold band on her finger. She hadn't meant to do this on her knees, but finding herself without the energy to stand up, she raised her head. "I want to apologize."

"Apologize?" he repeated. "For what?"

If he didn't remember, Meg thought, then maybe she should just keep her mouth shut. She then proceeded to silence that cowardly little voice. She was determined to get this over with despite his lack of cooperation. "What I said to you after the funeral," she reminded him, only to have him cut her off before she could finish.

"You didn't say anything you have to apologize for. It was a bad day for everybody."

"I'm not asking you to *excuse* it," she stressed because she'd meant exactly what she'd said. He remembered. She knew he did. For a fraction of a second that same stricken look she'd seen in his eyes that day flashed through them again. "I'm asking you to accept my apology. I'm sorry for the way I've acted toward you, Dave. I was wrong."

For several very long, very uncomfortable seconds he stood staring down at her. There was nothing in his expression to indicate that her words made any difference to him one way or the other, nothing definable in the gaze that held hers so steadily. "Maybe not," he said quietly. Spotting a pair of swim fins and a set of tanks in the corner, he turned away. "Are those mine?"

Meg saw Dave's mouth harden. Thinking the clench of his jaw implied impatience, she quickly told him they were. More than a little confused by his response, she was also terribly afraid that he wouldn't give her a chance to say anything else. He'd obviously wasted all the time he cared to listening to her and was now interested only in collecting his things and getting out of here. "Your wet suit's over here in the utility closet," she added, and with one hand on a box, she started to her feet.

She was halfway up when she felt a wave of heat wash over her. It hadn't come from the window. The breeze coming through there seemed to have died down completely. Raising her hand to her head, she tried to stop the spinning that accompanied the heat. But the spinning only increased, and the air, which had felt awfully warm before, was now stifling.

The deep breath she took didn't seem to do any good. She took another, hoping to relieve the swift sensation of claustrophobia, but the air filling her lungs only made her feel more light-headed. She shouldn't have stayed on her knees for so long. Or maybe, she told herself, she shouldn't have moved so quickly.

That last thought had barely registered when the floor tilted. Meg saw it coming toward her, and she tried to straighten. Then all she saw was black.

Two steps. That was all it took for Dave to reach her. The instant he'd seen the color drain from her cheeks, he'd taken the first one; the second had him beside her just as her knees buckled. Catching her by the waist, he let her fall against him, then bent to slip an arm under her legs to lift her. For a fraction of a second he hesitated, suddenly conscious of the roundness beneath her smock.

It was almost as if his brain didn't want to assimilate the information it was being fed. He knew what he felt, what his senses told him. But the fact didn't seem to register. That odd, slightly benumbed state evaporated in an instant, though, his whispered "My God" prefacing an assault of emotion that was nearly staggering in intensity.

The breath he drew to stabilize himself brought with it the scent of jasmine from her hair. He scooped her up in his arms. Even pregnant, she didn't weigh enough to cause him any effort. That was just as well. He needed to concentrate all his strength on the formidable control that managed to reduce the barrage of conflicting feelings to something he could deal with.

The concern he hadn't let himself show when he'd first seen her now manifested itself in the agonized tone of his voice. "Oh, Megan," he groaned, shifting her head to his shoulder. "Why now?"

There wasn't time for Dave to acknowledge how completely his guard had fallen at that moment. He was too busy feeling relief. Her lips, so frighteningly pale, began to warm with color. The fringe of her black lashes fluttered briefly, then flew wide, and her eyes darted wildly as she tried to reorient herself. Instantly her muscles stiffened, resuming their preparation for the fall he'd prevented.

"It's okay," he whispered, tightening his hold. "I've got you. It's okay," he repeated, and felt her relax against him.

She didn't hear him at first. Nor did she see the anxiety in his eyes when he sat down with her on the bench by the worktable. She was conscious only of cool fingers stroking the hair back from her forehead, of strong arms cradling her against an equally strong chest. There was security in those arms and, when she finally became aware of his voice, a wealth of tenderness in his quiet assurances.

Still disoriented, she wasn't conscious of the words she heard so much as she was aware of their deep, soothing tone. She knew only that something about the way he held her made her feel protected, cared for. It had been years since she'd felt anything like that—and it was rather disconcerting to find it was Dave who was making her feel that way.

"Are you all right?"

Nodding, she tried to pull back. Either she was still on the weak side or his hold was firmer than she'd thought. "I guess I got a little dizzy," she said, feeling a need to excuse what had happened. Confusion had quickly accompanied the return of consciousness, but that had already been overridden by embarrassment.

"Are you still dizzy now?"

"No."

"You sure?"

Again she nodded, succeeding this time in lifting her head from his chest and pulling her shoulder from the groove of his arm. The air didn't feel quite as hot now that her equilibrium had returned, but she still felt awfully warm.

"Put your arms around my neck."

She blinked up at him, sure she'd heard his request but failing to see its necessity.

"Put your arms around my neck," he repeated with a kind of patience he probably reserved for whatever encounters he might have with the mentally infirm.

"Why?"

"Because I'm going to carry you into the house."

"Oh, that's not necessary." Wondering if fainting always caused a slight acceleration in heart rate, she hurried on to add, "I'll walk."

"Like hell," he muttered, and stood up. Instinct had her arms around his neck within seconds. Satisfied with her compliance—however unwilling—he added a polite "That's better." And he turned sideways to get them both through the door leading into the house.

Chapter Two

Determined. That was how Dave looked to Meg as she clasped her hands tightly behind his neck and stared at the set line of his jaw. She'd forgotten how inflexible he could be once he'd decided something. He'd decided she needed to be carried, and like it or not, his decision was final. In her present position, her attempt to make him change his mind—an ambitious task under the best of circumstances—was quite ineffective.

"This really isn't necessary" she repeated when the screen door slammed behind them. "I'm okay now."

Dave, as he had a tendency to do when someone interfered with his purposes, ignored her. Rounding the corner from the laundry room, he muttered, "Watch your head," nudging it forward himself with his shoulder when it came precariously close to the wall. "Where do you want to lie down?"

His motion had tucked her head under his chin. His question brought it right back up again. "I don't want to lie down anywhere."

"How about the family room?"

"I don't *need* to lie down," she said, but Dave, his footsteps echoing on her white tile floor, didn't seem interested in her assessment of the situation.

Eyes straight ahead, he carried her through the kitchen and past the bay-windowed breakfast nook with its garden of hanging ferns and hothouse geraniums. Stepping onto the pale green carpet of the spacious family room, he pronounced flatly, "You do, too." And he skirted a three-foot brass lion by an eight-foot potted ficus.

Meg opened her mouth to question his assertion, then decided it wasn't worth the effort and closed it again. She wasn't quite sure why she felt so compelled to oppose him. He was being awfully presumptuous, but that didn't bother her as much as she thought it should. Possibly, she concluded, seeing the deepened furrows in his brow, it was because she found the concern behind his authoritative manner rather remarkable. Almost as remarkable as the conflict of wanting both to stay right where she was and to free herself from the arms that held her so easily. That ambivalence was very confusing and prompted her to renew her protest.

"Here," she said when he stepped between two pink-and-green striped chairs flanking a glass-topped table. "Put me down and I'll sit here."

He stopped in front of the sofa. "You need to put your feet up."

He was obstinate, too, she reminded herself. Determined and obstinate. "Dave, I'm fine now."

"I'm not," he muttered, bending to lower her to the cushions. "So humor me, will you?"

Meg was normally quite sensitive to other people's feelings, but the instability of her physical equilibrium had caused her to overlook its effect on Dave. Suddenly aware that having a person pass out right in front of you could be as frightening for the observer as the victim, she glanced toward him. "Oh, Dave, I'm sorry if I—"

Her sentence ended right there, as did her attempt to remove her left arm from around his neck. Dave had pulled his arm from beneath her legs, but the one behind her back was still securely in place. His face, she couldn't help but notice, was mere inches from hers.

"If what?" he coaxed.

It was with curiosity—and that same disoriented sensation she'd felt when she'd first found him holding her—that she watched his eyes darken. She felt certain it was only the reaction of his pupils to a reduction in light, but the phenomenon seemed to remove all expression, leaving only the stark intensity of the man himself. What she saw was someone she really didn't know.

There was something powerful in him, something raw and strong and potent. He was a man who could dominate if he chose, and few would dare question his right. But even more obvious, more compelling than the power was the maleness that confirmed his right to those formidable qualities. Masculinity was basic to him, and a very basic part of her wanted to respond to it.

Had he been anyone else, Meg would have been stunned by the heady pull she felt toward him. But because it was Dave, because he wasn't really a stranger, she could excuse her thoughts as the imaginings of a distressed mind. After all, she told herself, what woman wouldn't be distressed after she'd fainted?

"If I frightened you," she finally concluded, wanting to look away but finding that she couldn't.

He almost smiled. "Frightened?" She noticed his gaze move down to her mouth, his own parting slightly as he drew a deep breath. She wasn't sure, but she thought she did the same. "Let's not understate it, Meg. Frightened is what happens to little kids when you tell them about things that go bump in the night. What you did was scare the hell out of me."

His fingers flexed where they curved over her side. Her own seemed to mimic that motion, tightening against the smooth cotton stretched over his shoulders. A faint spicy scent clung to him, along with the clean smell of soap and fresh air. She'd noticed the combination before, but it only now registered—along with the thought that she should say something, anything, to break the odd and sudden quiet. All she could hear was the constant drone of the ocean filtering through the open windows of the house—and what sounded very much like her own soft gasp when Dave slowly raised his free hand to touch her throat.

"Your hair's caught," he quietly explained, carefully pulling the dark strands from beneath her collar. His eyes followed the motion of his fingers as he loosened the long curls behind her neck, then brushed the wisps away from her temples.

A single strand fell forward again. With the tip of his finger he drew it back, allowing his touch to stray along the curve of her mouth before he realized how far his thoughts had strayed from his purpose. It would be so easy to simply lean forward and taste the softly parted lips, to carry his touch down the elegant line of her throat.

In the brief seconds before Dave abruptly pulled his hand away, Meg noted two distinct peculiarities. She'd stopped breathing, and Dave was shaking. Yet when he quickly smoothed her hair back from her shoulders, the tremor was gone from his fingers.

"Are you okay now?"

She'd already told him she was. Several times. So she just nodded and, meeting his eyes when he drew his hand from her back, wondered if the tension that had permeated their relationship for so long hadn't just undergone a subtle shift. The thought, adding itself to the disturbing pull in her mid-section, caused her glance to dart to one of the clay stains on her smock. More than likely, she hastened to rationalize, what she felt could be blamed on her equilibrium. It was entirely possible that it hadn't quite returned to balance.

Dave straightened and, pushing his fingers through his hair, turned to the wall of floor-to-ceiling windows across from the sofa. Beyond the patio outside, low waves washed a sandy stretch of beach. Clear and calm, he thought. The exact opposite of his thinking. What was the matter with him? What had ever possessed him to touch her like that?

Automatically he reached for a cigarette, but before he withdrew the pack, his hand stilled in his shirt pocket. It probably wasn't a very good idea to smoke around a preg-nant woman, he decided. He had no idea what to do next—an interesting circumstance, considering his reputation for always making the right move.

Frustrated with himself, wanting a cigarette, he jammed his hands into his pockets. Meg was being awfully quiet. "You mentioned that there's another reason you asked me to come over," he reminded her, still looking out the win-dow. "But before we get to that, would you mind telling me something?" Without waiting for a response, he turned. "How far along *are* you, anyway?"

It hadn't occurred to Meg that Dave hadn't known she was pregnant. On the other hand, it hadn't occurred to her that he could know. She hadn't thought about it one way or the other. "A little over five months," she told him, just as she would have anyone else who'd asked. "The baby's due the end of October. And no," she added because she could see the question forming, "Ted didn't know."

To her relief, Dave didn't offer the sympathetic phrases that inevitably accompanied that bit of information. She wasn't after sympathy. Dave seemed to have accepted her apology, and now she wanted only to capitalize on his apparent willingness to suspend his own antipathy toward her. That willingness, such as it was, was there because of Ted. She was sure of that. Dave could be a fierce opponent or a loyal ally. If he did agree to help her, it would be out of loyalty.

"When did you find out?"

That was something else she'd forgotten about him. When Dave wanted to know something, he simply asked the question. "Just after the accident."

"Is everything all right?" He nodded toward her stomach. "With that."

"That," she told him, trying not to smile at his phrasing, "is a baby. And yes, everything's fine."

"Maybe in your opinion," he muttered.

"You have a different one?"

"Yeah. Do you want to hear it?"

The hint of disapproval in his tone tempered her curiosity. "Why do I have the feeling that I'm going to hear it whether I want to or not?"

"Feminine intuition, I guess." He leaned his shoulder against the frame of the patio door, his stance quite casual. It was a bluff. The events and revelations of the past half hour had shaken him far more than he wanted to admit, but he wasn't about to let his weakness show. "Tell me, Mrs. Reese, does your condition account for your sudden lack of good judgment?" At the swift frown clouding her delicate face, he obligingly explained, "It's like common sense. It's what tells you that a woman in your condition has no business moving heavy boxes in this heat. Didn't you realize that it's close to ninety degrees out there?"

"I know how hot it is," she said defensively.

"Do you do that often? Faint, I mean?"

"Of course not. It was just a little—" she started to say warm, but since that was his argument, she switched to "—stuffy."

"The doors were all open," he pointed out. "So was the window. It wasn't any stuffier in the garage than it is outside."

Sensing that she'd do no better scoring this point than she had the other, she sighed. Maybe he'd think it was exasperation rather than defeat. "Is there a point to this little lecture?"

"Pointing out the obvious is not a lecture," he countered, though she was obviously inclined to disagree. "Call movers, Meg. They'll come in and pack all this up and you won't have to do anything but direct traffic. And while you're looking into moving companies," he went on, his eyes sweeping the length of her slight frame, "I suggest you consider hiring a cook. Pregnant women are supposed to gain weight, not lose it."

Stifling the urge to ask when he'd become such an expert, she tried to acknowledge his suggestion with good grace. "Thanks, but I don't need a cook."

"You're right. What you need is a keeper."

Meg blinked up at him, more than a little stunned by his tone and his scowl. He looked genuinely irritated with her. Come to think of it, she realized, she was getting a little irritated with him.

She was also aware of something else. For the first time in weeks, she felt something other than numbness. Annoyance wouldn't have been her first choice for renewed emotion, but since it was there she used it to fuel the nerve she'd feared she might not have. Swinging her feet to the floor, the motion losing its intended defiance in its graceful execution, she placed one hand on the arm of the sofa and the other on her stomach. "What I need," she informed him as she rose, "is advice. And not about movers, or vacations, or my diet," she went on, figuring she might as well include most of the topics her friends had covered lately. "I need the name of a good, inexpensive accountant, and some-body—"

"Wait a minute," he cut in, stepping in front of her. "What happened to the accounting firm Ted was using?"

From where she was she could see only the stripes on his shirt, so she tipped her head back. Now she could clearly see the lines fanning from the corners of his eyes—the ones that added so much character to his face. "They quit. He hadn't paid them, and because I won't be able to pay them for a while, they won't work the account."

"Is everything tied up in probate?"

She shook her head, more comfortable with him now that the focus of his attention was where she wanted it. "Ted had put everything in a special kind of trust," she told him, and hurried on to explain as best she could everything the law-yer had told her.

Fortunately, Dave seemed to know exactly what she was talking about. He was even quite approving of what Ted had done to ensure that the Reese holdings wouldn't be tied up in the courts, as they would have been with a will. But after asking several questions she couldn't answer, Dave was at a loss to see why Meg had a problem.

"Unless," he stated, as one possibility occurred to him, "his mother's decided she likes what she's seen." His blue eyes grew cold, and his voice gained a harder edge as his loyalty slipped into place. Quite unconsciously, Meg took a step backward. "If that's it, Meg, you don't have anything to worry about. You were his wife. Even without the trust, that leaves everything to you. Legally that woman has no claim. As far as I'm concerned, morally she doesn't, either."

The aversion in Dave's tone sent a chill racing down Meg's spine. She couldn't find much fault with his obvious dislike of Ted's mother, since she shared the feeling. Ted had rarely mentioned his childhood, but what little he had related spoke clearly of a disrupted and unsettled youth. His father had walked out when Ted had been ten, and any sense of stability had walked out with him. His graduation present from high school had been the request that he find someplace else to live, because his presence 'irritated' his mother's then-current boyfriend.

Meg had often wondered if the reason Ted had been in such a hurry to marry her was because she'd represented everything that had been missing in his life. He'd put himself through Stanford on athletic scholarships and had been near the end of the year he'd allotted himself to travel when he'd literally bumped into her at an outdoor art show in Springfield. At the time, he'd been seven years older than her twenty. He'd been darkly attractive, with his neat beard and serious gray eyes, and much more worldly than the boys she'd been dating at the art school. She hadn't stood a chance when he'd turned on the charm. And he'd had plenty—along with a sense of humor she'd adored and more plans for the future than any ten people she'd ever met. Once he'd met her, he'd added more plans. After meeting her large and boisterous family he'd decided that, like her, he wanted to have a big family, too. And a big house, because a big family would need one. Within the month, Meg had fallen in love with his enthusiasm and with him. All she'd wanted was to be his wife, make that big house comfortable for him and fill it with his children.

Aware of Dave's indulgence as he waited for her to answer his question, Meg made a deliberate effort to shake off those memories. Bits and pieces of the last seven years had demanded thought in one form or another over the last couple of months, but now wasn't the time for dwelling on hindsights. "His mother isn't the problem," Meg said. She knew that even if the woman decided to become a problem—which wasn't likely—there was nothing for her to get from the estate.

The coolness left Dave's expression, replaced now by confusion. "If that's not it, then what is? You probably saved a bundle in estate taxes with the trust," he told her. "You've got immediate access to the investments, and you don't have to worry about a contested will." Having explained away any possible problem there, he got back to the matter he was sure he'd misunderstood. "Ted hadn't paid his accountant?" The first rule of business was to keep your lawyer and your accountant happy. Ted had known that.

"Or any of the insurance. Can I show you something? It'll explain why I can't afford to hire anyone who's going to cost a lot." She hesitated, hating to ask for the favor but seeing no way to avoid it. "Then, what I really need is for you to go through the files and, if you wouldn't mind, turn them over to a company that can take care of the properties until they can be sold. One of them is that little shopping complex in La Jolla that Ted wanted you to go in on. It's still being built, and I don't know what to tell the man from the bank. He keeps calling to ask what I want to do about the next advance on the construction loan."

The room Ted had used as his office was at the far end of the house. White-painted shutters covered the two arched windows, and Meg opened them to throw slanted streams of light across the mint-colored carpeting. On the desk sat a large pile of mail.

"My brother got after me to file the insurance claim forms a couple of months ago," she said, picking up one of the letters. "I got this about a week later." With a small shrug, she handed it to Dave. "I thought for sure there had been some mistake, so I called right away. But after I couldn't find any of Ted's canceled checks—" Not finding it necessary to complete the sentence, she grouped a few more letters together and held them out to Dave, as well. "It wasn't just the insurance on the boat that he let lapse. He didn't pay the premiums on his life insurance, either.''

Meg moved to the window, watching the breeze play with the hibiscus on the other side. Behind her she heard the rustle of paper as Dave read first one letter, then another. There was a certain irony in having Dave discover how irresponsible Ted had been. But then, Dave was probably the only person who wouldn't condemn him for what he had—or hadn't—done.

Dave wasn't in the proper frame of mind to be terribly understanding at the moment. Ted might have been his best friend, and damning the dead probably wasn't a very wise idea, but Dave was furious. Never, *never* had it occurred to him that Ted could have stretched himself so thin that he'd let his life insurance lapse. He had driven a Mercedes, for God's sake. And he'd sunk a forty-thousand-dollar sailboat! He could have gotten rid of either one and paid for enough insurance to keep Meg comfortable for the rest of her life.

The plea underlying Meg's statement ended his silent seething. ''I'd just as soon you didn't mention this to anyone. Okay?''

''Of course not,'' he muttered, then dropped the matter, which she shouldn't have felt she had to bring up in the first place. ''You got the final response on this three weeks ago?''

Nodding, she turned, pale tints of blue gleaming among the black curls framing her face. ''I put the house on the market the next day. I didn't see that I had any choice. I can't make the payments on it.''

''Has your realtor shown it?''

''She's brought a few people through, but there haven't been any offers.''

She looked so incredibly beautiful in the dimly filtered light, so fragile—though she'd have hated it if she'd known, because she was usually so resilient—rather helpless. Watching the shadows of the leaves outside the window move over her face, Dave allowed himself to feel just a little bit protective. The emotion was safe enough. It was also the only one he felt comfortable with around her.

"Would you stay here if you could make the payments?"

"No," she returned quietly.

"Fine. As long as that's your decision. You always have a choice," he said flatly, picking up on the statement she'd made moments before. "Don't ever forget that." He dropped the letters onto the desk, turning his attention to the file cabinet beside it. "Are all of Ted's files here?"

Meg's slow sigh was one of relief. Everything was going to be okay. Dave would put the situation under control, and she wouldn't have to worry anymore. She knew very little about the business world and was somewhat awed by its complexities. Her talents, if she'd let herself admit to them, lay elsewhere. She could appreciate line and form and color, and had no problem comprehending Keats and Shelley and Khayyám. With very little notice she could turn out exquisite French pastries by the dozen and enough lobster bisque to feed fifty. Her flower arrangements were the envy of the local florist. But when it came to things like contracts and deals, she knew just enough to know she'd only mess up anything she tried to handle.

Everything is under control, she repeated to herself, though this time she wasn't thinking of her financial circumstances. Somehow her thoughts had wandered back to how she'd felt in Dave's arms. The assurance didn't seem quite as certain when she realized that.

By Monday afternoon, Dave was dealing with a few uncertainties of his own. He stood by the corner windows in his Newport Beach office, his back to the stack of correspondence and reports hiding the top of his desk. Sometimes, when he was wrestling with a problem that defied easy solution, he wished he'd taken an office with an ocean view. There was something about contemplating the sheer magnitude of the sea and its constant, unalterable ebb and flow that helped him put things into perspective.

There was also something about looking out at the waves that made him want to bag work and go diving or sailing or windsurfing, which was why his suite of offices occupied the east half of the floor and faced inland. When Dave chose to exercise his self-discipline, it was extraordinary. But he wasn't into testing himself any more often than he had to. Avoiding a temptation was a lot easier than tormenting oneself with it.

That was why he'd steered such a wide course around Meg for so long.

"I'm off to lunch, Dave." Eunice Blair, her rimless half glasses dangling from her neck by a gold chain, dropped a stack of letters on his chair and put the tape she'd just transcribed in the tray by his Dictaphone. "Your father's secretary called to remind you that you're expected at home this weekend. I'll make your reservation when I get back. Do you want anything before I go?"

Dave stifled a groan when he realized he'd forgotten about flying to San Francisco this weekend, and his eyebrows rose questioningly as he considered the auburn-haired woman in the trim navy suit. Later he'd have to call either his father's or his mother's secretary and sweet-talk her into telling the appropriate parent, gently, that he wouldn't be able to make it—again. At the moment, though, it was *his* secretary, an eight-year veteran of the Elliott Company and Dave's self-appointed mother hen, he needed to deal with. She didn't look pleased.

"Is something wrong, Eunice?"

Never one to mince words—it was a quality Dave appreciated, because it saved time—she straightened the hem of her jacket. "I thought you were going to take the Ryker project," she said, pointing to the letter that indicated he was turning it down. "Just in case you didn't notice, I spent all last week rescheduling meetings and trips on your other projects to fit that one in. Do you want me to see if I can put everything back the way it was?"

Easing her pique by telling her something else had come up he took his pen from his pocket and the letters from the chair. A few minutes later he handed them over, read and signed. With them he relinquished a very handsome commission. His talent for putting the people with the money together with the people with the ideas to make more was always well compensated. "Send the ones to Ryker and his partner by overnight mail."

Propping her glasses on her nose, Eunice peered over the rims. It was what she did when he gave her an unnecessary instruction—or when he was being evasive. "Of course," she returned. "Is there anything I need to do about this 'something else'?"

"Not really. I'm just going to help...someone I know," he concluded, because he didn't really know what to call Meg. He couldn't call her a friend. It had been years since that term had fit. Yet 'acquaintance' wasn't accurate, because she was much more than that.

I never have been able to define her, he thought, avoiding Eunice's inquiring eyes by taking out a cigarette and searching his desk for his lighter.

When Ted had introduced Dave to Meg, only days before their wedding, Dave had thought her to be part child, part woman, but mostly elf; a beautiful, enchanting elf with long black hair, mischievous green eyes and the most incredible smile he'd ever seen. The impish light that had once danced in her eyes had disappeared over the years, and her beauty had grown haunting. But though he'd sensed a certain sadness beneath the calm and poised exterior she'd presented, there had been nothing Dave could do to bring her happiness back. It was like that when you wanted something you couldn't have.

Surprised to find that it wasn't as easy as usual to remind himself that the wanting had stopped long ago, he deliberately switched mental gears. He hadn't been able to do anything then, but there was something he could do for her now. Dave doubted very much that Meg had been happy with Ted the last couple of years. For one thing, he had rarely been home. But she was the kind of woman who'd try to make the best of any situation. She was also the kind of woman who would protect her husband's reputation, no matter what she had to do—even if it meant turning to someone she wasn't too crazy about to do it.

Dave knew it must have cost her a lot to ask him for help, but he understood why she had. Who else but Ted's closest friend could she trust with the knowledge that her husband hadn't been all he'd appeared to be?

"I'm going to help Ted Reese's widow with his estate," he finally told his secretary, who had joined the search for the lighter, finding it under a stack of computer printouts. "It might take a while, so I'll use the time you set aside for Ryker for her instead."

The quick lift of Eunice's eyebrows went unnoticed, as did the careful way she considered him when he turned back to the window. A moment later he heard her tell him she'd bring him a sandwich, and he mumbled his thanks just before the door closed.

Squinting through a haze of cigarette smoke, Dave picked up the worksheet he'd put together on Meg's property. Everything Ted had sacrificed so much for was listed there, including the deal that had caused the rift between the two friends to widen. Dave had tried to tell Ted that building a shopping center next to two others with vacant retail space wasn't such a hot idea. Ted hadn't listened, though, and after getting upset with Dave for not going into the venture with him when he ran into problems financing it, Ted had matched what funds the bank would lend him with his own.

Dave now knew how he'd been able to do that. He'd simply added a mortgage here and there and stopped making payments on his other obligations—probably, Dave figured, with the idea of reinstating things such as insurance later. The way he had everything structured would have worked out beautifully if he hadn't died.

Dave hadn't told Meg that yet. He hadn't been able to tell her anything at all on Saturday. After spending almost an hour with her trying to familiarize himself with the files, he'd decided the effort was a monumental waste. The faint scent of jasmine she wore had insisted on reminding him of how she'd felt in his arms. Small. Soft. And pregnant.

Deliberately he turned to the box of files on his credenza. It had been easier to bring them here than to try to concentrate at Meg's house. His eyes shifted to the left. Beside the box was another he planned on taking by Meg's tonight.

Dave rubbed the bridge of his nose. She'd asked for his advice, but he had a feeling she might not like what he was going to suggest.

"What's this?" Meg frowned at the book Dave handed her and watched him extract another from the box he'd carried to her kitchen table. The bouquet of sweet peas she'd picked that morning had been pushed aside to accommodate the stack of files he'd taken with him two days earlier. "Were these Ted's?" she asked, preparing to tell Dave to keep them if they were reference materials he'd borrowed.

"They're mine." Dave handed her another book. "Except for that one. It belongs to the library. You might want to read it first, since it's due back in two weeks."

Meg looked up uneasily. The title of this particular volume was *Analyzing Asset Disposition*.

"Besides being able to make an informed decision about what property to sell—" he pushed his hands into the pockets of his gray suit slacks and leaned against the table "—you should know something about accounting, depreciation, property valuation and building trends. I thought about having you read up on capitalization and funding, but we'll get to that later. Don't worry," he said lightly, seeing a flicker of panic streak through her eyes. "I'll explain it all to you."

Meg was far from relieved. Pulling out one of the white rattan kitchen chairs, she sat down at the glass-topped table and glanced toward the loosened knot of Dave's tie. He obviously hadn't understood the nature of her request at all. "I don't want to try to take care of this myself," she said, not knowing how to make it any clearer for him. "I want to hire a firm who knows what they're doing to do it. Can't you recommend one?"

Tipping her head in anticipation, she waited for what she thought would be a simple answer to a simple question.

Dave apparently found the matter a bit more complex than she did. "It isn't that easy, Meg. I'll give you the name of a management company who can handle the rental properties for a reasonable percentage, and of an accountant who'll help you straighten out the books. But there are a few things you're going to have to do yourself. Unless you know something about what's going on, you have no way of knowing whether or not your interests are being handled to your best advantage. Frankly, you can't afford the luxury of remaining uninvolved."

"But I can't just read a few books to figure out how to do this!"

The alarm in her voice had Dave adding a note of forbearance to his. He hadn't meant to overwhelm her. "You don't have to *master* anything. I'll just teach you enough so you can recognize problems. It could take you up to a year to liquidate your holdings, and if you don't know what to watch for, a lot could go wrong.''

A stained-glass butterfly hovered between the hanging ferns in the bay window behind Meg, the sunlight that poured through it streaking color on the white tile floor. The shimmering hues of purple and pink drew Meg's eye, allowing her to focus on something other than the man whose presence had effectively removed the lethargy she'd been fighting all day. He'd only been here for a few minutes, but even in that short space of time she'd noticed herself reacting to the difference in his manner. He seemed less guarded than he had in the past, more relaxed. She, on the other hand, was beginning to get a little nervous.

"Let me make sure I understand this," she requested, pleating creases in the hem of her pink smock. "You're offering to try to teach me all that stuff you were talking about?"

The ease of his smile was quite disarming and very unexpected. So was the teasing note in his voice. "You can't just read a few books to figure out how to do this. Someone needs to explain it to you. I'm a very good teacher. Excellent, in fact."

"Modest, too."

He'd made her smile. That was all he'd wanted to do just then. Remove the fear and make her smile. The doubt was still there, though, preventing pleasure from reaching her eyes. For no discernible reason, she seemed a little short on confidence.

"I know it sounds like a lot right now, but you can do it, Meg." He stepped directly in front of her. "You know that, don't you?"

She hadn't expected him to be so perceptive. Maybe that was why she felt so startled, so unnerved by the way he was looking at her now. No, she corrected, feeling oddly defenseless. Not *at*. *Into*. Standing over her, with his eyes intent on her face, he seemed to be looking inside her. What, she wondered, did he see?

"I'm not sure I do," she heard herself admit, her voice sounding far too small. "I've never even considered doing any of this myself. I don't know that I can."

"Listen to me, Megan." Placing his hands on the arms of her chair, he lowered himself in front of her. Though his tone was firm, something in his eyes prevented his expression from being harsh. "Ted made some good investments. He also made a few really stupid business decisions. I told you the other day that you always have a choice, and right now you've got one. You can do this right and make enough to feed yourself and Junior, or you can sit back and let some third party take most of your profits as their percentage. You'll be a lot farther ahead if you take the initiative and get some of these properties ready to sell yourself. I'll help you pull this all together if you want me to, but I can't do it for you."

"I'm not asking you to," she said hurriedly, marveling at just how much he was offering to do. "I know how busy you are."

"My time doesn't have anything to do with this," he replied. "Your independence does."

For several seconds Meg sat twisting her gold wedding band and trying to figure out why she wanted to put her arms around his neck and hang on for dear life. It was better when she was numb, because then she wasn't scared and she didn't have this ridiculous need to experience the security she'd felt when he'd held her before. She simply had to stop thinking about that.

"Independence, huh? How is my putting myself into bankruptcy going to make me independent?"

"When did you become such a pessimist?"

"Yesterday," she muttered, and when he smiled, she did, too. She hadn't remembered his grin being quite that charming.

As she forced herself to forget about the dimple she'd also somehow overlooked before, she had to admit that Dave wouldn't waste his time on her if he didn't think she was capable. Therefore, it was now a point of pride as well as survival that she prove herself worthy of that faith. "You say you're a good teacher?"

"The best."

"Do you still get as impatient as you used to?"

"What makes you think I was ever impatient?"

"I heard you every day for two weeks while you and Ted were trying to rebuild that dune buggy you guys bought."

"That was six years ago."

"That's not an answer."

"I'll try to be better," he promised.

Dubious but aware that, Dave's assertion to the contrary, she didn't have a whole lot of choice, she finally acquiesced. "Okay, Dave. You tell me what I need to do and I'll try to do it. Just remember that you offered to do this, and don't lose your temper if I don't understand everything the first time."

"You got it," he returned with a grin, and started to rise. The touch of her hand on his arm stopped him.

The sleeves of his white shirt were rolled back. Curling her fingers over his forearm, she was aware of the softness of the brown hair made golden by the sun and the feel of hard, disciplined muscle. The contrast was intriguing. "Why are you doing this for me?"

A seemingly indifferent shrug preceded his bland "Why not?"

"Don't do that, Dave. I'd really like to know."

No, you wouldn't, he thought. If he were to be honest he'd have to tell her that a large part of his motivation stemmed from guilt. He couldn't help thinking that if he'd gone in with Ted on the shopping complex, Ted would have handled things differently and Meg wouldn't have found herself in such a distressing position. He wouldn't speak of guilt, though. She didn't need to hear that.

Those thoughts were cast aside when he saw her smile at him. Her eyes were so wide and inquiring, and she seemed so accessible. It would be a mistake, he knew, but it would take no effort at all to reach up and test the softness of her skin again. One touch, he thought, almost able to imagine the satin smoothness of her cheek. His hands tightened on the arms of her chair. "I guess it's because that's what friends are for."

"You were Ted's friend," she reminded him quietly.

He, in turn, reminded her, "You and I were almost friends once, too."

"I know." She saw his glance move to where her fingers lay on his arm. Suddenly aware that her grip had tightened, she pulled her hand away and went back to twisting her ring. "A few centuries ago," she added when he straightened.

"Has it only been that long?"

"Cute, Elliott," she muttered, grateful that he apparently hadn't noticed anything odd about her actions. "So tell me. What do I do first?"

As she stood, Dave let his glance skim from her bare feet to the knot of gleaming black hair on her head. She had her hand at the small of her back. "That vacant strip of property just south of town," he began, watching her arch a little. "You can probably break even on it if you get the zoning changed to commercial. Otherwise you might have to sell it at a loss."

Get the zoning changed? He made it sound as simple as stopping by the bakery for a loaf of bread. "Are one of these books going to tell me how to do that?"

He shook his head, pulling off his tie at the same time. "Nope. I am." Dropping the tie on the table, he took the book she'd just picked up and laid that down, too. "We'll get to work in a few minutes. Does your back hurt?"

"Always," he heard her reply with a little half laugh that did something quite electric to the nerves at the base of his spine.

With a muttered "That's not good," he stepped behind her. "Come here."

Over the years, Meg had learned that Dave took no for an answer only when it was the answer he wanted to hear. She also remembered how silly a person could feel when she anticipated one thing and got something else entirely.

Chapter Three

Meg had definitely misread Dave's intentions a couple of nights earlier, but she knew she hadn't misinterpreted Annie's purpose in inviting her to lunch on Thursday. Lacking the energy to defend herself against the skilled plea her very transparent friend had no doubt planned to deliver, Meg stayed home. Strategy sessions for a charity ball rarely went as planned, and having served on her share of committees in the past few years, Meg knew the lunch might go on for hours. Today she was using her time and energy for more selfish purposes. Annie would fill her in, anyway.

The application for variance she'd picked up yesterday at the county courthouse—the one Dave said she had to file as soon as possible to get the zoning changed on the south-end property—lay on the coffee table in the family room. Next to it was the property file and a paper tube of soda crackers. The queasiness that someone had rather inaccurately dubbed *morning sickness* hadn't hit until noon today. Now, three hours later, it was gone. It seemed to have subsided in direct proportion to her growing frustration.

Dave had told her that the file contained all the information she'd need to complete the form. It probably did, she conceded, if a person knew what she was looking for. How was she supposed to fill the thing out if she didn't understand the questions it asked? What was a *land use permit*? What were *access* and *egress*? Why did she want Dave to hold her again?

"Oh, hell," she muttered, stuffing the application into the file just as the back door slammed.

"It's me," Annie announced as she entered the kitchen. "Where are you?"

Relieved by the interruption, Meg called, "In here." Too often she'd found her thoughts straying back to those disconcerting moments in Dave's arms. At least now, with Annie's arrival, she wouldn't have to wonder why.

"I brought you a salad. Fresh fruit with that poppy-seed dressing you like. I'll stick it in the fridge."

Bribery. Meg shook her head, smiling to herself. Was she really such a pushover that Annie thought she could be bought with a fruit salad? "Thanks, Annie. I'll have it for dinner."

In a swirl of brilliant fuchsia that made Meg feel rather frumpy in her white gauze maternity shift, Annie came to a halt beside the leafy potted ficus. Her mouth was open, as if she'd been about to say something, then had changed her mind.

Raising her eyebrows at Meg's unusual posture, she drawled, "That's a new one. Don't tell me. You decided to try Lamaze after all, and that's a new breathing position. No, wait," she hurried on, loath to lose her inspiration, "Vanessa was here and brought that guru she's been going to. She finally managed to convince you that the only way to cope with stress is to find nirvana. You're meditating. Right?"

Meg smiled. "Not hardly."

"I've got it!"

"What happened to 'eureka'?"

Annie ignored her. "You want your offspring to be a race-car driver. You're doing a little prenatal programming."

Meg supposed her position did somewhat resemble that of the Big Wheel racers who zipped up and down the neighborhood sidewalks. She was sitting on the carpet with her shoulders against the sofa, one of its thick bolsters at the small of her back and a large stack of throw pillows under her knees. What the position lacked in convention, it made up for in comfort. It was also quite practical. With her legs angled as they were, she could prop a notepad or a book against them.

"I think that subliminal suggestion stuff only applies with music," she said, her hand on her stomach as if she wanted to include the baby in the conversation. "At least, that's all I've read about."

Though the hypothesis might never be proved, Meg treated her unborn child to Strauss or Chopin or Mancini almost every evening. The purpose was twofold. If the theory worked, her baby might develop the talent for music she'd never had. All she could play was the radio. The music also helped Meg relax, sometimes even enough that she was able to sleep.

"How was lunch?" she asked when Annie just stood there staring at her.

"I'll get to that in a minute." Dropping down onto the far end of the sofa, Annie planted her elbows on her knees and cupped her chin in her hand. "Why *are* you sitting like that?"

"It's comfortable," Meg returned, and proceeded to elaborate. "Dave said his sister always had back problems when she was pregnant. Sitting this way seemed to relieve them." With a slight shrug, she added, "It works."

Dave hadn't just told her about the position the other night. He'd put her in it. Despite the physical contact required, which she'd noticed he kept to a deliberate minimum, his manner had been totally impersonal. Before she'd caught on to what he was doing, Meg had thought he'd meant to rub her back. It was no wonder he'd seemed so puzzled when she'd insisted it wasn't necessary.

"Dave's sister?" Annie inquired.

"Mmm." As she pleated the fabric covering her knees, Meg's glance slid toward the window. The position she was in had one distinct disadvantage. She couldn't see the ocean from here. "She's got three boys."

"How'd you two get to talking about her? When I left you guys I thought for sure he'd just get his scuba gear and leave."

"Oh, this wasn't Saturday." Still looking at the window, she stifled an inner moan. Now that she'd said that, she'd have to do a little explaining—at least enough to satisfy the curiosity she saw in her friend's widened eyes. "You know how good he's supposed to be at real estate," she went on, still unable to heap Dave with the praise Ted had so freely bestowed on him. "So I asked him if he'd mind looking over Ted's business to make sure everything was in order. He's already found a couple of little things that I need to take care of."

There was no way Annie could know how drastically Meg had understated what Dave had found. And if she found it hard to believe that Meg would ask such a favor of Dave in the first place, she didn't say so.

"That sounds logical. I suppose it's wise to have an expert check your holdings, and you could certainly trust a friend of Ted's over some stranger." Picking up her purse, which she'd set on the coffee table next to the crackers, she grinned. "I just wouldn't have thought Dave would have any expertise about pregnant women with backaches."

"It does sort of alter the image," Meg agreed, watching Annie rummage around in the huge straw bag. "He sounds awfully close to her."

"To his sister?" Seeing Meg nod, Annie frowned and kept digging. "Why shouldn't he be?"

"It's not that he *shouldn't*. It just surprised me a little. I've never pictured him as being close to his family."

"Do you know much about them?"

"Not really." Mildly curious about what Annie was hunting for, Meg watched as a wallet and an appointment book were tossed onto the sofa. "His father's a judge, and his mother is a professor of some kind. English, I think." Ted had given her the rundown on the Elliott family when he'd introduced her to Dave. Until a couple of years ago, he'd also kept her up to date with occasional bulletins about any Elliott accomplishment—such as when Jan, Dave's sister, had been accepted as a research fellow following her marriage to a prominent pediatrician.

"I'm impressed," Annie mumbled, flipping through a small folder she'd extracted from her handbag.

Ted was, too, Meg thought absently, remembering how she'd once wondered how Dave had felt about being raised in such an obviously goal-oriented environment. She'd never had a chance to find out. About the time she'd felt she knew Dave well enough to ask such a personal question, she'd realized that Ted's increasing absorption in his business was being fueled by Dave's own success. Her resentment toward Dave over the changes taking place in her husband had soon removed any desire she'd had to know anything about Dave or his background—and had ultimately blocked out any redeeming quality he'd possessed. She'd seen him only as a law unto himself, an enigma whose influence could create or destroy. To her, the movers and shakers—or those trying to be—diverted their affections to more profitable alliances than mere relatives. She was sure Ted had learned that lesson from Dave.

"I just hadn't thought he'd have time for anything like family," Meg offered. Annie was still engrossed in her search. "He's always so busy."

"If something's important enough, a person will make time."

Meg was careful not to glance away too quickly. The remark had merely been an observation, but the reminder stung.

"I suppose you're right," she returned, telling herself that it didn't matter anymore. Though Ted had been dead for only three months, she'd really lost him long before that. She'd even come to terms with the fact that she hadn't been important enough for him to want to come home more often.

Meg gave a soft, rather disgusted sigh. There was absolutely nothing to be gained by dwelling on her shortcomings as a wife. More productive matters beckoned.

Tugging the pillows out from under her knees, she stood to stretch out the kinks. The other night, after Dave had propped her up in front of the sofa, he'd very carefully explained what Ted had left in the way of assets and liabilities. He'd then exhibited more patience than she'd thought he possessed as he explained which files she should keep and what needed to be done on them, and which should be turned over to a management company. Those two hours had convinced her that no matter what tactics Annie tried to use on her today, she'd have no choice but to refuse any involvement with this latest benefit. She simply wouldn't have the time.

That had been before Annie had unintentionally reminded Meg of the emptiness she was trying desperately not to feel. "I'll chair the publicity committee if you want."

The sheet of paper Annie had finally found in her note-book fell to her lap. "You will?"

Meg's nonchalant "Sure" seemed to bring a hint of dis-appointment to Annie's stunned expression, but then the astonished blonde broke into a beaming smile.

Meg's own smile was slightly apologetic. She hated cheating her friend out of what was probably a well-rehearsed plea, but she couldn't have held her former ground with any conviction. She wanted to stay so busy that she didn't have time to think. Given the commitment she'd just made, along with everything Dave had mapped out for her to do, keeping herself occupied shouldn't present a problem.

If Annie was thrilled with Meg's easy capitulation, Dave, Meg was soon to discover, was not. He called that after-noon to tell her he'd pick her up for her appointments with the bank and the management company the next day. Then, sounding just as hurried as he probably was, he brushed off her insistence that he needn't chauffeur her to the meetings and asked how she was doing with the rezoning applica-tion.

She could tell he was busy, and not wanting to keep him— and feeling terribly grateful for his willingness to attend the meetings with her—she said the application was coming along just fine. Dave, chuckling, told her he doubted it, and arrived on her doorstep at six that evening. As on Monday, he came straight from his office. And, as on Monday, he almost immediately shed the more cumbersome compo-nents of his suit when he got to the kitchen.

Meg couldn't help allowing herself to feel a little relief when he muttered, "What a day," and stopped by the table to drop his jacket over a chair back. She'd been afraid that his companionable nature the other night had been a fluke, that the next time she saw him he would resurrect the awful strained formality that had existed between them for so long. Obviously, she thought watching him take a cracker from the box she'd brought to the counter but hadn't gotten around to putting away, she needn't have worried. He seemed as much at ease as he had when he'd made himself at home in her kitchen while waiting for Ted to show up.

Relying on that sense of normalcy to soothe her lingering apprehensions, she headed to the refrigerator. It wasn't right that he should be more comfortable in her kitchen than she was. "Do you want some cheese with those?" she asked, referring to the remaining crackers.

The shake of his head was accompanied by an absent "I had a late lunch." He took another cracker and turned his back on the package. "Thanks anyway."

"How about something to drink?"

"Yeah, sure. Whatever you're having is fine." Loosening his tie he frowned at the papers lying on the table. "What's all this?"

A tray of ice cubes in hand, Meg peered around the open door of the freezer compartment. Dave, chewing thoughtfully, had his head bent over the papers she'd taken out after Annie had left. "Last year's publicity for the South Coast Women's Shelter benefit. I was looking for my mailing list so I could update it with new donors. The benefit isn't until October, and I've got a couple of months before the mailings go out, but I don't want to wait until the last minute." Ice in one hand, a pitcher of cold tea in the other, she headed to the white ceramic-tiled island in the center of the kitchen. "Is iced tea okay? If you'd like a mixed drink, there's—"

"Tea's fine," Dave cut in, feeling a sizable portion of his good mood slip into oblivion. She wasn't really going to work on that benefit, was she? Hadn't she listened to what he'd said the other day?

Convinced that he was right, that she did need a keeper, he lifted the cover of the art pad she'd left under a small folder full of correspondence. "And the sketches?"

He wasn't surprised when she hesitated before saying, "Logo roughouts for this year's theme." She'd always seemed a little shy about her work, though she needn't have been. Even her most elementary drawings, such as the sketches he now perused with his usual analytical detachment, contained a purity of line that was unique—even if the subject matter wasn't. There were only so many ways two hands reaching for each other could be drawn. Meg had, however, added a touch of originality by superimposing them over a silhouette of a woman's head.

"You're doing the artwork, too?"

This time there was no hesitation, only the briefest flicker of uncertainty in her eyes at the flatness of his tone. "That's the part I wanted to do," she said. Sensing that he wasn't very pleased by her response, she reached into the wire basket of fruit hanging beneath one of the oak cabinets. It was then that she glanced back to see him replace the folder on the pad and noticed in his expression what she'd heard in his voice. Disapproval. Very distinct, and more than a little unsettling.

Dave's stance was deceptively casual as he watched her busily pour the iced tea into the cut-crystal tumblers and place a slice of lemon on each rim. He had always enjoyed keeping her company when she'd prepared hors d'oeuvres and drinks before the many meals he'd taken at her table. He'd found a very comfortable pleasure in watching her add the little touches that turned something ordinary into something special. He might have felt that pleasure now if he hadn't been so exasperated.

Any sane person in her position would figure she had enough to do without taking on more right now. To Dave, she already seemed as fragile as the Dresden dolls he knew she collected, but it was none of his business if she wanted to run herself ragged. All she wanted from him was advice about how to run her financial affairs. Since advice was all he was prepared to give her, the arrangement, he supposed, should work just fine. It would if she'd listen to him, anyway. It seemed as if she needed to be protected from herself as much as from anyone or anything else.

The deep breath he drew spoke of his internal agitation. On the surface it appeared to be nothing more than a way to check impatience. "I thought you didn't want to do the benefit this year."

Puzzled, and growing even more uneasy as he moved toward the island, she set one of the glasses within his reach. "Where did you get that idea?"

"From you. You seemed upset with Annie when she left last Saturday because she wouldn't take no for an answer. Remember?"

"I wasn't upset," she said dismissively, as if the idea were absurd. "I just knew she'd do what she always does and try to talk me into it. I hadn't decided—"

"She succeeded, obviously."

Not liking either Dave's tone or the way his inexplicable displeasure was making her feel, Meg's reaction was to ignore both and hope they'd go away. Now, though, having learned that ignoring reality didn't change it, she prepared to meet Dave's problem—whatever it was—head-on.

That thought was fine. Putting it into effect was another matter entirely. She didn't quite know what to say. She'd never been very good at confrontations, but she hoped inspiration would strike by the time she'd wiped the drops of water from the gleaming ceramic surface.

Dave was not about to be put off. Reaching in front of her, he flattened his hand on hers, stilling the brisk back-and-forth motion of the towel. The contact also brought her head up, her expression startled as she met the quiet determination in his eyes. "Megan," he said, refusing to be ignored, "why did you let her talk you into it?"

Her confused expression made Dave reassess his approach. He was going about this all wrong. His personal feelings about her decision aside, there was a point to be made here. Meg needed to learn how to stand up for herself, something he doubted she'd ever done in her life. He wished he hadn't gotten quite this close to her, though he could clearly see her wariness as she glanced from his face to his hand and back to meet his eyes. He felt her fingers flex beneath his, then relax, as if she'd meant to pull away. He was a little surprised when she didn't.

Pulling back had been her first reaction. Her second reaction had been to ask him why he was making such a big deal out of such a little matter. Then she'd looked up at him.

The pressure of his palm on the back of her hand had immediately eased, and she was now more aware of its warmth than of its weight. But she couldn't seem to look away from his eyes. She knew it would be infinitely safer to find somewhere else to focus, to pull her attention away from those compelling blue depths. With him touching her, with him so close that she could almost feel his solid strength, he was no longer just Dave. He was the stranger she'd met only briefly, the man who'd lifted her in his arms and made her feel so secure. Only now it wasn't security she felt. It was response.

The pull she felt toward him caught her so off guard that she could only think of breaking the contact that had elicited the startling phenomenon in the first place. She turned her head and withdrew her hand. She was too confused by her reaction to Dave to try to rationalize it. She only knew that if Dave felt anything toward her at all at the moment, it was irritation.

"Look," he said, his tone as daunting as his scowl, "a few days ago you seemed convinced you wanted to turn

Annie down. Now you've agreed to take on something that's going to demand more time than you've got. Besides learning about a business that's damn near falling apart at the seams, you've got to sell this house, find an apartment and try to find some time to take care of yourself. I'm not trying to tell you how to run your life, but it seems to me that your priorities are a little messed up here."

He stepped back and pushed his fingers through his hair. Getting upset with her wasn't going to help him make his point. All that did was make him wonder why he seemed so bent on getting a real reaction out of her. Any complete emotion, anything but the apathy that drained the life from her smiles and frowns. She went through the motions so well that anyone who didn't really know her might not realize how much vitality she'd lost. But he knew.

He thought it best to get to the point. "You're a little too easygoing for your own good sometimes. You can't let people walk on you anymore, Meg. And believe me, they're going to try when it comes time for you to start negotiating on some of your property. Unless you're presented with a valid and profitable reason for changing your mind about something, it'll play havoc with your credibility to back down on a decision. Once it's apparent you can be manipulated, it's all over."

Curious to know what kind of thumbscrews Meg responded to, Dave pressed the issue. She'd be eaten alive by his peers if she didn't learn how to hold her ground. "What was the trade-off?" he asked. "What do you get in return for the time you'll have to put into this?"

Annoyed with herself for feeling intimidated by the way he was glaring down at her, Meg forced herself to meet his eyes. She didn't think Dave was really unhappy with her. He merely wanted her to see that she had to learn to be firm. But because Dave was only doing the job he'd taken on for himself—making her independent—she didn't have to tell

him that the 'trade-off' was the preoccupation that left her
unable to think too much.

Quite unexpectedly, she smiled. ''In return for my time I
get the dubious privilege of listening to three other women
tell me how happy they are that they didn't get stuck with
the job, while behind my back they're criticizing everything
I do. I also get to put a few hundred miles on the car running back and forth to the printer because either the invi-
tations or the posters—probably both—won't be done right
the first time. Then there's the task of trying not to alienate
any of the other volunteers who aren't doing their job fast
enough or who have forgotten to do it at all.'' It was important to her that he realize she wasn't beyond redemp-
tion. She also wanted him to know that she didn't hold his
overbearing methods against him, even if she did find them
a bit annoying. That was why she let her smile settle in her
eyes and added, ''Sounds like almost as much fun as a mi-
graine, doesn't it?''

Dave watched her raise her glass to him, then take a
swallow and head into the family room. Picking up his own
glass, he followed, his eyes moving restlessly over her loose
cotton shift. The woman moved like a dancer; she seemed
to drift rather than walk. And her eyes... When she smiled,
a man could find himself as enchanted by those mesmeriz-
ing green depths as the ancient mariners had been by the
songs of the sirens.

With a grudging respect for her evasive tactics and a certain appreciation for what Odysseus's men must have gone
through, Dave watched Meg pick up one of the papers on
the coffee table. Sighing, she held it out to him.

''Speaking of headaches,'' she said, and saw him frown
at the application.

He had to hand it to her. When Meg wanted to avoid an
issue, she exhibited all the skill of the most seasoned tacti-
cian. She hadn't given him a single clue as to why she'd

agreed to chair that committee. It was apparent that no amount of probing on his part would provide one, so he didn't press the issue. Answers, he knew, could be found in a more indirect manner.

It didn't take Dave long to help Meg finish the application for variance and to explain what she could expect in terms of delays for the rezoning. As he had the other night, he paced as he spoke, his hand occasionally straying to the pack of cigarettes in his shirt pocket. His voice was clipped and concise, his manner totally impersonal. If she didn't understand a term or phrase, he patiently explained it. If she couldn't quite grasp a concept, he formed an analogy to assist her comprehension. He didn't talk down to her or belabor a point once she'd grasped it, and not once did he brush a matter off as something beyond her intelligence.

It was his concession to her intellect that was most unexpected. So many times in the last couple of years she'd asked Ted to explain a project to her. Not because she'd had a great interest in real estate, but because she'd been interested in saving her marriage and had thought the subject would give them something to discuss. Ted's whole existence had revolved around his projects, and she'd known that if she wanted to be a part of his life she'd have to converse with him about things that held his interest. His answer to her questions, though, had become a standard evasion: "Some other time, honey. It would take too long to explain right now."

After getting that response for the better part of a year, she'd had little choice but to decide that her husband didn't think her capable of comprehending his complex business life. What had hurt more, though, was that he hadn't cared to waste his valuable leisure time enlightening her about them.

It was that thought that made Dave's presence even more remarkable. He didn't owe her anything, yet he was spending *his* very valuable time helping her.

Since it was impossible to think that Dave's actions were prompted by anything other than the affection he'd held for Ted, Meg made herself alter the course of her mental wanderings. Dave's time and patience were gifts to his friend's memory. What he was doing had little to do with her personally.

"Is there anything else I need to know?" she asked when he cut back across the room again. His pacing made it difficult for her to concentrate. She wasn't sure if it was his pacing or his presence that made her nervous. She did know, however, that the room felt much too small when he was in it.

"On the rezoning?" The slow shake of his head seemed distracted. "No. That's about it for now. You're going to have to move on that shopping complex in La Jolla right away, though." Pushing his hands into his pockets, he retraced his path across the family room. Turning when he reached the two striped chairs, he headed toward the patio door again. "Now that we know the bank isn't going to continue advances, your chances of coming up with backers before it calls the loans are pretty remote."

Dave's hand clenched, a conscious reaction to the urge to reach toward his shirt pocket. With his cigarettes so accessible, they were too much of a temptation. He should have left them in the car, as he had the other day. "I'd recommend putting it on the market before the end of the month and selling it to the first party who can assume the loans. You need to see what the bank has to say tomorrow before you make any real decision, though."

"What about the money Ted put into it himself? You said he had to have put up thousands of his—our—money to get the bank to loan him the rest of it. Can't I get that back?"

"I doubt it," he answered honestly, and stopped in front of her. This was the moment he'd dreaded. There were questions he needed to ask before they went any further with this discussion. Earlier, she'd evaded his inquiries. Now he couldn't let her. Unlike his earlier questions about why she'd taken on the volunteer work, these were questions he wasn't sure he really wanted the answers to. "I think we've come to the hard part," he said, finally reaching for a cigarette. "There are a few things I have to ask you that you may not have considered yet, but you need to make some decisions fairly soon." He dipped his head toward the deck. "Let's go outside."

Moments earlier, Meg would have welcomed his suggestion, if for no other reason than that it would give him more room to pace. Now she felt herself trying to wall herself behind the protective numbness she'd learned to rely on.

Dave's expression was brooding as he headed toward the door. "I'll be out as soon as I get us some more tea," she answered, groping for a reason to delay.

"You wouldn't happen to have a beer, would you?"

The beer was produced from a six-pack that had occupied her refrigerator for months. Joining Dave at the rail surrounding the flagstone terrace, Meg offered it to him in the bottle because she remembered that he preferred it that way, and looked out toward the ocean.

The tide was out, and the waves were low. On the horizon, the sun waned above the gray-green water, its descent rather unspectacular. A sunset was always more impressive when there were clouds to catch its color. "Do you still run on the beach every morning?"

Watching the breeze carry away the smoke he exhaled, Dave propped his elbows on the waist-high rail. The question had, no doubt, been prompted by the two joggers visible in the distance. "Whenever I can," he replied. "I usually make it four days out of seven."

That explained the hard, corded muscles she'd felt when he'd held her. "I stopped running last month. Walking's easier."

Meg turned into the breeze so that it could move her hair away from her face. Dave was now directly in her line of vision. He was looking straight ahead, the corners of his mouth pulled tight. He didn't seem in any great rush to get on with the subject—whatever it was—either. "I imagine it is."

Looking away from his strong profile as he took another draw from his cigarette, she forced her attention to the rock escarpment several hundred yards down the beach. She often sat out here in the mornings and watched the gulls congregate. Sometimes they flocked in such numbers that they nearly obliterated the craggy gray boulders. Now, she knew, the rocks were occupied only by mussels and land crabs, which were too small to be seen from where she stood.

"I need to know what you want, Meg."

Meg glanced at Dave. Seeing his gaze still riveted on the horizon, she turned her own to the rocks again. "Why?"

"Because I can't really help you unless you tell me what you want to accomplish. You have to have some goals. Short-term. Long-range. The best way for me to understand that is for you to tell me what really matters to you."

She supposed he had a right to know where she wanted to go from here so he could give her the proper advice. But for all his reputed financial wizardry, he couldn't wave a magic wand and change her future into one she'd be comfortable with. Nothing would ever be the same again. The life that had become so familiar had been irrevocably altered by Ted's death. Where she'd once awakened each morning knowing what was expected of her, she awoke now with a vague sense of panic and the feeling that what remained of her once-comfortable world could come crashing down around her any minute. She'd lived at home until the day she'd been married. From then on, she'd always been a wife and a homemaker, a woman whose existence had revolved around making a house comfortable for a husband and someday, she'd hoped, children. Now she didn't know what she was. She felt as if she were floundering. And Dave, secure and certain of who and what he was, wanted to know what her goals were. If she hadn't been so frightened by that unknown future, she'd have laughed.

She knew Dave would tell her it was impossible, but she spoke her wish anyway. "I want everything to be like it was."

"At which point in your life?"

His response caught her completely unprepared. "I don't remember you being so perceptive."

"It surprises a lot of people," he returned in a wry, self-mocking tone. "Don't let it throw you."

Dave looked over at her. When it became clear that she wasn't going to answer the question he'd asked, he took one last draw on his cigarette and stubbed it out. "He changed, didn't he?"

"We all change," she offered, having known that they would speak of Ted eventually. "Some of us just don't do it as well as others."

"You don't have to defend him to me, Meg."

"No," she replied quietly. "I don't suppose I do. You probably knew him better than I did." Oddly, she didn't envy Dave for that. Not now. "He wanted to be just like you, you know."

It was one thing to suspect something, quite another to have your suspicions confirmed. There had always been a healthy competition between Dave and Ted, though Dave had noticed a tougher edge to it during the past couple of years. He'd tried to overlook the times Ted had exhibited more rivalry than friendship. He understood about pres-

sure and the desire to succeed. He knew all about the heady
rush that came with winning, and he knew how a man was
measured by the amount of power he wielded. He'd been
there. He was there now. But for some people—such as his
parents, he thought without rancor—even that wasn't
enough.

"Is that why you disliked me so much?"

Her first reaction was to utter a denial. Stunned, though
she shouldn't have been, since she knew Dave could be em-
barrassingly frank when it suited his purpose, Meg drew a
preparatory breath. The cynicism in Dave's eyes stilled the
lie. He'd know how she'd felt about him. There was no reason to insult his intelligence.

"I used to think it was all your fault," she admitted quietly. "I used to think," she went on, unable to hold the cool
blue of his eyes, "that if it hadn't been for you, everything
would have stayed like it was in the beginning. But after he
died I finally faced the fact that he'd have become just as
obsessed with his work with or without a role model."

Blunt honesty didn't come easily for Meg. She'd been
raised to soften hurtful truths, to keep ugly thoughts or
feelings to herself. A lady never offended or hurt someone
knowingly. Something about Dave invited her to drop that
pretense and encouraged her to admit to him what she'd finally admitted to herself. "Hating you was just a way of not
hating him."

Dave, his elbows resting on the railing, stared at his
clasped hands. At one point in his life her admission would
almost have destroyed him. But that had been before he'd
stopped telling himself he could handle how he'd begun to
feel about her. Once he'd realized how utterly foolish it was
to continue torturing himself, he'd distanced himself from
her. Meg's growing coolness had helped build the wall he'd
so frantically constructed. Whether that wall had been to
protect himself from her or her from him, he'd never really

known. It hadn't mattered. What had mattered was that with her unwitting help he'd finally managed to bury his thoughts of something that could never be. He'd also buried part of himself. He preferred it that way. Now, when he let himself care about a woman, he didn't experience the total absorption that could interfere so mercilessly with his concentration, and he didn't wake in the middle of the night wanting so badly that no number of cold showers or runs along the beach could relieve the ache. Thanks to her, he was always in control.

Because he was in control, he could keep his thoughts channeled in their proper direction. This conversation was, after all, really about business. He knew how important it was to maintain a certain image when liquidating property. Commanding top dollar was always easier when it wasn't obvious that you needed the money. The minute it was suspected that you had to sell, the more incentive the other side had to offer less. Dave doubted that Meg's reason for keeping the seriousness of her financial situation to herself was due to any sophisticated strategy on her part. More than likely, her reasons were much more personal.

"You're still trying to protect him, aren't you?"

"I have to," she returned, thinking that Dave, of all people, should appreciate that. "All that really mattered to Ted was what other people thought of his accomplishments. You know that. He worked so hard to prove himself... to be the best, to have the respect of his peers. He had that respect, and that's what I want to protect for him."

"Why?"

To anyone else she would have said, "Because I loved him," and let it go at that, since she'd never admitted to anyone that her marriage hadn't been quite the fairy tale so many people believed it had. But Meg hadn't loved Ted for a long time. She suspected Dave was shrewd enough to recognize any shading of the truth. "I was his wife," she said to the darkening sea. "I'm carrying his child."

Seconds passed, silent but not strained. It was the night air that caused her eyes to sting, or so she told herself as she blinked to ease the burning.

"Were you happy with him, Meg?"

"I wasn't unhappy."

"Did you ever want more?"

"Sometimes. Lots of times," she corrected, sighing softly. "I think more than anything, though, I wanted him to want me. To need me." She raised her hand to brush the blowing curls from her cheek. The motion was unconscious, and her thoughts were far away as she stared out into the gathering darkness. "They say a marriage is only good if the people grow. We grew, Dave. We really did. But not together."

To Dave she seemed lost in some inaccessible place that defied intrusion. There was pain in her voice, but the pain sounded of guilt. He cursed himself for wanting her to feel when it was apparent that feeling hurt her so much.

"It was going to be different," she said. "We were going to start over. At least I'd thought we were."

"But he died before you got that chance," Dave supplied, trying to understand. He wished he hadn't brought any of this up.

"He never really took it."

"What do you mean?"

She didn't answer until she'd watched the red light of an airplane disappear into the night. When she did reply, her voice sounded a bit husky. "I didn't even know he'd gone sailing."

The phrase was spoken so simply that it was a moment before Dave realized how much she'd just told him about the state of her marriage. It was more than he'd wanted to know.

How empty it must have been for her, he thought. Before he could think better of it, his hand curved over her shoulder.

Meg felt the touch of his fingers and obeyed the gentle pressure he exerted to turn her toward him. She didn't bother to question what she did. She simply stepped into his arms and let herself absorb the comfort he offered.

With her eyes closed, she stood enveloped in his strength, letting herself imagine for a moment that her world hadn't shattered into a million tiny fragments—and that somehow, when she let herself acknowledge again that it had, she'd know how to pick up the pieces.

Chapter Four

Meg sat quietly in a red leather wing chair, one of two positioned in front of a fastidiously neat mahogany desk. Rich dark paneling served as a backdrop for the ornately framed oil paintings that hung on the far wall, and heavy damask draperies bracketed a set of tall windows. Beside her was a row of low polished-wood file cabinets. The decor, Meg supposed, was intended to give an impression of staid solidity, a perfectly logical image for the Inter-Pacific Bank to want to convey. Even the man behind the desk, Mr. Quentin W. Caldwell, seemed the product of design. His compact frame was fitted into a three-piece pin-striped suit, complete with gold pocket watch and chain. His rather thin brown hair was conservatively cut, and he wore small wire-rimmed glasses, which he peered over as he steepled his fingers.

Staid solidity. The impression was definitely there, along with a hint of intimidation Mr. Caldwell no doubt intended. But it was Dave's air of quiet authority that permeated the atmosphere and diluted the banker's effectiveness. Mr. Caldwell's subtle attempts to assert his dominance over the meeting hadn't gone well, and Meg could tell he didn't appreciate Dave's silent but powerful presence.

Once he'd learned that the prominent Mr. David Elliott wasn't there on behalf of an investor who wanted to take the doomed property off the bank's hands, he'd made it clear that the loan on the project in La Jolla was a matter strictly between Mrs. Reese and the bank. Dave made it equally clear that if Mrs. Reese wanted him to leave, he would. Meg, of course, wanted him right where he was, a circumstance Mr. Caldwell could do nothing about. He did, however, speak only to Meg as he outlined the bank's position on the loan, which was pretty well as unyielding as Dave had told her it would be. At the moment, though, Mr. Caldwell was on the phone, impatient for the information his secretary was to have brought him before Meg and Dave had arrived.

Meg glanced toward Dave, wanting some kind of reassurance that this would be over soon. However, his attention was focused on the toes of his brown Italian-leather shoes.

He occupied the chair beside her, his long legs stretched out and crossed at the ankle. In deference to the warm weather, he'd abandoned his customary business suit in favor of a linen sport jacket and slacks, and he seemed as at ease in the stuffy and sedate surroundings as he'd been in the starkly modern ones of the management company they'd left an hour ago. Meg looked at her wedding band, twisting it around her finger. Her experience at the management office had been much more pleasant.

Her rental property, which consisted of two thirty-unit apartment buildings and several small duplexes, was now in the hands of Four Seasons Management. Bob Hastings, the

company's owner and a personal friend of Dave's, had
promised to contact the resident building managers that day
to advise them of the change in reporting procedures and to
check on the rent deposits for the last three months. When
Dave had looked over the statements for the apartment bank
accounts—to which the resident managers deposited the
rents—one set of figures had seemed short. Since the funds
to pay the mortgages on the buildings came from those accounts, the matter had to be taken care of as soon as possible. The last thing she needed was to fall any farther behind
on those payments.

Meg had felt neither relief nor concern when she and Dave
had left Bob's office. None of what they'd spoken about felt
relevant yet. She'd known she owned things with Ted, but
because he'd moved their investments around so much, she
hadn't been aware of exactly what those things were. She felt
that same sense of disassociation now. She'd never seen the
shopping mall Ted had wanted to build so badly, so she
couldn't relate to it as something tangible. She had, however, been aware of the project. Her signature on the loan
papers attested to that.

Clearing his throat as he replaced the receiver, Quentin
Caldwell glanced expectantly toward the door to his left. It
opened immediately. A young and obviously flustered
woman hurriedly deposited a sheet of paper on his desk,
then departed just as quickly.

"Sorry for the interruption," Caldwell said, appearing
more satisfied than apologetic as he quickly glanced at the
sheet.

Taking her cue from Dave, Meg didn't acknowledge the
shallow apology. Considering that the interruption appeared to have provided him with something that put a very
unholy gleam in his eyes, she certainly wasn't going to say,
"That's all right."

"It appears that you have some income property in Los Angeles. The Windmill Apartments and Twin Palms Townhouses," he went on, still studying the page. "Our title check shows several other deeds in the name of you and your late husband. Odd," he mumbled to himself. "We didn't know about them when this loan was approved."

Before Meg could ask what he was talking about and why he had a list of her holdings, she became aware that Dave had reached over and very calmly touched her arm. Just as unhurriedly he withdrew his hand, keeping his eyes on the little man behind the desk. Dave was telling her not to say anything yet.

She was beginning to learn that there were times when silence could be a subtle form of control.

Caldwell obviously expected her to say something. He had the look of someone with a swift reply prepared. When she said nothing, he seemed to suffer a moment's disappointment. Then he quickly cleared his throat. "The checking account you have with us here has a balance of eleven dollars and three cents," he informed her. "That account, I believe, was the one used to disburse funds from our loan to the contractors and suppliers employed on the mall project. Mr. Reese had at one time indicated that he'd be opening a savings account, but our records fail to show that ever being done." He tapped the corner of the page against his desk. "You don't use this bank for your rent deposits, do you?"

Her soft "No," sounded a bit reluctant, but not because she was unsure of her response. Her hesitation was due to the distinctly unsettling feeling that somehow she was trapping herself.

"Where do you have those accounts?"

"The Union Bank and Trust."

"Does that institution have any interest in the complexes themselves?"

"I . . . I don't think so," she replied, turning to Dave for confirmation.

His expression was completely devoid of any helpful reaction to the conversation. All she got from him was the slow shake of his head, which Caldwell didn't see. He was too busy writing down "UB & T" and putting a big black line under it.

"As I've indicated, Mrs. Reese," he continued, peering over his glasses at her again. "When a project we're financing is no longer viable, due to cost overruns or labor problems or the kind of unfortunate circumstance you've found yourself in where the principal partner is—" he lowered his voice ever so respectfully "—deceased, then we have no choice but to minimize our losses as best we can.

"But we're not without heart," he hastened to assure her with an unctuous smile that threatened to revive her morning sickness. "It shouldn't be any problem for you to move those accounts from Union Bank to ours. In fact, we'll take care of it for you. All you'll have to do is sign a couple of forms and you can consider it done." He made the gesture sound quite magnanimous, and he looked every bit as impressed with his generosity as he apparently expected her to be. "After that, I believe I can get the loan review board to hold off calling the loan for another six months. That should give you time to find a buyer for the project."

So far, Dave had kept out of the discussion, offering Meg his support simply by being there. She didn't realize how much his presence nettled Caldwell until Dave leaned toward her and said, "You don't want to do that, Meg."

The banker seemed to understand the reason for that advice, and immediately went on the defensive. Meg, who was marveling at Dave's rather hard expression and Caldwell's sudden high color, looked from one man to the other.

For the past several minutes she'd had the awful feeling that the bank wasn't going to give her enough time to straighten things out. Dave's inscrutable expression had seemed to indicate that he didn't share her concern. Now, having heard the offer, Meg actually felt relieved, but Dave wasn't looking particularly pleased. What, she wondered, had she missed? She saw nothing wrong with the proposition Caldwell had offered. It didn't make any difference to her which bank the rents were deposited to, and if moving them to this one would buy her more time to sell the property and possibly recover some of her own money from it, then what was wrong with that?

When Dave didn't explain, she turned to Mr. Caldwell again. His agitation didn't make any sense, either. He also refused to look anywhere but at her. "The transfer of those accounts is the only way we will consider any kind of an extension," he informed her flatly. "The alternative is that the loan is immediately declared delinquent. We will then file suit to repossess the property and obtain judgment against you for the deficiency. I understand your home is for sale. It would be a shame for you to have to give up your equity by having a judgment lien attached to it."

To her credit, Meg didn't allow her composure to slip. She'd been ready for a hard line, but she certainly hadn't been prepared for such an ultimatum. Certainly not from Mr. Caldwell, who'd been so nice to her on the phone.

"That would be a shame," she agreed, her reasonable tone bringing a thin smile to Dave's lips. "When do you need my answer?"

Mr. Caldwell folded his hands on the gleaming surface of his desk. He'd obviously expected something other than her composed and rather placid response. Capitulation, perhaps? Or possibly a touch of hysteria? "I believe ten days is quite generous, considering the time that's passed on this already. I'd advise you to consider transferring your accounts, despite whatever advice you'll receive to the contrary, Mrs. Reese." The oblique reference to Dave didn't go unnoticed. "We'd much rather work with you than against you, but we can't go giving away hundreds of thousands of dollars—even to attractive young widows such as yourself."

Meg rose gracefully, not even aware that Dave had stood with her or that his hand hovered protectively at the small of her back as she turned to the door. She didn't understand any of this, but she knew the importance of a dignified exit.

The roundness protruding against the front of her neatly pleated navy maternity dress made her carriage no less regal than usual. The public always saw her as poised and assured. What they were really seeing was a well-rehearsed act. The fact that she carried it off so well just then prompted a sense of satisfaction in knowing that Mr. Caldwell hadn't been pleased with their meeting's outcome.

Satisfaction was actually the least of what she felt. But as she and Dave joined a young man with a mail cart in the elevator, that small sense of satisfaction was enough to keep her from thinking about her more unpleasant sensations. Irritation. Panic. Confusion.

Definitely confusion.

"I know something went wrong," she said when they reached the ground floor. "Would you please tell me what?"

"Nothing went wrong, Meg. You just didn't do what he expected." There was approval in Dave's tone, and she liked that. Just as she liked the way his hand rested lightly on her back as they headed for the exit. His stabilizing touch was something she welcomed. It kept her from feeling as if she were in this all alone. "It's obvious enough he didn't think you had any idea what was going on, and my being there wasn't in his game plan. Somehow I got the feeling I kind of cramped his style."

Dave's wry remark was a deliberate understatement. He knew that if he hadn't been there, Caldwell would have done everything short of getting down on his knees to get Meg to sign those account transfers. Such extremes wouldn't have been necessary, though the strategy he'd chosen would have worked just fine. He'd made his sly suggestion sound reasonable, and Meg, who barely knew enough to qualify as a novice at this point, wouldn't even have realized what she'd done.

"It's like hunting doves in a cage," he muttered. She wouldn't have had a prayer.

"What did you say?"

"That I don't like your banker's tactics," Dave said more audibly, nudging her ahead of him.

"Well, he did give me ten more days."

"He gave you those ten days because he had to," Dave pointedly informed her. "Not out of the goodness of his heart. You've probably got a ten-day notice provision in the agreement. Don't be surprised if you get it in writing tomorrow."

The glass doors parted with a whoosh. Before they were through them, he was shaking a cigarette from a half-empty pack. By the time they reached the first of the six steps leading to a large bench-encircled fountain and on to the multistory parking lot, a cigarette was between his lips and he'd pulled his lighter out of the pocket of his slacks. "When you get home this afternoon, I think you should go through the loan agreement on this." Flame touched tobacco, and a pale whiff of smoke drifted off behind him. "You've got an offset clause in there that allows them to apply any moneys on deposit with them to any outstanding debt. I remember reading that, but I don't remember whether they've already got a security interest in the rental income. Do you remember anything about an assignment of rents? Nah," he went on, more to himself than to her, which was fine because she didn't know what he was talking about anyway, "Caldwell would have been sure to mention that if they did."

If you say so, she said to herself. She had no idea whether Caldwell would have done that or not, and she didn't even try to figure it out. She thought she was doing well to understand the part about the bank using the apartment rent money to apply to the construction loan.

"Can they do that? Take money out of another account like that?"

He gave a slight shrug, taking her elbow as they descended the steps. "You told 'em they could."

Meg was aware of his light grip on her arm, the gentle pressure of his palm against her skin. As it had been when he'd guided her outside, his touch was unassuming, polite. But it mattered somehow. Just as it had mattered when he'd held her for those few moments last night.

That thought was just a nebulous observation floating in the back of her mind. At the front of her mind was what Dave had just said. Knowing she would have recalled such a statement, she prepared to tell him she'd done nothing of the sort.

"In the contract you signed," he said, just as she opened her mouth. An instant later she closed it, dismay replacing certainty. "You didn't even read it, did you?"

The reproach and disappointment shading his flat question told her he already knew she hadn't. She wasn't the only wife who'd always signed whatever her husband had asked her to, but Meg knew that such a defense wouldn't hold much water with Dave. The man would listen to reason, but he wouldn't tolerate excuses. "I trusted Ted," she told him. To her that was reason enough.

"Of course you did." Dave had no desire to discuss Ted at the moment, and he felt strangely unwilling to point out how foolish he thought that blind trust of Meg's had been—

or how lucky Ted had been to receive that kind of faith. "From now on, though, don't sign anything until you've read it and understood every word. Got it?"

She had no intention of signing anything that she didn't show to Dave first. Keeping that assurance to herself, she mumbled a dutiful "Yes, sir," and silently thanked him for not giving her a lecture on the subject. After everything they'd gone over last night and their meetings this morning, there were so many details on her mind that she simply couldn't have assimilated any more information.

They'd reached the huge gray concrete fountain. Tall and tiered, its cascading water muted the conversations of the half-dozen office workers who occupied the bench on the far side. A couple of them were eating sandwiches from brown paper bags; others were reading books or papers. Meg expected to walk right on past them. Dave, however, had come to a halt when he'd released her arm, and he was scowling at her through the stream of smoke he'd just exhaled.

"Do you understand why you shouldn't move those accounts?"

"No, but you seem to think it's a bad idea. That's good enough for me."

At any other time, Dave would have felt pleasure at the trust that implied. But it was what prompted that trust that tempered his ego's reaction. The more time he spent with Meg, the more convinced he was of her intelligence. But her lack of aggressiveness was going to destroy her.

Not only was she failing to understand what Caldwell had tried to pull a while ago, she hadn't even asked Dave to explain why he thought the proposal was such a lousy deal. She'd simply given in to what she perceived as his authority.

"No, Megan." He all but groaned as he stuffed his cigarette into a sand-filled pot behind him. A touch more exasperated than he wanted to be, he put his hands on her shoulders and gave them a gentle squeeze. He'd told her he'd try to be patient. That was why he didn't shake her. "This isn't going to work unless you understand. You can't understand unless you ask questions. The whole purpose of my helping you isn't to have you depend on my judgments. It's to have you depend on your own. You can't do that unless you know what's going on."

He was getting that tutorish look again. The one that drew his eyebrows together and made his blue eyes seem so very dark. The problem was that the more intense his expression became, the more aware she became of how much character was carved into the lines of his face. With his hands resting on her shoulders, his head bent to look down at her, she was also aware of what countless other women had no doubt noticed. He was a man who could make a woman feel small and soft and feminine simply by standing beside her.

"Well?" she prompted him, letting herself absorb the experience. It seemed harmless enough. "Are you going to stand there frowning at me, or are you going to explain what *is* going on?"

He must have known she was teasing, because she could see his amusement. Then suddenly the smile in his eyes was gone, and Meg had the distinct impression that he didn't like what he was about to say. For someone who seemed bent on delivering a dissertation, Dave became awfully quiet.

Dave was definitely not too crazy about what he had to tell her, but that wasn't why he'd gone silent. He'd deliberately stilled himself to keep from doing something stupid—such as pulling her into his arms.

That thought usually occurred when he wasn't in a position to do anything about it, but now was the perfect moment. She stood only a foot away, and he felt no resistance beneath his hands. It amazed him that she so freely allowed his touch, though he had to admit that what contact he'd managed had been far from intimate. He wished he could say the same for his thoughts. They'd been playing pure havoc with his sleep.

Her teasing had faded, and her green eyes were somber now as she studied his face. "Dave? What is it?"

He could tell that his silence had frightened her. Hard telling how she'd have reacted to it if she'd known he was wondering how her lips would feel against his naked chest instead of thinking about the bank's little proposal.

Stepping back, he let his hands slip from her shoulders. When they were safely in his pockets, he was once again in control. Meg was the only woman he'd ever known who could so completely destroy his concentration.

"I'm just trying to figure out how to explain this and have it make sense," he told her, because that was what he was doing at the moment. Having decided on an approach, he wasted no time implementing it. The picture he was about to present was not pretty, and there was no point in pretending it was.

"The bank has offered you six months in exchange for a couple of accounts. That sounds harmless enough, but it isn't. You're already in default under the terms of the loan agreement, and once they get the accounts there's nothing to stop them from calling the loan due and payable. Which," he added when she started to say that that was hardly fair, "means that they pick up twenty or thirty grand to apply to the loan by taking the funds in your accounts prior to foreclosing on you."

"But what about the six months they promised?"

"They didn't promise anything. Caldwell said he'd talk to the board *after* you signed the account transfers, remember? Anyway," he went on before she could respond, "once they've taken that money you're out at least a month's worth of receipts, which means you can't make the mortgage or insurance payments on the apartments or pay the resident managers. You've got two pieces of property that could potentially give you enough cash to make up those payments. The south-end property, which isn't ready to sell because of the zoning, and possibly your house."

He crossed his arms over his chest. Meg would have once thought the posture arrogant. Now she knew that he was only involved in what he was saying, too occupied with complexities to be conscious of his mannerisms. That was what gave him an edge over his opponents. They had to concentrate on what came naturally to him.

"But even if your house or the south-end land sells before the holder of the apartment mortgages starts screaming about a missed payment and your managers walk out and the insurance gets canceled, it won't do you any good because the bank will have a judgment against you for thirty times that much, and every other piece of property you own will also have a lien against it. Their legal department probably has those papers ready to file with the court right now. It's like a little snowball that starts rolling down a hill, Meg. Once it starts, it just keeps getting bigger and bigger and—"

She held up her hand. She didn't need his analogy. Even if she didn't quite comprehend the details of the scenario he'd outlined, his meaning was clear. If she wasn't very careful, she'd lose everything. She might have started that snowball rolling a few minutes earlier—if Dave hadn't been there to stop her.

It took an enormous amount of knowledge to pull off the balancing act this kind of financial game required. Ted had known how to do it, and for years he'd continued to build what might have become quite an empire—if only he'd survived his attempts to create it. But she certainly didn't have that kind of savvy. What she did have was access to someone who was unselfish enough to show her how to keep from getting tangled up in the ropes. Just now, he'd kept her from hanging herself.

It wasn't until that very moment, as she stood there, barely conscious of the people and the noisy fountain and the bright sunshine, that she realized just how much she owed him.

"Oh, Dave." His name was little more than a whisper, a whisper made that much quieter by the rush of water beside her. She wanted so badly to put her arms around him. "You're doing so much for me, and I haven't even asked how I can repay you." It was so foreign to her nature not to acknowledge any type of kindness, let alone something of this magnitude. "What can I do? Is there even anything I can do?"

Since Dave's mind had been occupied with the logistics of a countermaneuver to Caldwell's proposition, it took him a moment to come up with an answer.

"As a matter of fact, there is." He was relieved to see the expectation that entered her eyes. It removed the anxiety that had been there only moments before. He didn't want her to feel bad because of him. "Do you remember the peanut-butter cookies you used to bake?"

Expectation was replaced by exasperation. "Come on, Dave," she said, struck again by the ease with which he minimized what he was doing for her. "I'm serious."

"So am I. I teach you what you need to know, and you keep me supplied with peanut-butter cookies."

She'd forgotten how he liked to eat. His mention of the cookies made her recall what he'd once done to a pot roast that she'd intended to serve for two meals. It was little enough to do for him, and being a bachelor, he might appreciate them.

Suddenly, she decided to ask him to dinner tomorrow night. One meal wouldn't make so much as a dent in the obligation she felt, but it was a place to start. It was also something she'd enjoy doing. It would be fun to spend a day in the kitchen again, and even nicer to have someone there who'd appreciate her efforts.

It was quite obvious to Dave that whatever had just occurred to Meg had pleased her enormously. Animation slipped into her smile, giving her features a brightness that hadn't been there for quite a while. He was rather surprised by the change and very curious about what had caused it. Just as she started to speak, though, a female voice intruded.

"David!" A striking platinum blonde strolled toward them. "What are you doing here? I've been trying to call you."

The woman's smile remained in place when she glanced at Meg, growing wider when she'd finished a once-over that somehow encompassed her wedding band and her obvious pregnancy in the blink of an eye. Meg knew that look—she'd been dismissed as no threat. She'd been guilty of subjecting other women to it herself.

"I left a message with your secretary," the woman said, turning back to Dave. Placing her hand on his lapel, she kissed him on the cheek. Meg couldn't help but notice that Dave's arm had automatically slipped around her back. "Did you get it?"

Under any other circumstances, Dave would have thought little of Susan's casually possessive greeting. Seeing the spirit drain from Meg's soft smile, though, and wishing she hadn't been interrupted, made him rather annoyed with Susan's presumption. But then, Susan had been presuming an awful lot lately.

Still, now was not the time to think about why he'd declined her invitation to go to Catalina last week or why he wasn't really looking forward to their date tomorrow.

Telling her that he hadn't received her message because he hadn't yet been to his office, he ended any further discussion by drawing Meg forward. He didn't like the way Susan seemed to be ignoring her. "Meg, this is Susan Hennessey. Susan," he went on, pretending not to notice her puzzled glance, "I'd like you to meet Megan Reese."

Susan, Meg quickly learned, was an old family friend, as well as an attorney with a firm whose offices were in the bank building behind them. She was on her way to a lunch meeting, then on to a hearing which, she told Meg with a grimace that did nothing to mar her very professional appearance, was bound to be an absolute bore. The woman was beautiful, apparently very sharp and obviously quite interested in Dave. She also appeared to have a date with him tomorrow evening.

"Call if you're going to be late," Susan said, going up on tiptoe to kiss him again—this time on the lips. "I can meet you at the restaurant."

When he nodded, she smiled at Meg again and hurried off through the thickening crowd. Judging from the number of people exiting the building, it had to be close to noon. Two young men brandishing briefcases—their badges of entrée into the business world—sauntered past, followed by a small swarm of men and women that quickly overtook them. Dave and Meg fell into step with everyone else, and Dave, making no mention at all of Susan, continued as if she hadn't shown up at all. "What were you going to say before?"

Meg didn't have to be reminded to know what he was referring to. She left the invitation unissued, though. "You'll get your cookies," she told him, and was trying to smile when he muttered a terse and quite succinct expletive.

Dave was positive that she hadn't been thinking about the cookies. Something else had brought that momentary vitality, and he wanted to know what it was. If only Susan hadn't shown up.

Aware that his thinking was as much a reaction to Susan's irritating possessiveness as to the fact that Meg wasn't leveling with him, he gave Meg a sheepish grin. Later, he'd think about Susan and his relationship with her, which his family insisted on encouraging. Meg was more important right now. She was staring up at him as if he'd just grown antlers.

"Sorry," he mumbled. "I just remembered I've got a one-o'clock meeting." He hadn't actually forgotten the meeting, but that was the only thing he could think of to excuse his language a moment ago. "Why don't you wait here while I run over to the parking garage? I'll bring the car down and meet you on the corner."

"I told you I should have brought my own car."

"Maybe next time I'll listen." He grinned as he took off. "But don't count on it."

Meg smiled back at him, then stole a glance in the other direction. Susan stood at the crosswalk waiting for the pedestrian light to change. Her long jacket, with its fashionably squared shoulders and matching pencil-slim skirt, was a style Meg herself would have worn up until a couple of months ago. And her hair, while its shining pale color was as far removed from black as one could get, was worn in nearly the same casually tousled style Meg preferred. She was probably even right around the same age. Certainly no older than thirty. Yet she had an air of confidence, a kind of sureness about her, that Meg never had felt.

As she thought about it—since she didn't have much else to do while she waited for Dave—it occurred to Meg that every woman she'd ever seen Dave with had that quality. Seeing Dave with Susan just now had made her realize how naive she was being. Why would he want to have dinner with her when he had a girlfriend? How silly to think he'd enjoy another evening with her when he could be doing heaven only knew what with someone like Susan.

She didn't know why that thought suddenly made her feel so terribly lonely.

Chapter Five

Meg stood by her front door, her hand at the base of her throat as she listened to her realtor's car pull out of the drive. She probably looked like an idiot standing there all alone with a smile plastered on her face. She didn't care. She'd just sold the house—and most of the furniture.

"I can't believe it," she whispered to herself. Amazement was accompanied by a strangled laugh. "I really can't believe it," she repeated, looking again at the copy of the purchase money agreement she held. The long goldenrod-colored sheet with all the signatures on it was tangible enough. It was just taking a moment for the reality it represented to sink in.

A few days earlier, Norma, her realtor, had called to tell Meg she had a couple who were very interested in buying her home and to keep her fingers crossed. Since Norma had called the week before with the same news but for a different prospect, Meg hadn't let herself get too excited. It was

better not to anticipate. That way, when something didn't
work out, there was less disappointment. Besides, a few
other matters had required her attention lately.

Annie had found a printer who'd agreed to do the charity ball's posters for free provided he could have the artwork by the end of the week. July was apparently his slow
month. That had meant Meg had to put aside her study of
Winning through Negotiation and *Real Estate: The Fun Way
to Make Money* and create the two-by-three foot charcoal
sketch she'd delivered to Mr. Neufbaum of Neufbaum's
Print and Office Supplies yesterday. She hadn't been particularly pleased with the result, but Annie had liked it.

Yet Meg wasn't remembering yesterday's events, nor was
she thinking three days ahead to her next meeting with
Quentin Caldwell. At that moment, she was simply feeling
a little numb as she stared beyond the tiled entry into the
high-ceilinged living room. Norma had said it wasn't the
house so much as what Meg had done with it that had
cinched the sale.

The first thing a person noticed when they entered
through the double doors and turned from the ten-foot
arched mirror in front of them was the baby grand piano at
the far end of the living room. Ted had bought it for Meg's
birthday a few years ago—after learning that Joe Paulson
had bestowed one upon his wife the month before. It sat
beneath a chandelier. The piano was ebony lacquer, as were
the occasional tables placed strategically beside or in front
of the various pieces of oyster-colored overstuffed furniture. A two-foot-wide strip of black bordered the pale cream
carpet.

Striking. That was the only way to describe a room that
was completely black-and-white except for an enormous
bouquet of red silk poppies in the crystal bowl on the coffee table. The effect of positive and negative interrupted by

a splash of brilliant color was exactly as Meg had intended. She'd loved every minute she'd spent decorating her home.

Drawing her fingers through her hair, she looked once more at the paper she held. Very soon the majority of the things in that room and the rest of the rooms in the house wouldn't be hers any longer. Only the personal items—pictures of family, gifts from friends—could she take with her. She'd never thought of it before, but leaving this house would be a rite of passage. A transition from an old life to a new one. She supposed she should feel a certain sadness, and at some point she probably would. But now she felt excited and happy and maybe just a little bit free. She felt like celebrating.

But a celebration for one—or one and a half, she thought with a wry glance at her increasing bulk—didn't sound like any fun at all. She could call Annie, but Annie and Larry were looking at wedding rings this afternoon. Chances were she wasn't back yet.

There was an answer at her parent's house, and since her brother Mark and his family were there for the day, she spent almost an hour listening to their congratulations, assuring them that she was feeling fine and catching up on what had happened with everyone in Springfield during the past week. She endured her mother's repeated admonitions to eat properly and get enough rest and exercise, teasingly telling her she was only pregnant, not recovering from a major illness. At that point her father cut in to ask how her car was running. Since he was a couple of thousand miles away, there wasn't a thing he could do even if there were a problem, but everyone in the family had his or her area of concern. It was a typical call, and Meg always found it satisfying to touch bases with her family. But within minutes of hanging up, she was feeling oddly restless.

She wanted to *do* something. And not by herself.

She flipped through her address book, only to close it the minute she realized whose telephone number she was looking up. She'd stopped at the *E*s. Lucy Bevins was nearly always available to go to lunch. Jennifer O'Malley had told her dozens of times to call whenever she felt like getting together. So why had she thought only of Dave?

Because he's the only one who can appreciate the monetary significance of the sale, she told herself—and groaned when she realized she was beginning to think the way Dave talked. She'd go ahead and call him just to tell him her news. He was probably busy today, anyway.

Suspicion confirmed. She got his answering machine.

"This is Dave Elliott. I'm not available to take your call at the moment. If you'll leave your name and number at the tone, I'll get back to you as soon as possible." Three seconds later came an electronic beep.

"Dave?" she began, though she knew she was talking to a mechanical device. "It's Meg. I just wanted to let you know I sold the house. And the furniture, too. Now I won't have to call the auction place you told—"

A barely audible click preceded an exuberant "Hey, that's terrific!"

Meg blinked at the receiver. Leave it to Dave to have an answering machine programmed to deliver an appropriate response.

"Meg? You there?"

"Dave? Is that you?"

His chuckle was deep and throaty. "Yeah, it's me. I had the machine on because I was working."

"Oh, I didn't mean to disturb—"

"You didn't disturb me," he cut in. "I picked the phone up when I heard it was you. Congratulations."

It perplexed her a little to discover that she didn't want to let him go even though, since he was busy, she knew she should. She wanted to tell him all about the terms of the sale. The buyers wanted to close quickly because they'd been living in a hotel since the husband's company had transferred them here last month. She also wanted to tell him that she'd bought the peanut butter to make his cookies, and to ask when she could bring them to him. Instead, she murmured her thanks and said, "Well, I'd better let you get back to work. Will I see you before Wednesday?" Wednesday was her meeting with Caldwell. Dave had said he'd get together with her before then to figure out how to respond to the bank's ultimatum.

"You can see me this afternoon if you'll let me buy you an ice cream cone."

"Ice cream?" she repeated, feeling herself smile.

"Champagne would actually be more appropriate to commemorate this event, but ice cream is better for a woman in your condition. Why don't I drive over, and we can walk down to Swensen's? The exercise wouldn't hurt you."

"I thought you were working."

"I just finished."

"Liar."

"Okay, so I'm taking a break. It will be here tomorrow. See you in half an hour."

As Meg replaced the receiver, she felt almost certain that Dave had known she wanted to get out for a while. He'd even put aside his work for her.

That thoughtfulness made Meg overlook the way he'd so firmly announced how they'd celebrate her sale. She knew that walking was good exercise. That was part of the reason she was down on the beach nearly every day. She also knew that alcohol wasn't good for her baby and was avoiding it during her pregnancy. Dave, though, kept informing her of how she should take care of herself and what she should and shouldn't do, as if he had a vested interest in her offspring.

That's just Dave, she concluded, prepared to excuse another of the faults she'd once found so unforgivable. He'd always been pretty opinionated—though she had noticed how carefully he seemed to consider both sides of an argument—and it had become more obvious than ever that he was accustomed to having his way.

He's also going to be here in a few minutes, she reminded herself, not at all sure why she felt so pleased at the prospect of an ice cream cone. She hurried up the stairs to her bedroom. What she was wearing—a pale coral smock with white bands at the sleeves and hem, and white shorts—was fine. It was her hair that needed attention. She had it wound up in a knot. Now she wanted the wavy shoulder-length curls down and free.

She should have left her hair up.

An hour later she sat on a bench outside Swensen's, holding her hair back with one hand to keep the breeze from blowing it onto her ice cream. She licked the drips from her cone as she waited for Dave to come out. As was typical on weekends, the combination ice cream parlor and restaurant was jammed with locals and tourists. After running into several elbows, Dave had suggested she wait outside while he paid. The elderly woman sitting beside her was doing the same thing—waiting for her husband to fight his way to the cash register while the warm breeze melted her marshmallow-and-caramel sundae.

"With nuts," the silver-haired lady went on to explain, having already identified the contents of her paper dish to Meg. Her voice dropped secretively, and she leaned closer. The scent of roses clung to her blue-and-gray flowered dress. "I'm not supposed to eat them. But this is our vacation, so I'm indulging. There's not that many on here, anyway." She tasted the forbidden fruit—or rather nuts. Seeming satisfied with the quality, if not the quantity, she leaned back to study the view across the street.

Meg turned her smile to her cone and, content with her scoop of chocolate, did the same.

The Coast Highway in Laguna was an ordinary multi-lane street, as it was in many of the cities and towns it passed through between Rockport and Capistrano. On the other side was a huge, grassy park area, and beyond that, forming a slight crescent, were the sand and the sea. Shops, restaurants and art galleries stretched in both directions, and people wandered everywhere. It was the children who captured Meg's attention, the little ones who bobbed by on stubby little legs, clung to an adult's outstretched hand or were carried on a daddy's shoulders. Their innocent faces held so many emotions: delight, curiosity and, as with the little boy whose sister wouldn't give him a pail, frustration.

When her baby was old enough, Meg told herself as she caught another drip, she'd bring him here. She had no idea what would happen to them between now and then, but she wasn't going to let herself think of that right now. She'd think only of the two of them and how she'd buy him ice cream cones and they'd wade in the ocean and play in the sand.

A faint smile touched her lips. With kids it was more like eat the sand and play with the ice cream, but she wouldn't mind that. Ever since she could remember, Meg had adored children and had wanted dozens of her own. Fortunately, with maturity had come a certain sense of practicality. The dozens had decreased to three or four, but the desire had grown stronger than ever. She'd just managed to repress it—until the need could no longer be denied and Ted had finally realized he was losing her.

That recollection was shoved to the back of her mind. If it hadn't been for the promises he'd made then, she wouldn't be pregnant now. But she didn't want to think about those broken promises or about all the others that had preceded them.

The woman beside Meg sighed deeply. "This weather sure is lovely."

"Yes, it is," Meg agreed. The weather. That she could think about. "It's perfect."

"Darn near. We're from Yuma. Over in Arizona, you know," she added, just in case Meg hadn't heard of the place. "It's so hot over there this time of year you can't breathe. Heard on the news yesterday that it was a hundred and sixteen. I keep telling Lester we ought to sell and move over here somewhere, but he just keeps dragging his feet." She punched her spoon into her bowl so that it stood straight up, and glanced at Meg over the top of her rimless glasses. "Where are you from, honey?"

Meg had no qualms at all about carrying on a conversation with this friendly little woman. After all, they'd already revealed their favorite flavors of ice cream to each other, so it was almost as if they were on intimate terms. "About a ten-minute walk from here," she replied. The lady seemed to want to talk, so she asked, "Why doesn't Lester want to move?"

"Oh, he'd die before admitting it, but the thought of uprooting scares him silly. He's never lived anyplace else, you see. It's not easy leaving behind everything that's familiar to you and starting over again. That's Lester, though. Me, now, I like trying something new. I had no idea what I was going to do when my sister and I left Maryland back in 1930. Didn't know what I was going to do when I left her in Chicago in 1934 to come out this way, either. But it all worked out just fine. Things always have a way of doing that, you know...even if we ain't got a clue as to how it's going to do it at the time." Extracting her spoon, she eyed the dripping caramel. "When you due, honey?"

Thinking the woman's philosophy well worth remembering, though she really identified better with poor Lester's plight, Meg pulled back the strands of hair the breeze had blown across her face. "In about three months," she returned, and was wondering if it would be rude of her to ask what had prompted all those moves when the woman gave her an assessing glance.

"This your first?"

At Meg's nod, she appeared satisfied. "Thought so," she said without elaboration. "Lester and I have two. Brats, both of them. Enid retired from the school district last year, and all she can do is complain about her retirement pay. Lester, Jr., hit his midlife crisis just a couple days shy of his fifty-ninth birthday and took off with the secretary down at the lumberyard. Now, most men go through that in their forties, you know, but not Junior." She gave her head a disgusted shake and plowed into her sundae again. "That boy always was slow."

Since the woman was now quite involved with her marshmallow-and-caramel concoction, Meg was left with nothing to do but repress a grin while trying not to choke. Thus occupied, she didn't notice Dave until he was right in front of her.

"Are you okay?"

His question was no doubt prompted by her somewhat pinched expression. Clearing her throat, she straightened her shoulders and tried to look dignified. The attempt probably would have worked if she could have kept the corners of her mouth from turning up. "I'm just fine. Why?" The last thing she wanted to do was offend the dear lady on her left by laughing.

For a moment, Dave seemed to doubt her response. Then, apparently deciding she knew what she was talking about, he held out his hand to help her up.

"Take it easy with those nuts," she said to her bench companion.

She received a smile and a wink in response. Dave merited only a glance. The woman spoke to him, but her words were directed to her paper bowl. "You take care of your wife now, sonny. She's a real nice little girl. Most of you young 'uns pay no mind to us old folk. She listens. Could stand some meat on her bones, though. Feed her more. She needs fattening up."

Out of the corner of his eye, Dave saw Meg's mouth open. But before she could correct the woman's erroneous assumption, he said, "I'm working on it." He put a proprietary hand on Meg's shoulder. Turning her around, he said, "Eat," and bestowing a polite smile on the woman on the bench, escorted Meg down the sidewalk.

"Friend of yours?"

"I just met her. She was waiting for her husband." The word *too* almost slipped out, but Meg caught it. She was already a bit puzzled by Dave's behavior. She didn't want to have to start wondering about her own.

Her puzzlement showed. Twice, as they stood with the other pedestrians waiting for the light to change, Dave caught Meg looking up at him. And twice she immediately glanced away when he turned to her. He still caught her open curiosity.

"Something the matter?" He posed the question in the blandest of tones, then took a bite of his ice cream.

Was he smiling to himself? "No," she told him. "Everything's fine." I guess, she thought.

A few seconds later, they'd crossed the street. By then Meg had concluded that what Dave had done wasn't really all that odd after all. His actions had merely been practical. The woman had made an understandable mistake in thinking that Dave was her husband. It had just been simpler to let the error stand. But Dave had stepped into the role so easily it had surprised her. Her feelings about that were actually more cause for concern, but there wasn't time to consider that at the moment. Dave wanted to know what she'd meant when she'd warned the woman about the nuts, so she had to tell him all about her conversation with the little lady from Yuma, Arizona.

Engaged in that easy dialogue, they dodged the surfboards carried on the heads of teenagers and avoided the Frisbees which seemed invariably to be followed by a loping dog. The grassy park area gave way to sand, and having finished their cones and discarded their napkins in the trash, they abandoned their shoes.

"I can't remember the last time I did this." Tennis shoes dangling from his left hand, Dave waited while Meg balanced herself against him and pulled off her sandals. "About all I ever do on the beach anymore is run."

Meg wanted to ask if he brought Susan down here at sunset, or later for a moonlight stroll. She wasn't sure she really wanted to know, however, or why she preferred ignorance.

Falling into step beside him as they headed to the water's edge, she decided she might as well ask. After all, they had to talk about something. "Don't you ever bring Susan down here?"

He shot her a quizzical glance, but she missed it. She was too busy pretending nonchalance.

"Susan isn't overly fond of sand."

"It does have a tendency to get into everything."

"I don't think she'd know. She won't go near it."

Meg gave a skeptical little laugh. "I can't imagine you dating someone who isn't as crazy about the ocean as you are . . . or were," she corrected, thinking she might have assumed too much. It was entirely possible that he'd tired of the sports that had once taken up his and Ted's weekends and vacations.

"Are," he confirmed, and promptly dropped any further reference to Susan. "I don't think there's anything quite like the feeling of freedom you can get from the sea. When I'm sailing, I don't think about anything else. And with diving there's even more freedom. It's a release."

"Release?" Ted had liked to dive, but he'd never spoken of it in such terms. And though she loved the water, she'd never cared to strap tanks on herself and go play with fish. "I'm not sure I understand what you mean."

"You know. Letting go." Dave's glance darted straight to the corner of her mouth. "Look back up here for a second."

Obediently she raised her head. A moment later, his fingers curved under her jaw and his thumb slid to the edge of her mouth.

"Ice cream," he explained, slowly wiping away the tiny dab. "It's like when you make love," he went on, seeming quite fascinated with her lower lip, though his tone remained bland. "You know that feeling of being totally involved? Of not being aware of anything beyond that moment? Everything is focused, and for however long it lasts, nothing else matters. Afterward, there's this kind of exhilaration. Exhaustion," he added with a chuckle, "but exhilaration, too. Release."

He pulled his hand away, and they resumed their pace. Absolutely nothing in his expression revealed the slightest interest in what he'd just done.

Not that he'd done anything. He'd simply removed the ice cream her napkin had missed. And he was talking about diving, Meg reminded herself. About descending underwater in a rubber suit with weights and regulators and all that stuff. The fact that he chose to compare the experience to lovemaking was something she really should overlook— especially since the idea of him being that "focused" was creating images she had absolutely no business considering. Dave was an extremely attractive man. His person in the nude would indeed be a sight to behold.

"Do you know what I mean now?"

"Yes," she replied, wishing he could have chosen a less graphic analogy. She also wished he'd worn something other than the blue muscle shirt that revealed his very tan stomach and the white cutoffs that clung to his hips and thighs. He was much easier to take in a business suit.

"Have you ever tried it?"

"Of course I have." She was pregnant, wasn't she?

"Really?" Dave sounded quite pleased all of a sudden. "When? Ted never mentioned it."

"Why would—? Oh, good grief," she groaned when she caught Dave's slightly wicked grin.

"Diving, Meg. I'm talking about diving."

"You're terrible."

"And you're kind of cute when you blush. I didn't think women did that anymore. Now where were we?"

"We were discussing your love affair with the sea," she reminded him. She liked it when he teased her. "And Susan's aversion to it. She's a friend of your family?"

If Dave regarded her curiosity as odd, he did nothing to betray that thought. Quite amiably he confirmed what Meg remembered from her introduction to Susan, and went on to tell her, "The Hennesseys and the Elliotts have known each other for years. My father and Kenneth Hennessey— that's her father—went to Stanford together."

"That's where Ted went to school," Meg said. When she saw the droll smile forming on Dave's mouth, she realized how unnecessary the comment had been.

"I know. That's where I met him. In fact," Dave went on, picking up a small gray shell as they walked, "my father met him before I did. Ted had been assigned as my roommate, and Dad insisted on talking to him alone before he'd let me move into the dorm. He wanted to be sure that Ted was the proper sort of person for me to associate with.''

"You're kidding.'' She'd never heard that before.

The shell was sent sailing out over the water. "Nope. Between my father and my mother, there wasn't a whole lot of room for making your own decisions or picking your own friends. Don't get me wrong. They're terrific people. But they had some very rigid ideas about raising kids. They've still got some very definite opinions about what I should do with my life,'' he added, thinking about the anything-but-subtle way they kept promoting Susan's various qualities. "But they've also realized that they can't plan my life for me anymore. I think my dropping out of law school had something to do with that.''

As they shuffled through the warm sand, then braced themselves against the chill water to trek along the edge of the surf, Meg thought she detected a rebellious note in Dave's voice. Recalling that she'd once wondered how he'd felt about being raised in a goal-oriented environment, she was fairly certain now that he'd resented it. "Why did you drop out?''

"I wanted to get my master's in business.''

"Were your parents upset?''

Dave's quiet "Very,'' had a definite ring of understatement. "I was breaking an Elliott family tradition. My great-grandfather was a barrister in England. My grandfather is retired from the District Court, and my father's a state Superior Court judge. The plan was that I'd join the firm my father and Ken Hennessey started. Susan's a junior partner in the firm's Newport office,'' he added. "She's always been more malleable than me.''

Meg wasn't interested in Susan at the moment, only in Dave and the amazing ease of their conversation. She'd always thought he'd be such a difficult man to get to know. "Why didn't you want to be a lawyer?''

"It's just not what I wanted," he replied, sounding as if he thought settling for less was an unpardonable sin.

"We can't all have exactly what we want" was her instinctive response. "Sometimes we have to think about the other people in our lives."

Dave glanced over at Meg and saw the same conviction in her face that he'd heard in her voice. It was just like her, he thought, to subscribe to the philosophy that others came first. There was an inherent flaw in that ideal, though. A selfless person had a tendency to get walked on, which in turn made him or her ineffectual. He was hardly an advocate of hedonism or unbridled selfishness, but he did want her to understand why he'd had to disappoint his parents.

"I care a great deal about my mother and father," he told her. "But being a lawyer was their dream, not mine. Since I was the one who had to live with myself, I figured I might as well like what I do for a living. I also refuse to get married just because they think it's something I should have done by now, or run for political office—which is my mother's latest notion."

Overlooking his statement about marriage because his tone hadn't invited any more questions, she watched him cup his hand around his lighter to guard the flame while he lit his cigarette. It was a little easier now to see why he felt so strongly about personal independence. Apparently he'd had precious little of it as a child.

Meg felt a major preconception she'd held about Dave fly away on the gentle breeze whipping around them. Earlier this morning, as she had many times in the past, she'd thought that Dave must be quite accustomed to getting his way. It hadn't occurred to her that he'd had to fight for it.

"I don't think you'd make a very good politician," she said teasingly, hoping to bring back his smile. "You're far too blunt most of the time."

Feigning superiority, he sent her a narrow glance and slipped his lighter into his pocket. "I'll have you know that I can be the epitome of tact when I need to be. Do you remember the first time you ever saw the ocean?"

"What?" she said with a light and puzzled laugh.

"Do you remember the first time you ever saw the ocean?" he repeated, then gave her the smile she'd hoped for. "That's a tactful change of subject, by the way... just in case you didn't recognize it. So," he prodded, "do you?"

She most definitely did. And while she related the story of her family's first trip to Florida—and the hurricane that had ruined it, since Dave wanted all the details—she and Dave covered almost a mile of beach.

The water rolled around their ankles, pulling the sand from beneath their feet as it drained back again. Above, wispy white clouds streaked through a pale blue sky. It was just this kind of calm that had so completely fascinated the nine-year-old Megan. She'd witnessed the fearsome destruction of the waves; then, with the sun, had come the soothing tranquillity of a peaceful sea. She'd been utterly captivated by the contrast.

And Dave found himself quite captivated with her. Her green eyes sparkled as she recalled how she and one of her brothers had come home from that vacation and shown all the kids in the neighborhood how to play hurricane. Her mother hadn't been overly thrilled when the men from the fire department had brought them back to the house after they'd unscrewed the nut on the fire hydrant, but the game, she told him, had been fun while it had lasted.

Dave knew the mischief in her eyes was there only because of a memory, but he liked the way it brightened her face. The wind teased her hair, and the sun scattered its ebony darkness with blue and silver. She was, at that moment, the lovely woman-child he'd first met. There was a guilelessness about her that had drawn him since the beginning—and, as he had since the beginning, he had to remind himself that she was off limits.

"Speaking of your family," he cut in after she'd gone silent, "what did they think about your news?"

"About the house? How did you know I'd even told them?"

"I just figured you would have."

There were times like these when it felt as if he'd always been there for her. She liked the fact that she could talk to him about things she didn't want to discuss with anyone else.

"They're happy about it," she told him, pressing her hand to the small of her back. "They all agree that a smaller place would be more practical. Mom doesn't like the idea that I don't have an apartment yet, but it shouldn't take that long to find one."

"Do they know about your financial situation?"

A gull sat perched on a rock just beyond the shoreline. With a great flap of his wings, he rose suddenly, Meg's gaze following his graceful flight. "Not really. I didn't want them to worry."

You don't want them to know how badly Ted screwed up, Dave thought. "I imagine they're pretty concerned as it is."

"Why do you say that?"

"I met your mother once, remember? When your family was here for Thanksgiving a few years ago." The light of recollection flashed in Meg's eyes, prompting him to continue. "She reminded me a little of my mother when she's around my sister. If my sister were in your position, Mom would be on the phone at least once a week to make sure she was taking care of herself. She did that with Jan anyway, and her husband was there. Not that being her husband counted for much when the kids were born," he added. "Mom took a leave of absence from the university and just sort of moved in and took over. She let Tom hold the baby, of course, but she wouldn't let *me* near the first one until he was a month old.''

As they continued along the beach, Meg couldn't help but think that a few months ago she couldn't possibly have reconciled the picture Dave created of himself with the one she'd had of him. Even now, knowing he wasn't the monster she'd made him out to be, it was hard to imagine this big, overwhelmingly masculine human being holding a tiny baby. That visual image was powerful. The emotional one was even more so. Strength and dependence. Toughness and vulnerability. Those contrasts were the type of elements she tried to capture in her art, the kind of counterpoints that balanced each other so beautifully on canvas.

Could any woman capture this man? she wondered, realizing she wasn't thinking about art anymore, but about the man himself.

The more she knew of him, the more of a stranger he became. The thought made sense somehow, but it was her reaction that caused her heart to pound as heavily as the surf that beat against the craggy rocks ahead.

She turned away from the smile in his eyes. She had no business being attracted to another man, yet she was most definitely attracted to Dave. It had only been four months since her husband had died, and though she hadn't really loved Ted, she owed him...what? The consideration he hadn't shown her?

It didn't matter that she couldn't come up with anything concrete at that moment. She was carrying Ted's child, which in itself was reason enough for Meg to set aside any attraction she felt for Dave. It wasn't that it was wrong. It just wasn't right. Besides, what she thought she felt toward Dave was probably only the result of her emotional and physical condition. The diving analogy he'd used hadn't helped matters much, either. She'd read somewhere that pregnant women often noticed feelings of heightened awareness, and that they also had a tendency to experience feelings of vulnerability and dependency. Under ideal circumstances, the child's father would be the beneficiary of those emotions. Under less-than-ideal circumstances, she thought wryly, the recipient was the father's best friend.

He was her friend, too. She absolutely couldn't let herself think of him any differently.

Even having come to that conclusion, she wasn't quite prepared for the warmth of his hand folding around hers. He'd never held her hand before. But as with any other time he'd touched her, he seemed to think nothing of it.

"Do you want to take the path or the stairs?" he asked, angling them out of the surf and onto the hard-packed sand.

"The path."

Her feet, she'd noticed, had developed the very unglamorous habit of swelling in the afternoons. They didn't hurt yet, but she didn't want to add more mileage than was necessary. The stairs were another quarter of a mile north. If they took them, they'd then have to backtrack.

Instead of zigzagging between the bleached tree trunks scattered above the shoreline, he led her up and over the smaller ones and skirted only those she couldn't step up on. Then they came to the driftwood that had washed up to the embankment.

"Terrific," she drawled, trying not to notice the friction of his skin when he slipped his fingers through hers. She slowed, but he pulled her forward.

"It's just a little log," he said, stopping when she did.

"David, that log's not little."

The path had been clear a few days ago, but they'd had several high tides lately, which explained why there was a three-foot-thick chunk of tree completely blocking the opening in the five-foot-high embankment. If she hadn't been pregnant, Meg wouldn't have been any more pleased with the prospect of climbing over it, but she wouldn't have hesitated. Six months along, she wasn't quite as agile as she had once been.

"I won't let you fall."

The timbre of his voice drew her eyes back to him, but she saw none of the quiet sincerity in his expression she'd heard in his voice. He was smiling at her, much as one would when indulging a perplexed child.

Certain she'd read more into those deliciously deep tones than could possibly be there, she gave him her most challenging look. It was the same one she'd been practicing to use on Caldwell. "How?"

"It's quite simple, really." He stepped behind her and put his hands on either side of her waist. "I just lift you up."

The instant her feet left the ground, she grabbed for the stubby limb sticking out of the trunk and scrambled to get a toehold on the gnarled wood. Hoisting herself the rest of the way, and still holding on to the limb for balance, she watched Dave jump up beside her. Before she could say a word, he'd landed on the other side. "Then," he said, reaching up under her arms, "I lift you down."

Again he didn't wait for any sign on her part that she was ready before proceeding. His presumption annoyed her at times. It might have annoyed her now if she hadn't been so busy telling herself that it only *seemed* as if he were lifting her down more slowly than was necessary. Just as it only seemed that the smile in his eyes had given way to the thrilling intensity she'd seen before. Just as he only seemed to be focusing on her mouth as her hands gripped his shoulders and he lowered her in front of him. It had to be her imagination that caused her to feel the tightening of his hands when she knew he really must be easing the pressure to let her go. And it had to be nothing more than an illusion that everything had suddenly gone completely still.

It wasn't Meg's imagination at all. Dave was quite aware of how he'd deliberately taken his time to lift her down.

He'd wanted to be careful with her. But he'd also wanted the contact she was allowing him. A while ago, he'd taken a chance when he'd taken her hand. That risk had paid off; she hadn't pulled back. There was no doubt in his mind that what he was contemplating at the moment wouldn't be so easily accepted.

"I think you've gained weight," she heard him say, and the illusion vanished.

Chapter Six

Illusions. All her life, Meg had lived with one illusion after another. Creating fantasies was a talent she'd perfected as a little girl.

Being a middle child in a large and busy family, she'd had a tendency to get a little lost in the shuffle. The fact that she'd lacked the assertiveness of her older siblings and hadn't been as demanding as her younger ones hadn't done much to earn her any attention, though her quiet personality had probably been a godsend for her harried mother. To make up for the lack of individual attention that came from simply being caught up in the flow, Meg had learned early on to pretend that tomorrow things would be different. Tomorrow, someone would really *look* at a picture she'd drawn before mumbling an absent "That's nice, dear," and patting her on the head. Tomorrow, someone would notice how pretty her cake looked before it was devoured without comment. Such silly, incidental things when one thought back on them as an adult, but even the seemingly inconsequential can make an impression on a child. Meg had always been impressionable, and no one had influenced her more than her father's mother. That diminutive ball of fire ruled the Flaherty clan with her keen wit and profound wisdom. Even now, in her eighties, her lively green eyes could sparkle like dew-covered shamrocks when she laughed or grow dark and stormy like the thunderheads her father said built beyond the lea back home in county Cork. Meg had adored her.

Grandma Kate maintained that a person's happiness was of her own creation. Therefore, if a person was unhappy, it was her own fault. Always wanting to please, and fearing that her grandmother would think her quite wretched if she wasn't happy, Meg had accepted the family matriarch's proclamation without question—and perfected her skills of self-deception. Instead of dwelling on troubling circumstances, she simply told herself that things would be better tomorrow, or next week, or when it rained, or when the sun came up.

That Scarlett O'Hara approach had proved quite effective in the past, and it wasn't an easy one to give up. Now Meg couldn't help but think that her life would finally get back on course once she moved. That would be a starting point, a place to begin again. All she had to do to get from here to there was wait.

In the meantime she stayed as busy as possible, tried not to worry about how she'd pay her pending hospital and doctor bills because worrying wasn't good for the baby, and gave everyone the impression that she was scaling down her style of living by choice and not out of necessity.

Maintaining the image Ted had worked so hard to create really wasn't all that difficult, since all the trappings were still in place. It also helped that time passed. The novelty of his death had worn off among the people he'd most wanted to impress, and they'd moved on to other things.

With the exception of the committee meetings that put her into contact with Buffy Cunningham and Vanessa Mc-Millin, Meg rarely came in contact with the members of the "in crowd." Since she no longer played tennis at the club in the morning and hadn't kept up with the gossip she'd always tried to avoid anyway, Vanessa now seemed to feel that the only topic left to discuss was how much money Meg's obstetrician—an outsider by her standards—made annually. Buffy, on the other hand, avoided any conversation that wasn't really necessary. There seemed to be a stigma to being widowed. It was, Meg supposed, not unlike being divorced. Women suddenly either saw you as a threat—which Meg considered a totally ridiculous idea, given her very obvious condition—or a reminder that it could happen to them.

One's friends—like one's enemies, she supposed—all eventually proved how true they were. That Buffy and Vanessa had chosen to limit their association with her came as no real surprise—or loss, for that matter. But never would Meg have expected Dave, the person she'd once regarded as an adversary, to become such an ally.

Annie, who rarely passed up a chance to offer advice when the situation presented itself, apparently thought Meg sadly lacking in initiative in terms of that friendship with Dave. "I can't see where he'd mind coming with you," she announced from her position atop a chair on Meg's deck. "Why don't you just ask him? The worst he can do is say no."

Meg knelt on the wooden planks in front of her, a tape measure draped around her neck. Removing one of the straight pins clamped between her lips, she mumbled, "I don't think so."

"Why not? He's over here half the time anyway."

Lord, how you exaggerate, Meg thought, spitting the rest of the pins into her hand so she could tell Annie just that. Dave wasn't around all *that* much. During the past couple of months, she'd seen him only when he'd accompanied her to business meetings. Of course, there were also the hours he spent drilling her on such fascinating topics as working capital funds flow statements and how to read a balance sheet. He usually attended to her "lessons" in the late afternoon, and more often than not he left before seven because he had a meeting or a date with Susan. He had sort of stuck around once, though, to help her bake his cookies. The other batches, three of them so far, he'd picked up on his way home from work. And he had spent the whole Saturday afternoon before a reception given by Susan's law firm fixing the leak under the downstairs bathroom sink so Meg wouldn't have to pay a plumber. She'd picked his suit up from the cleaners for him so he wouldn't be late getting Susan, and she still shook her head at the memory of what she'd heard before he'd realized she was back. His language, she'd noticed, hadn't improved one iota from the time he and Ted had rebuilt that dune buggy.

"He was only here once last week," she finally said, not mentioning that he was due to arrive any minute. He was bringing back a file, the one on the La Jolla property. At their meeting with the bank in July, Mr. Caldwell had backed down from his ultimatum and advised Meg that the loan committee had agreed to let her advertise the property for ninety days before taking any further action. Apparently the committee had realized they would have just as much trouble selling it as she would but that *she'd* put more effort into finding a buyer than someone in their collection department. Dave, who'd been instrumental in bringing that fact to their attention, had taken the file to show to a developer he knew. He'd already told Meg on the phone that the man wasn't interested.

Intent on keeping her growing sense of panic to herself, she gave Annie's hem a tug. She still had another month before the bank filed the suit that would take everything—including the money she needed to pay her doctor and hospital bills. Most of her other creditors had been placated with the promise of payment as soon as the sale of her house closed in two weeks. Her hope now was that she'd have enough left to live on for a couple of months after the baby arrived. She had no idea what would happen after that. Right now, she just needed to get through September. "Turn around a little. This piece here doesn't hang straight. Why didn't you have the bridal shop do this over again?"

"I did, and this is what I got. I couldn't stand hassling with them anymore. Besides, you do such good work."

Meg ignored the compliment and frowned at the ankle-length handkerchief hem of Annie's dress. The dress itself was a gorgeous confection with long sleeves, a high neck and a slim skirt, created from white organza and covered with tiny crystals and seed pearls. The beadwork was what made fixing the hem such a pain.

"I'll have to take these little guys off first," she said, referring to the pearls. "Then I can whack off about an inch, turn this up and put them back on again. How does that sound?"

"Very unprofessional. You know, if I didn't know you could sew, I think I'd be getting nervous about this."

"If you're getting nervous, it's only because you're getting married tomorrow."

"Which brings me back to what we were talking about a minute ago. There's no reason for you to feel awkward about coming to the wedding alone. I know telling you that doesn't make any difference, but it's true. You have to make an appearance at a social event at some point, and being the humble person I am, I'd just as soon it be my wedding."

"I didn't say I wasn't going, Annie. I just said it's going to feel odd—"

"Going alone. Yeah, I know. Everything always seems to be set up in pairs, and you've been half of a couple for so long that you've forgotten how to function as a single. Nobody said you *have* to come by yourself," Annie added, attempting to stand up straight while at the same time trying to see what Meg was doing to her hem. "Ask Dave to come with you."

"Come with you where?" came a pleasantly deep inquiry from the edge of the deck.

The pin Meg held missed the fabric. Instead, it stabbed her finger. "Damn," she muttered.

"Hi, Dave," Annie said, glancing down in concern. "Did you get blood on my dress?"

Mumbling an absent "No" to Annie, Meg turned her frown to Dave. Almost immediately, the lines smoothed from her brow. It had been a week since she'd seen him, and for some reason she couldn't begin to explain she found herself anxiously scanning his face. She had no idea what she hoped to find in his expression, or why she felt so disappointed when he gave her what was little more than a perfunctory smile. She knew only that he was finally here—and that was what had caused her to start when she'd heard his voice.

The frown replaced itself in the moments before she offered him a quiet "Hi" of her own and stuck the pins she held into the tomato-shaped pincushion beside her knee. She knew she'd looked forward to seeing him. She always did, because when he was around everything felt more vital somehow. But had she been anticipating his arrival that much?

Deciding that the question was hardly worth worrying about, she watched him lay down the file he was carrying on the patio table and then cross the deck. Her perspective was somewhat slanted, since she was sitting back on her heels, but as his easy strides brought him closer, the effect of his imposing presence seemed magnified. Maybe it was because he was wearing a tank top, and all that exposed muscle made him look so... masculine, she thought when he glanced up at Annie. More practically, it was probably because she had to tip her head back so far to look up at him.

"Tomorrow, huh?"

Annie nodded in response to Dave's question, then shoved back her newly cut hair. The boyishly cut bangs flopped down over her forehead again. "At six o'clock. Want to come?"

Meg was absolutely certain that the last place Dave wanted to go was the wedding of a woman he barely knew. She told herself she'd deal with Annie's lack of subtlety later and gripped the seat of the chair so she could stand up. She'd given up trying to be graceful when she'd entered her seventh month. Her goal now was simply to keep from being completely awkward.

"Sure," she heard Dave say as his hand folded around her upper arm.

"You do?" she asked, too surprised to notice how quickly he removed his hand when she'd gained her footing. "Tomorrow's Saturday. Don't you have a date with Susan?"

"No," he answered blandly. "Don't you want me to take you?"

"I didn't say that." Actually, she liked the idea of going out with Dave. Not, she hastily corrected, that she'd really be "going out" with him. It wouldn't be like a date. That was a whole other area, one that Annie would undoubtedly bring up when she felt a suitable length of time had passed. The present matter was merely one of convenience; of two people who'd been invited to the same place simply accompanying each other. Why, she wondered, did she feel this sudden and immediate need to rationalize? "If you want to go, that's fine. But what about Susan?"

"What about her?"

"Excuse me," Annie interrupted. "Who's Susan?"

"His girlfriend," Meg said.

"A woman I used to take out," Dave corrected.

A small "Oh" formed on Meg's lips. For a moment she didn't know what to say, and Dave's enigmatic expression didn't offer any clues as to an appropriate response. Susan had seemed nice enough, Meg supposed. But it didn't exactly break her heart to learn that Dave wasn't seeing her anymore. At least, she told herself, she wouldn't be displeased as long as Dave wasn't hurt. She didn't want him unhappy. "That explains why you're available," she finally said.

"It could. But I could also be available because the lady I'm seeing now had already made other plans," he pointed out reasonably. There was amusement in his voice, and a hint of it was visible in his eyes. "Do you want a ride tomorrow or not?"

The twinge of sympathy she'd felt at his news evaporated. She should have known better than to think Dave would let himself get so involved in a relationship that he might actually suffer if and when it was over. For as long as she'd known Dave, he'd always had a female friend or two waiting in the wings. Unless he'd changed drastically—and this breakup with Susan seemed to prove otherwise—he either couldn't settle down or didn't want to. That was why Meg wasn't all that surprised that he'd implied he was seeing someone else. She was, however, a bit perplexed to find herself so concerned with his activities. The current status of his love life was none of her business, and if he was any kind of a gentleman at all he wouldn't say anything else about it.

"I would, thank you," she replied.

Acknowledging the conclusion of the matter with a nod, Dave walked over to where he'd left the file and picked it up. "I'll put this in the office. Is there any mail you want me to look at?"

"The confirmation of my last conversation with the bank is in there. I told them that the ads were still running and that I've put one in the Houston and Chicago papers now, too." Aware of Annie's open curiosity, Meg chose her words carefully. It was no secret that she was selling off her property, but she still guarded the circumstances behind the liquidation of her husband's business. The way things were going, it appeared possible that all she would have left when this was over was the tenacity that kept her from admitting defeat. "And the statements came from the management company. I've got a couple of questions about them, if you wouldn't mind. It looks like the reason that one account was short is because a utility bill was paid twice."

"I'll go take a look."

"There's beer in the fridge."

"Thanks," he muttered as he headed toward the patio door. A moment later, he'd disappeared inside the house.

Meg turned back to Annie's hem. "A couple more pins and you can go in and take this off."

Annie said nothing, which bothered Meg. Annie's silence meant she was thinking, and that was always dangerous. The woman didn't jump to conclusions. She fairly leaped to them. Right now, if Meg were to be objective about the scene Annie had just witnessed, there were plenty of conclusions to be drawn. Dave had just waltzed into her house, and after asking if there was any mail, helped himself to a beer. At this very minute he was clearly visible through the kitchen window, reaching into the cabinet next to the refrigerator for a box of crackers. He seemed to have developed a taste for them during the first weeks he'd been around. Her morning sickness had finally passed, but Dave invariably looked for the crackers she'd always left out in the first months of her pregnancy.

He was obviously quite comfortable here, and Meg didn't mind that at all. She'd always wanted her friends to be comfortable in her home, and Dave was a very special kind of friend. He'd become her mentor. Her confidant. Someone she could talk to when it felt as if no one else wanted to listen. She knew she probably relied on him a little too much at times. But she assured herself it was only because he knew so much more than she about business. She was also very careful not to ask more of him than was necessary. His friendship was becoming too important to her to ever have him think her a burden.

"He's a nice man," Annie said from above her. "I imagine he's been indispensable in helping you with Ted's business."

"Yes, he has" was all Meg would say. "There. It's going to take a while to rehem this. I'll do it tonight while Dave is explaining leveraging to me."

One hand on Meg's shoulder, Annie gathered a handful of fabric in the other and stepped down from the chair. "Leveraging?"

"That's this week's lesson," she explained, wondering why her friend wasn't making more of what she'd seen. She hadn't expected Annie to be rational. "Or is it negative and positive cash flow? Oh, well. You'd better get going. You don't want to be late for your rehearsal."

"I'm always late," Annie said. After pausing a moment to study Meg's slightly preoccupied expression, she walked off with a very perplexed look on her face.

"Annie just left. She said she'd see you tomorrow," Meg announced when she went into the family room to find Dave there. He was sitting on the sofa, his long denim-clad legs stretched out on the coffee table as he scanned a copy of *The*

Wall Street Journal he'd brought for her to read. She paused beside him, curiosity vying with hesitation. After a two-second struggle, curiosity won. "Did you really break up with Susan?"

Dave's answer was a vaguely preoccupied "Uh-huh."

"Do you mind if I ask why?"

"It was time."

"That's it?"

"You sound just like Jan."

"You talked to your sister about Susan?"

"No. She's always asking about who I'm going out with, though. When I stopped by to see her while I was in Seattle last week she wanted the update, so I gave it to her."

Encouraged by that explanation, Meg waited for him to expand on the other. Dave was usually very straightforward, and she thought it a bit strange when he fell silent. "Well?" she prodded.

"Well what?" he asked, his eyes still on the newspaper.

"What was the update?"

"That I'm not seeing Susan anymore," he returned, trying to suppress a grin.

Eyeing him dully, she felt a slow smile spread over her face. It was good when he was here. "Do you know that you can be rather frustrating at times, Mr. Elliott?"

"It's been mentioned before," he chuckled, and because it always did something very strange to his insides when she smiled at him like that, he turned his attention to something less disturbing. "You ready to get started?"

"Not until you've answered me."

"You really want to know?"

"Yes, David. I really want to know."

"So did Jan." He gave the paper a snap. "I didn't tell her, either. Read this," he went on, indicating an article on the IRS's position on accelerated depreciation.

"David."

"Yeah?"

He looked totally innocent. Quite an accomplishment for a man of his maturity and experience. "Never mind," she mumbled, taking the paper from him. If he didn't want to tell her what had happened, she shouldn't pry. And she also wouldn't ask about this new woman in his life. She'd probably meet her eventually, anyway.

"She just wanted more than I could give her. Okay?"

"Okay," Meg returned softly, dutifully turning her attention to the article he wanted her to read. A while ago she'd been inclined to think that Dave was a bachelor by choice. Now, because of the defensiveness she'd heard in his voice, she leaned more toward the other possibility. Maybe it wasn't just Susan. Maybe he couldn't give anyone enough of himself to make a real commitment. Even as she tried to absorb the words in front of her, she couldn't help wondering why that might be.

Dave leaned back on the sofa, his eyes on the view beyond the patio doors as Meg sat beside him concentrating on the paper. He should let the matter rest, he knew, especially now that she'd dropped it—but he liked talking to her.

"Susan was my parents' idea of the perfect wife for me," he heard himself tell Meg. "Or I should say she became their idea of the perfect wife when she broke up with her fiancé last year. Her parents' influence didn't help. She gave me the impression they were all for it."

Meg laid down the paper. "All for her breaking up with her fiancé or for you as a son-in-law?"

"Both."

"She wants to get married?"

"That's what she said."

"And you don't?"

"No."

"Because your parents are pushing the idea? Or because you don't love Susan enough?"

"I'm not in love with Susan at all," he replied.

"Then I guess it doesn't matter whether or not you're just reacting to being pushed. From what you've told me about your parents, I could see where you might balk at an idea of theirs."

A bit puzzled by the way her face had brightened a moment ago, he said flatly, "I'm not rebelling against my parents." He really wasn't. He just didn't want to commit himself to a loveless relationship. Seeing the changes in Meg over the years, he'd come to understand what that lack could do to a person. "If and when I get married, it will be because it's the right thing to do. I'm just not in the market for it right now."

He actually hadn't been interested in anything permanent for quite a while, thanks to his thoughts of Meg. The consistency of those same thoughts lately also made him wonder if his involvement in her life wasn't prompted by more than guilt. He wasn't prepared to delve too deeply into that, but he felt something for Meg. Actually, he felt a lot, but he couldn't drop the barrier that kept him from caring too much. He'd worked too hard to erect it. If she felt anything for him beyond the friendship they'd finally managed, it was only dependence. That would be short-lived. But for now it was better than nothing.

Having faced those truths, he'd also faced another. No matter how he tried to ignore it, no matter how he tried to excuse it, his physical attraction to her left him unable to respond to anyone else. More than his ego was suffering on that score. He didn't dare think about that too much. When he did, he forgot all about being a friend to her, and a friend was what she needed right now.

It was the friend in him who ignored the scent of jasmine that invariably evoked the memory of how her head had once nestled against his shoulder, and how soft her skin felt when she put her hand on his and told him she was sorry his relationship with Susan hadn't worked out. It was the friend who, over an hour later, was trying to make her understand that by taking the money from the rezoned property her realtor had just sold and using it to pay down the mortgage on the duplexes, she'd increase her liquidity and make that property more attractive to another buyer.

"But I don't want to spend that money," she stubbornly maintained. "It's all the cash I have."

"You'll have more when the sale on your house closes in two weeks. Right now you've got someone interested in those duplexes, and you can sweeten the deal by making the loans on them cheaper to assume."

"But I'll lose my money!"

"No, you won't. You'll be getting more. Half with his down payment and the rest, plus interest, on a note that he pays to you over the next two years. Besides making money on your money, you'll have a regular income of a few hundred dollars for the next twenty-four months."

"But . . . oh, geez," she moaned, dropping her head into her hands. "Einstein couldn't make sense of half this stuff. How am *I* supposed to understand it?"

"You're doing fine," Dave assured her hastily. Thinking he might be pushing her too hard again, her wandered over to where she sat in front of the sofa and squatted down in front of her. "Just remember that the more attractive you can make a deal up front, the more you can push for on the other end."

He smiled at the top of her head, thinking she'd probably hit him with a throw pillow if he patted it, and started to simplify his explanation. But Meg wasn't listening. She'd straightened—rather slowly—and now she was pressing her hand to her stomach. She'd gone completely still.

"Meg?" He said her name quietly, not at all sure what to make of the intense concentration furrowing her brow. Like most men, he was reluctant to admit to any form of alarm.

Seeing a pregnant woman holding her stomach that way, though, could instill a fairly healthy sense of consternation in the uninitiated. She wasn't going into labor, was she? It was too damn soon! "Are you all right?"

She gave an impatient nod, her soft smile one of utter delight. "Give me your hand."

Moving beside her, he did as she'd asked, wondering at the same time what had prompted such a request. She placed his hand against her smock and covered it with hers. "There," she said. "Can you feel it?"

She looked up at him, her features more luminous than the sunlight filling the room. Her smile held an ethereal quality, a Madonna-like essence that made him feel that any verbal acknowledgment on his part would be totally inadequate. Her eyes fairly glowed with pleasure, and beneath his hand he could feel . . . life.

Dave spread his fingers a little wider, wanting to feel more of her baby's gentle rolling motion. He could see her excitement, could actually feel some of the wonder she felt as she moved his hand with hers, repositioning it so he could follow the tiny arm or leg or whatever it was that poked against his palm.

Even as he watched Meg concentrate on the movement within her, he had to acknowledge that the child wasn't as real to him as it was to her. Admittedly, there was something special about feeling a child stir in its mother's womb, but he wasn't the type to get philosophical over the miracle of life. That task was best left to the poets. What was important to Dave was that Meg felt comfortable enough to share something as intimate as this with him.

It was that very intimacy which, a few seconds later, prompted the thought that he should pull back now. That was what a friend would do. But he couldn't move away from her, not without offering something in return.

The ease Meg had felt when she'd reached for Dave's hand was diminishing rapidly. In its place came embarrassment over her impulsiveness and a vague sense of having crossed into a forbidden territory. All she'd wanted was for Dave to experience her excitement. So many times she'd felt the life stirring within her when there had been no one to whom she felt close enough to share that wondrous phenomenon. She hadn't even realized how close she felt to Dave until just now.

With that awareness came other feelings. A warmth had seeped into her where Dave's hand pressed to her stomach—the same warmth that seemed to be spreading through her as he turned his hand palm up and slipped his fingers between hers. The gesture was simple, yet its impact on her was so complex that she couldn't begin to examine the feelings it evoked. He searched her face, seeking the answer to some question he hadn't asked. She would have answered if she could. But as it was, she could do nothing but wonder at what thoughts caused his eyes to darken.

"Thank you," he whispered, lifting his free hand. The tips of his fingers felt rough against her skin, but his palm was smooth as he cradled her face. His head inched forward, his breath teasing her cheek. "Thank you," he repeated, and gently brought his lips to hers.

Meg's eyes drifted closed. The pressure of his mouth against hers was exquisitely tender, almost reverent. Her throat burned suddenly, the feeling of tightness increasing as his lips lifted to hover and nip, caressing first one corner of her mouth and then the other.

Oh, don't do this, she prayed silently, knowing even as she did that she needed his kiss very much. Long seconds passed. She knew only that she needed the warmth he could give her. Ached for it. She'd felt so cold for so long. Ignoring that emptiness hadn't made it go away, nor had pretending that she didn't need anyone.

He held her with his palm curved at her jaw, the fingers of his left hand entwined with hers. It wasn't enough. She wanted his arms, needed the strength she knew she'd find there.

A groan, deep and muffled, came from within his chest when she leaned closer. The kiss deepened, his hand moving behind her neck to tip her head back. A moment later, his mouth opened over hers. The first touch of his tongue caused her breath to catch, and she had to consciously release it. His quest gentled further, allowing her to decide the pace. There was no urgency behind his unhurried exploration, no demand. Just the heady taste of him and the promise that there was more if she wanted it.

She wanted him to stop holding back and make the chill inside her go away. She wanted him to make her forget about the stinging behind her eyelids. It was the surge of emotions battling inside that caused the moisture building there. She didn't want to cry, but that was what she felt like doing right now. "Please hold me," she begged in a broken whisper, and within moments she was in his arms.

He hadn't meant to kiss her that way. The instant he'd felt her respond to him, Dave realized that he'd forgotten all about denial and succumbed to the temptation. He'd frightened her by asking for more than she could give, but she hadn't withdrawn. Instead, she'd sought his arms. More relieved than he would ever have thought possible, he drew her against him, cradling her head against his shoulder and slowly stroking her hair.

Meg's hand curled on his chest, her eyes closed against the burning. It was okay now. As she had all the other times, she managed to keep the tears from falling. All crying ever did was make your nose red and give you a headache. It changed absolutely nothing.

Taking a few deep breaths, she waited to feel the protectiveness she'd experienced when Dave had held her before.

He'd offered her comfort once, that night an eternity ago when they'd talked long after the sun had set. That was what she'd hoped for this time, but instead she felt only sensations and longings and confusion.

Dave felt the tension entering her body. She was withdrawing from him, mentally as well as physically. He didn't blame her. She was going through enough without him rushing her toward something she wasn't ready for. He was only human, though, a fact attested to by the dull ache centered in his loins.

Having wanted her for so long, he'd expected the desire he felt. But nothing had prepared him for the physical impact she'd had on him. He'd felt passion before and was no stranger to the urges and demands of his body, but never had he simply kissed a woman and felt such hunger. It was, he had to admit, a little unsettling.

So was the way she leaned back, her head bent as she twisted her ring. Her wedding band. When was she going to take it off? he wondered.

Now didn't seem the appropriate time to ask or to indulge in any jealousy if she was thinking about the man who'd given her that ring. More urgent matters beckoned. He had to do something to diffuse the tension filling the room and get her mind on something else.

He set her back before she could move completely away from him. "Nice try," he announced, standing over her with his hands on his hips. His voice was as firm as he could make it. "It isn't going to work, though."

Bewildered, as he'd intended her to be, she raised her head. "What won't work?"

"Trying to change the subject."

"The subject?"

He gave her a look of extreme indulgence. "The one we were talking about before you sidetracked me with Junior's calisthenics. The deal you're going to make on the duplexes, remember? Now..." Leaning over the coffee table, he rifled through the papers spread over it and handed her a yellow pad.

One form of uneasiness gave way to another. "You're going to be at the meeting, aren't you?"

"If you want me there. You're going to do the talking, though. Better take some notes."

Meg took the pad, her expression a bit flustered as she watched him turn away. He'll start pacing any second now, she thought, and he did.

She couldn't believe it. He was acting as if nothing had happened—as if he hadn't just taken the one constant in her life and completely rattled her faith in its nonthreatening image.

Half of Meg was relieved at Dave's nonchalant attitude. The other half wasn't sure how she felt. Dave didn't give her any time to consider the matter. All he allowed her to do was get Annie's dress so she could hem it during his lecture. He'd be a nice guy, he told her, and write down what she needed to remember.

Chapter Seven

I won't forget," Meg promised Annie, slipping the note she'd just written to herself into her patent-leather handbag. She stepped aside to allow one of the hotel's employees, who carried a tray of punch cups, to pass. Annie and Larry had exchanged their vows in the terraced garden of Dana Point's most luxurious hotel. The small reception was now in full swing in the same flower-bedecked area. "I'll call the band's agent first thing Monday morning and tell him the deposit's on its way. Now stop worrying about the benefit," she scolded. "It's bad enough that you're thinking about work at your wedding. Just don't let it ruin your honeymoon."

"Not a chance." Larry Thurman, newly graduated doctor of psychology and Annie's husband of a little over an hour, slipped his arm around his wife's waist. Dashingly attractive in his gray cutaway, he gave Meg a wink, his smile growing sly as he whispered something that was undoubtedly provocative in Annie's ear.

"Really, Larry," the not-quite-blushing bride teased, fanning herself. Her voice lowered as, leaning toward Meg, she patted her own hair to make sure the baby's breath was still in it. "You can't *imagine* what's he's proposed to keep my mind off of work."

"Can't I?" The lift of Meg's eyebrows gave a certain worldliness to her already sophisticated appearance. She'd worn black, not because she subscribed to any old dictates about periods of mourning but because the color was becoming. The dress, with its tailored shoulders and the slash of turquoise across the upper bodice, was as stylish as the "non-pregnant" clothes hanging in her closet, but it wasn't anywhere near as expensive as it looked. She'd made it herself after surreptitiously studying the designer original at a maternity boutique. "Would I be too far off to suggest that he wants you to sleep until noon, have brunch in bed, then spend the day in a deck chair reading?"

Larry's leer disappeared. "How did you know?"

"Maybe it has something to do with the fact that we've lived together for three of the five years we've known each other," Annie offered.

"Could be." Larry grinned. His hand cupped over the swirls of white beads and crystals covering his wife's shoulder, he leaned forward and pressed his lips to her forehead. "I'm going to find Dr. Trainer before he leaves. I didn't get a chance to talk to him before I left the clinic yesterday."

The same softness Meg heard in Larry's baritone entered Annie's voice. As she touched the pearl in his cravat she seemed to have forgotten all about her own work and worries. "I think you need to get away even worse than I do."

"So you've said," he told Annie quietly. He gave Meg an engaging smile and took his leave as two other guests approached.

Meg relinquished her position so that the members of Annie's office staff could get a closer look at her dress. Even as she did, she couldn't help but notice how Annie's gaze lingered on Larry. Their concern for each other was as evident as their affection. It was that concern, that caring, that had been missing from Meg's marriage. Meg fervently hoped that it would always be part of her friend's relationship with Larry.

Frowning, she glanced toward the fifty or so people crowding the sun-dappled terrace. All during the short ceremony, while she'd listened to the vows and promises Annie and Larry made to each other, Meg had been oddly aware of Dave. He'd sat right next to her, so naturally she'd been conscious of his proximity. But there had also been a mental awareness she'd recognized, a sort of enlightenment that awakened a strange restlessness within her.

When Larry had promised Annie that he'd always be there for her, Meg couldn't help thinking of Dave and how freely he gave her his support. As Annie had vowed to stay by Larry's side through good times and bad, Meg had had to credit Dave's willingness to stand by her while she'd tried to piece her life together. And when Annie and Larry had pledged first and foremost to be one another's friends, Meg had begun to wonder at how very much she wanted to sustain her friendship with Dave. She needed it badly. Until last night, it had felt safe.

She wished she knew how Dave felt about what had happened last night. Beyond the slight edginess she'd sensed in him right after the ceremony he hadn't given her a clue. They'd been too rushed before their arrival for her to search for insights, and he'd excused himself from her and her friends within minutes of the bride and groom's departure from the carnation-covered arch. The last she'd seen him, he'd been standing beside Lucy Bevins's husband, Ansel.

Spotting Lucy by the punch bowl and thinking that her
husband, and therefore Dave, must be nearby, Meg went
over to her, avoiding the crush of people in the middle of the
terrace by skirting the wall of early-blooming chrysanthe-
mums. She needed to put her mind at ease, to assure herself that Dave wasn't trying to avoid her.

The brightness in her voice effectively hid her disappointment when she came up behind Lucy. Dave was nowhere to be seen. "You've been abandoned, too, I see. Nice
of them, isn't it?"

The gregarious woman turned around in a whirl of pale
lilac silk. "Meg! I was hoping to talk to you." Lucy's smile
was genuine, her genteel Southern drawl as sweet as the ic-
ing on the now-dismantled wedding cake. She waved her
hand lightly. "Don't pay no mind to the men. They're off
talking business somewhere. Ansel's in on that import deal
Dave's putting together. Surprised the daylights out of him
to see a familiar face, though I must say he stopped pout-
ing about having to come to a wedding when he saw him."
Lucy stepped back. The profusion of enameled bracelets on
her wrist clanking lightly, she pressed her hands together and
touched the tips of her fingers to her chin. "You look absolutely wonderful, darling. And that dress. It's just precious. Adolfo, isn't it? I never could find anything on the
rack when I was expecting. Don't know what on earth I'd
have done without Mama's seamstress, God rest her soul.
She passed on last year, you know. My mama, not Miz
Hattie. Now, tell me what on earth you're doing here with
that gorgeous man," she demanded, her eyes fairly glow-
ing with anticipation.

Anyone who didn't know Lucy might have thought her
both pretentious and addlebrained. Deep down, the petite
brunette with the magnolia skin and the dreamy blue eyes
was a lovely woman who'd simply absorbed her environment too well. *To the manor born* described Ansel Bevins's

wife to the proverbial T. She was a true Georgia peach, cultured, well-bred and from very old money. Her husband, however, had discovered a new kind of gold in California—silicon chips—and his computer fortune had demanded entrée into the inner circles of local society. There Lucy had had the dubious honor of meeting the Vanessa McMillins and the Buffy Cunninghams of the world. They'd exposed her to the elitist games played by the nouveau riche, such as the tricky art of one-upmanship Ted had so quickly mastered, and how to escalate an innocuous rumor into the ruinous sort of gossip Meg was trying to avoid by maintaining the image Ted had created of himself. Unfortunately, Lucy had proven a quick study.

Meg knew how to play the games, but Annie and Larry's friends and relatives were not, with a stray exception or two, part of the circle Ted had chosen for them to associate with. It was because of that, and Meg's tendency to regard the more harmless affectations of snobbery as something of a joke, that she didn't feel too threatened by Lucy's nosy inquiry as to why she was here with Dave.

"We're attending Annie's wedding," Meg returned, deliberately keeping her agreement with Lucy's earlier description of her escort to herself. Dave was extremely attractive, she admitted, in a very physical sort of way.

"I know that," came the flat reply. "I mean, are you...well, you're not, ah...keeping company, are you?"

"He and Ted were good friends, Lucy. You know that. Haven't you heard that he's helping me with Ted's business?" Surely the rumor mill hadn't broken down that much since she'd removed herself from the mainstream.

"Well, I guess I hadn't. The children and I just got back from seeing my daddy, and before that we'd spent a month on St. Croix while Ansel was in Japan. I really haven't had a chance to catch up on what's been going on, I mean, naturally I was aware Dave and Ted knew each other. Heavens, they played golf together enough," she said, as if Meg hadn't been aware of that particular fact. "I just didn't know you'd hired Dave. But then, a woman in your position would have to be careful about who she selected to take care of all that property. There's all kinds of unscrupulous types out there, and you being widowed and all—" She cut herself off, tsking at the horrors that could befall a poor defenseless female. "Oh, well, you're in good hands now," she concluded, and charged on to yet another topic. "By the way. How are you feeling? I've been meaning to call ever since I got back. Did that recipe for comfort tea I gave you help your morning sickness? That was my mama's recipe, you know."

Meg really did like Lucy. But she'd have given anything at that moment to be able to pull her plug and walk away without appearing rude. The more she thought about it, the more convinced she became that Dave was sorry he'd come. He really didn't know anyone here. And though she'd tried to include him when people she hadn't seen for a long time had come up to say hello, she couldn't help but notice his coolness toward her. An even more disquieting thought struck her. It was virtually impossible to disappear in such a small crowd. Had he already left?

Dave was still there. Not out on the terrace but inside the bar overlooking it. Ansel had suggested something stronger than the punch they were serving outside, and Dave had thought a bourbon sounded like a hell of an idea. The twenty minutes he'd spent suffering curious stares while Meg had introduced him to some of the women she'd volunteered with at the shelter hadn't really bothered him. It was the fifteen minutes before that. For a quarter of an hour he'd had to sit inches away from the woman who'd robbed him of his sleep last night while a minister had expounded on love and loyalty and she had absently twisted her ring. He wished she'd take it off.

Knocking the ash from his cigarette, he picked up the aged Kentucky blend he'd ordered and nodded at the man occupying the chair across the table. Bevins didn't want to talk business, which was fine with Dave, since he had other things on his mind. The wealthy Georgian with the thinning hair and the shrewd gray eyes simply wanted to avoid what he called "all that fawnin' and fussin'."

"Much obliged," Dave said, raising his glass before taking a sip.

Bevins returned the toast. "You never did say what you were doing here."

"I guess I'm sort of a friend of the bride's. You?"

"Not sure. My wife's a friend of somebody's. The bride, too, I think. They work on some kind of committee, or she does volunteer work with her. Hell, I don't know. I just go where she tells me when it comes to this kind of thing. That's Reese's wife you're with, isn't it?"

"Widow," Dave corrected. "Yeah."

"Too bad about him. Her, too. Expecting a kid and all. Kinda got to feel sorry for her."

"Yeah," Dave muttered, taking another sip. "Who do you think's going to the World Series?"

To Dave, the change of subject was glaring. Bevins didn't so much as blink. "Too soon to tell. You putting money on anybody?"

"I don't bet."

"Know what you mean. Stock market's risky enough for me."

The safe conversation was welcome. Dave hadn't expected to know anyone here. He was little more than an acquaintance of Annie's, and he hadn't met the groom until he'd made the obligatory pass down the receiving line. Running into a business associate had saved him from having to stay with Meg. She was doing fine without him.

The thin stream of gray-blue smoke Dave exhaled snaked toward the ceiling as Bevins began to recall previous pennant battles. Dave was more than happy to let him talk, and kept him going with an appropriate nod every now and then. His thoughts, though, were light years away from baseball.

Meg had been almost reserved when he'd first picked her up. He'd been afraid of that, but he'd also been prepared for it. He'd purposefully arrived five minutes late, then promptly announced that they had to stop at a mall so he could buy a wedding present. By grilling her for gift suggestions and pleading helplessness in the bedding, bath and gift-wrap departments of the Broadway, he'd had her so concerned about being late that she'd been back to normal in no time.

Too bad he couldn't come up with something to create such a diversion for himself. All he seemed capable of thinking about was how he'd felt when he'd looked over at her during the ceremony. It was the way he'd felt last night after he'd kissed her. Only this time there had been nothing to keep him from dissecting the unpleasant mix of emotions he felt.

He told himself he had no right to feel anger or jealousy or resentment toward Ted, but he felt them anyway. He also felt guilt, though probably not as much as he should have. Meg had belonged to Ted. She'd been his wife. She was, at this very minute, pregnant with his child.

That, Dave told himself, downing the remainder of his drink in one swallow, was what bothered him most. It was why she was still off limits.

"You want another one of those?"

I'd like several, Dave thought. "No, thanks," he told his companion. "I'd better get back out there. Meg might be wanting to go soon." He hoped.

"No need." Bevins raised his drink to the window, indicating the two dark heads bobbing along the garden wall, following them until they disappeared through the doors leading into the hotel. "That's Lucy with Mrs. Reese. They've got to be heading one of two places. The ladies' room or here. Lucy knows me." The last statement was accompanied by a bland glance at Dave's empty glass. "You sure?"

"I'm sure," he returned with some reluctance.

Crushing out his cigarette a moment later, he looked up to see Bevins's wife crossing the room. Dave vaguely recalled having met her once or twice before, and he was on his feet by the time she reached the table. But even as the charming Lucy returned his greeting, Dave's glance swung to the arched doorway.

Meg stood there, seeming a little unsure of what to do. Dave could appreciate that. He felt the same way himself. He'd brought her here because he'd wanted to be with her. Having experienced the taste and feel of her, he knew now he could no longer be with her without wanting her. The barrier created from his sense of honor and his respect for both her and his best friend had developed a major crack. He had no one to blame but himself.

A heavy hand clapped him on the shoulder. "Well, buddy," he heard Ansel say with a sigh. "Guess it's time to go. Lucy says the bride's getting ready to pitch her posies. How about you and Mrs. Reese joining us for dinner after this little soiree's over? Hear the Bennington group's moving into California with a little investment capital. Like to talk to you about that."

"That would be wonderful," Lucy chimed in, appearing as pleased with the idea as Dave was disinterested. "Meg was telling me this is the first time she's been out. I mean, of course, she's been out before, just not to anything social. She and Annie are quite close, you know, so she really couldn't miss her wedding. It might do her good to make a night of it. Dinner with friends is perfectly acceptable, don't you think? It's got to be so lonely for her in that big old house.''

"She keeps pretty busy," Dave returned, avoiding the issue of dinner as the three of them weaved between the tables. A quick reassessment of his situation with Meg was in order before he spent any more time with her. As for any potential business with Bevins, that could be taken care of during the work week. "She might be getting tired."

She did look tired, Dave thought when he saw Meg's tentative smile at their approach. Or perhaps she was worried, he amended when they reached the doorway where she was waiting.

"I was wondering what had happened to you," she said, quickly scanning his face.

With no apparent contrition, Ansel spoke up. "Led astray by me, I'm afraid."

If Meg hadn't felt so anxious, she might have smiled at that. As decisive and as single-minded as Dave could be, she doubted that anyone could influence him without his permission. She couldn't make herself smile again, though, not when she could practically feel the tension radiating from Dave. Pleading genuine fatigue and a threatening headache, she politely declined Lucy's dinner invitation. Since she'd already offered her best wishes to the bride and groom, she also told Lucy that she'd have to miss the throwing of the bouquet. Dave, she noted, though she was sure neither of the Bevinses noticed, actually breathed a sigh of relief.

Other than to mumble, "I guess I'd better get you home," after Ansel and Lucy took their leave, Dave said nothing else until they were heading down the highway. The only reason he spoke then was that Meg wouldn't let him stay silent any longer.

"What's wrong?" she asked quietly.

Mired in his dark and brooding thoughts, Dave snapped a terse "Nothing." He immediately regretted the sharpness of his tone. She didn't deserve to be treated that way. He was fighting demons she knew nothing about, yet she was bearing the brunt of his anger with himself while he waged that battle. He was being very unfair. "Sorry," he offered.

The discouragement in his voice drew her eyes to him. In the fading light, his features were shadowed. "I really wish you'd tell me what's bothering you. If I did something to upset you, I'd like to know about it."

"Maybe I just need to be fed."

She tried to match his halfhearted smile. "If I'd known that earlier, I wouldn't have turned the Bevinses down. I was under the impression that all you wanted to do was leave."

"That is all I wanted."

They were heading north on the Coast Highway. The view through her side window was of darkened hills against a fading twilight sky. "I shouldn't have asked you to take me."

"Don't worry about it."

Adding to her concerns was the last thing he wanted to do. He was behaving like a selfish idiot. He'd told himself in the beginning that he was only going to help her get back on her feet. When had he lost sight of that objective? That was what was important—not this insane urge he had to pull the car over and kiss the troubled lines from her brow, to take her in his arms and make her ache for him the way he—

He had to put the brakes on either the car or his thoughts. Good sense dictated application to the latter.

"Did you get a chance to look for an apartment last week?" he inquired, trying to decide between a cold shower or a run along the beach when he got home. "I meant to ask last night, but . . ."

Wonderful, he drawled to himself. He did not want to think about last night.

Neither did Meg, which was why she jumped in the instant he hesitated. "Yes. With Annie. I won't know for sure until Tuesday, but I think I've got a place in her complex. The rent's a little more than I wanted to pay, but I think I can handle it for at least six months. Since I've got to be out of the house in a couple of weeks, I really can't afford to spend much more time looking. And it's not like I have to stay there forever."

"Does it have a place for your kiln?" He knew how much she'd once enjoyed working at her potter's wheel and glazing and firing her creations. After she was settled, she'd probably want to get back to her artistic pursuits. It would be good for her.

"I sold that."

"When?"

"Last month," she answered, breathing a little easier with the return of more normal conversation. "The guy from the secondhand store bought it when he came out to buy Ted's power tools and the freezer."

It made no sense to her that Dave should look so displeased. But then, nothing between them had made much sense in the past twenty-four hours—least of all his sudden insistence that he wanted to see her apartment before she moved in.

"What for?" she asked, puzzled by his clear determination. "It's just your basic apartment. Two bedrooms. One living room. A bath and a kitchen. It doesn't even have a view of the ocean. It's in the canyon."

"I just want to see it. That's all."

"Fine," she said, thinking she liked him much better when he wasn't so defensive. "If I get it, you can see it."

"Fine," he returned, gripping the wheel more tightly. "And let me know what day you're moving so I don't schedule anything else."

"I can't ask you to help me move. You've already done—"

"You didn't ask. I volunteered."

"Well, you don't have to do it."

Yes, he did. Part of getting her back on her feet was getting her settled where he didn't have to worry about her. "I'm going to anyway," he informed her.

The day Meg moved into the small apartment wasn't an easy one. For weeks she'd been telling herself she was looking forward to this day, if for no other reason than that she'd finally be able to start decorating the baby's nursery. That in itself was tangible evidence that the future held something worth anticipating. Up until now, she'd felt as if she were in limbo—simply waiting for something to happen that would provide the impetus she needed to move forward. Now, standing in the middle of a strange living room surrounded by packing boxes and what furniture she hadn't sold, she felt neither that impetus nor any sense of accomplishment. She felt like crying.

"Later," she told herself, swallowing past the burning in her throat. Spotting what she'd come into the room to find—the broom—she headed back into her new, decidedly smaller, kitchen. Activity, she'd learned, was the best antidote for melancholy.

Yesterday, after signing a six-month lease, she'd lined all the shelves in the kitchen with bright yellow paper and brought over her smaller potted plants. This morning, Annie had helped her put away the pots and pans and dishes while Larry and Dave had carted the heavy stuff inside. It was now six o'clock. Annie and Larry had left about an hour ago—after the four of them had polished off an enor-

mous pizza—and Dave was due back soon from the storage
company where Meg had rented a small space for the be-
longings she didn't have room for here. Meg, having taken
a few enforced breaks during the afternoon, was still going
strong. As soon as she swept up the sugar she'd spilled while
refilling the sugar bowl, she'd start on her bedroom. She
needed to feel as though she belonged here, and that
wouldn't happen until she'd made her surroundings more
familiar.

Pictures would help. After making her bed, she opened
the box she thought contained her collection of family photos, the collages she'd put together from the huge box of
snapshots she and her sisters had sorted through one
Thanksgiving a few years ago.

The box she opened didn't hold the anticipated photographs. It was full of books. Telling herself she should read
the labels she'd stuck on the boxes instead of relying on their
shape—and that she'd wait until tomorrow to put the books
away on the shelves in the living room—she thought she'd
finally struck pay dirt.

There were pictures in the next box she untaped, but not
the right ones. This container was full of old photographs
she'd intended for storage. Photos of her and Ted on their
honeymoon, Ted battling with their first Christmas tree,
Dave and Ted looking like two vagabonds as they grinned
at a big bluefish.

Slowly she closed the lid.

Mercifully, the doorbell rang.

"It's really getting nasty out there," Dave announced,
handing her the storage locker key as he closed the door.
"The wind's really starting to come up."

Dropping the key into the pocket of her turtleneck smock,
she watched him comb his fingers through his tousled hair.
Several wheat-colored strands promptly fell back over his
forehead. "It must be pretty sheltered here," she said, re-

ferring to the wooded hills rising around her. "I hadn't noticed. Is it going to storm? It's been overcast all day."

"It could. I had the radio on in Larry's pickup, but the announcer didn't say anything about it." Stepping around both her and the ficus she hadn't decided on a place for yet, he wandered over to the short hallway and picked up a handful of wadded-up newspaper. The paper was tossed into an empty box by her bedroom door. Hands on his hips, he turned around.

The furniture from her old family room had been placed more or less where she wanted it, but the bare white walls and the standard off-white apartment drapes covering the windows lacked the character he was pretty sure she'd soon give the place. If the way she'd pushed herself all afternoon was any indication, it wouldn't take long for her to accomplish that task.

"I thought you were going to rest."

"How did you...?" The remainder of her question trailed off. When he'd left a while ago the mattress and box springs had been set on the frame, but the blankets and sheets had still been in boxes. "I had to make the bed," she finished reasonably.

"You didn't have to put that perfume and stuff out on the dresser tonight, though."

He sure didn't miss much, she thought, and tried to smile when she realized he was watching her a little too closely. Her nerves felt raw, her emotions too near the surface to bear his scrutiny. It would probably be best if she thanked him now, told him how much she appreciated his help today and let him get on with his evening. This was the first time since Annie's wedding that they'd been alone together. It was easier when other people were around, because they seemed to absorb the subtle tension she could feel building now in the too-quiet room. Her awareness of Dave was just one more thing she lacked the energy to cope with.

But while half of her wanted very much for him to leave, the other half dreaded the moment when he did.

"I had to do it sometime," she told him.

Dave's gaze narrowed on her pale features. He'd noticed a suspicious brightness to her eyes the instant he'd set foot inside the apartment. Her smile didn't fool him for a minute. She looked tired and tense and very much in need of some rest.

If he thought she'd truly go to bed when he left, he'd be gone in a second. It was too hard on him to stand there wondering what thoughts caused the strain in her delicate features. But he didn't think she'd call it quits. All day she'd been a little obsessed with the idea of putting the place in order. Even now she was walking past him to rifle through another box.

"What do you think you're doing?" he asked, crossing his arms over the ancient football jersey he wore.

Rummaging around in a carton that belonged in the pantry, she sighed heavily. "Hanging pictures. Have you seen the hammer?"

"Yes."

When five seconds passed and he said nothing else, Meg blew the strands of hair from her face and glanced up. "Well? Where is it?"

"I don't think I'm going to tell you."

"Why not?"

"Look," he muttered, silently cursing himself for not deciding he'd done enough today and walking out the front door. He couldn't leave her to handle this mess alone. "I'll make you a deal. I'll get the hammer and nails if you'll take a few minutes and put your feet up. Then I'll hang the pictures wherever you tell me to."

"You don't have to do that."

"Megan."

Not wanting to argue with him, she dismissed her earlier intention. "I'm not sure where the pictures are, anyway. If you wouldn't mind, there are some books in the bedroom that belong in here. Would you carry them in for me?"

Dave said nothing when she moved past him to indicate one of the cardboard containers along the wall in her bedroom. He simply followed and with a shrug of his broad shoulders bent to hoist the heavy box to his knee. One more surge of lean muscle brought it to his chest, and he moved easily out into the hall. Meg wandered out of the room after him, her eyes drawn to the power revealed in his arms. Outlined by the taut pull of his shirt over his back, his muscles tensed again as he lowered the box to the beige carpet.

Meg was still watching him when he faced her. He was pleased to see that she actually had a little trouble looking away. "What are the chances of you waiting until tomorrow to tackle the rest of this place?"

"I'm not going to do it all tonight," she explained, extracting a couple of books to place in the wall unit. "But I can't see any point in sitting around staring at the mess, either."

Taking the books she held, he pointed to a spot on the floor beside the box. It took more patience than he'd thought he possessed to protect her from herself at times. "If you'll sit down there and hand the books to me, I'll put them away. It's not good for you to reach up that high, anyway."

Before she could decide whether or not she wanted to go along with his suggestion, Dave had removed a few more volumes from the box. After scanning their titles, he easily stuck them on one of the higher shelves. She'd have had to stand on her toes to do it.

It probably wouldn't hurt to sit down for a few minutes, she told herself, smiling a little. Dave was now reading the titles aloud, and he seemed quite impressed by the variety of topics covered in her small library.

"*The Complete Herbologist*," he read, taking two more hardbacks from her. "And *Les Misérables*. We'll put those right here by *A History of Renaissance Art*. Now this is one everybody should have," he went on to proclaim after he'd filled the top shelf with some popular fiction. "*Stocks: The Other Option*. Whoever bought this has excellent judgment. The author really knows his stuff."

"That one's yours."

"Thought it sounded familiar. Next."

She handed him two more, appreciating what he was doing far more than he realized. He wasn't being overt, but she knew he was trying to lighten her mood. She was glad she hadn't said anything about his leaving. It was almost always easier being with him.

"And here we have a leather-bound copy of Shake-speare's sonnets and...*Human Sexual Dysfunction*. This is getting better," he said, grinning. "Shows true diversity in reading habits."

Meg could feel the breath she'd just drawn trap itself in her lungs. Dave had added the Shakespeare to the shelf, but it didn't appear that he was going to put the other book away. It did look as though he were about to open it.

"Give me that." She half laughed, half choked, and could have kicked herself for not noticing the title sooner. She'd be utterly mortified if he started flipping through the pages and found the ones she'd marked.

Suddenly suspicious, Dave held the book up out of her reach. "Why?"

With a shrug that didn't feel anywhere near as indifferent as she'd intended, she mumbled, "No reason." She was only an arm's length away from him, but still much too far to rescue that damning book.

"No reason?" Squatting down in front of her, the closed volume held between his knees, he looked into her eyes. "Mind telling me why you won't look at me, then?" When she didn't answer, he tried again. "Megan?"

"Can I have it?" she requested weakly. "Please?"

She glanced up then, the trepidation in her eyes betraying her growing distress. Seeing the very real discomfort in her features, he held the book out to her just as she reached for it.

The collision of their hands sent it to the carpet with a soft plop. Most books will fall open to the pages where the binding is most worn. This one was no exception. There, in bold black letters that all but screamed the word, was the chapter heading: Frigidity. Beneath that, carefully highlighted with yellow marking pen, were the sentences Meg had all but memorized.

She couldn't move. As badly as she wanted to cover that awful word, she could do nothing but stare at it with a morbid fascination. Why hadn't she thrown the book away? It belonged to a part of her life that no longer existed.

Dave was unbearably quiet as he slowly turned the page. The only sound in the room more audible than the rush of wind past the windows was the sound of the pages turning. It was obvious that the entire chapter had been thoroughly read.

It seemed like an eternity before Dave spoke. When he did, his voice was restrained. "Meg," he began, his hesitation a clear indication that he was choosing his words very carefully. "Did Ted buy this book?"

She couldn't look at him. Not yet. Her gaze settled on the blue-white threads of his jeans. "No," she whispered.

"Did you?"

"Yes."

He sighed slowly. "Did Ted think you—? I mean, where'd you get the idea you were frigid?"

Her shrug was almost imperceptible.

"Did he actually *say* that to you?"

The shake of her head wasn't much stronger than her shrug had been. "No."

Dave knew he should drop it, for his own sake as well as hers. Meg's sexual relationship with Ted was the last thing he wanted to hear about. But she obviously thought the problem had rested with her, and for that reason he had to know why. "You must have gotten the idea from somewhere."

It had been more than an idea. Ted's disinterest in her had been a fact. It had shaken her confidence when she'd realized that discussing mergers with his buddies turned him on far more than she did. What sex they had had the last couple of years had been perfunctory—and usually after he'd had a few too many at a dinner party.

"I just didn't feel anything when he touched me," she heard herself admit. Even the last time they'd made love, after Ted had come as close as he had in the last two years to convincing her that this time things would be different between them, she'd felt nothing. She'd pretended. If the marriage was going to work, she had to do her part. She'd *wanted* the marriage to work. Ted had been a good man, if not the most devoted husband. He'd provided for her, met her every possible material need. He hadn't chased other women or drunk heavily or physically abused her. She'd had nothing to complain about. Her friends and family had always told her how lucky she was. They'd constantly remarked about how much she had to be grateful for. She would have appeared quite selfish and petty to complain.

But God, she'd felt so empty. "I guess that's where the idea came from. When love dies, a lot dies with it."

There was no way Dave could keep from feeling an enormous sense of relief when he heard her soft admission. He'd just been given a fighting chance. Feeling more hope than he dared acknowledge, he kept his relief to himself. His concern for her, and the blame she'd apparently placed on herself for her lack of response, took precedence.

He closed the book, leaving it facedown on the carpet. Hesitating for only a moment, he reached over and folded her hands in his. "You don't still think you are, do you?"

His hands felt warm against her cooler ones, gentle and reassuring somehow. But it was the touch of anxiety in his voice that turned her bleaker thoughts inside out. Here she was discussing the most personal of subjects with the very man who could quite probably refute her self-diagnosis. Maybe that was why Dave's concern struck her as just a little bit funny.

"I've been pretty restricted lately, so I think it's a little soon to tell."

He smiled. "It's never too soon. Look at me."

Warily she raised her head.

"You're not."

"You don't know that."

Something in his seductive blue eyes told her that no matter how she argued the matter, he'd never be convinced. His gaze never wavering, he slowly raised her palm to his lips. Her eyes widened at the contact, her breath coming in a sharp, near-silent gasp. Satisfied, he let his fingers slide from hers. "Close your eyes."

She wasn't sure why she was so quick to obey his gentle command. A moment later he knelt in front of her, his knees touching hers. She sensed rather than saw that he was moving forward. She felt rather than sensed the faint tremor in his fingers. The hair touching her left cheek was pushed back, and his lips, warm and soft, brushed just beneath her ear.

Willing herself to be perfectly still, she was aware of a faint tingling sensation as he grasped her earlobe between his lips, tugging gently before he traced a feather-light path

down the side of her neck. Her head tipped, exposing the
arch of her throat to his quest.

"What do you feel when I do this?" he whispered.

Though she was certain of little else at the moment, Meg
knew he expected an answer, would demand one if she
didn't respond. But how to describe what she felt?
"Warm," she breathed.

He continued a path to her temple, her eyelids and finally her mouth. He wouldn't kiss her, though. He just held
his lips over hers as he spoke. "I don't want you to think
about anything but what I'm doing. Concentrate very hard
and just think about what you feel."

The heat that had begun somewhere in the pit of her
stomach spread to every limb as his tongue slowly played
over her bottom lip. He moved to the top one, dipping behind its softness to taste the warmth within. With infinite
tenderness, he coaxed her into a sweetly erotic sparring, his
tongue sliding over and under hers, teasing its tip and
plunging deeply again.

She wanted to touch him, to mold the masculine lines of
his face with her fingers. She wanted to know the feel of the
silvering hair at his temples, to caress the strong cords of his
neck. Instead, she dug her fingers into the tops of her thighs,
willing herself to do only what Dave had asked—concentrate. As she did, her lips grew more pliant, her tongue more
bold. Dave was leading. Teaching. And she'd never realized how ignorant she'd been. Never had she imagined a kiss
could be so sensual.

Dave drew back just far enough to focus on her flushed
face. His eyes held hers as he touched the hollow at the base
of her throat, the throbbing there echoing the frantic pace
of her heart. When he saw that she wasn't going to stop him,
his hand continued downward, coming unbearably close to
one hardened nipple as it slid to the side of her rib cage. His

thumb pressed lightly below the fullness of her breast. She ached to have him touch her there, but he had grown still.

There was no smile to lighten the smoldering in his eyes, no teasing to remind her that this was Dave and therefore she had nothing to fear. This was the stranger she'd glimpsed before—the man who'd aroused long-dormant needs and desires and caused her to feel so restless. Those personalities seemed to merge for her when she saw him glance down to where the side of his hand rested against her rounded abdomen. When he looked at her again, and his gaze fastened on her mouth, she knew that there would be no separating them.

She felt the pressure of his hand increase as it moved upward, and heard the long, low sound of his indrawn breath. His thumb slipped up to roll over the swollen peak of her breast. Something hot shot inside her, magnifying the warmth already burning in her soul.

"I don't think you have anything to worry about," he whispered thickly. "But I sure do."

Uncurling her fingers, he drew her hand to him. A deep involuntary groan escaped his lips when he pressed her fingers beneath his. "See what you do to me, Megan?"

It was difficult enough to deal with the trembling ache he'd awakened in her. The knowledge that she had somehow created the same need in him made the struggle to deny what was happening a complete impossibility. He wanted her. And he wanted her to know it.

The thought was frightening and intriguing and compelling. And completely amazing, considering the shape she was in.

Pulling her hand from beneath his, she took a stabilizing breath. "Dave, I—"

"You don't have to say it," he cut in. "I'm no more prepared for this than you are."

"I don't understand."

"You don't have to understand anything right now. Just don't worry about it . . . and let me hold you."

At his tender words, she felt the burning in her throat, the angry sting at the back of her eyelids. These emotions came on top of leaving the place that had been her home for seven years, on top of facing a future so frighteningly different from the one she'd envisioned for herself. "I don't think that's a very good idea."

There was a catch in her voice, a definite evasiveness in the way she lowered her head. "Hey, I didn't mean to—"

"It's not you," she tried to dismiss, though his gentleness wasn't doing anything to alleviate the tears wanting to be shed. Blinking hard, she stared down at the carpet. "It's just . . . I'm . . ."

She tried to move back. Dave wouldn't let her. Smoothing the hair back from her cheek, lifting her chin with his finger, he made her look at him. "It's just what? Does my wanting you make things that much worse?"

"Yes. Maybe. Oh, Dave, I don't know."

How could she answer him when she couldn't even answer that question for herself? Her thoughts were as jangled as her nerves. "I'm not sure of anything anymore," she admitted, her voice very small. "Everything is so confusing, and I want so badly to make some sense of all this. But every time I try, it only gets worse until you come along and tell me it's going to be okay. I don't know it's all going to be okay, though. And sometimes I don't even care if it ever is . . . all that mess with the bank and the property. All I really care about then is the baby. God, if anything happens to it, I'll . . ."

For a moment Dave didn't recognize the strange sensation in his gut when her voice trailed off. Then, seeing the anguish in her glistening eyes, he realized what it was. Fear.

"Meg? The baby's all right, isn't it? Has the doctor told you something?"

Thick black curls tumbled around her face as she shook her head. Every woman worried about her unborn child, but Dave apparently didn't know that. She hadn't meant to alarm him. "No. No. The doctor says everything's fine."

"Then why are you crying?"

"I'm not."

"Oh, Meg," he said with sigh, and slipped his arms around her.

She wished he hadn't done that. His gentleness made it that much more difficult to make the ache in her throat go away. His whispered words made it impossible.

"It's all right, honey." The deep, husky tones of his voice soothing her, he cradled her against him. "Let it go. You've probably needed to do this for a long time."

Her emotions were already unstable, and she was frightened by the intensity of what Dave could cause her to feel. The tears she'd held back for so long finally started to fall. Once they did, they didn't want to stop. Feeling completely powerless, as if nothing in her life would ever be right again, she took what Dave offered. More than anything at that moment, she wanted to feel the security only he could give her.

For long minutes she sat with her head against his shoulder while he smoothed the back of her hair. And when the pain refused to abate, he carried her to her bed and stretched out beside her on the comforter while she quietly sobbed against his chest. As the wind pelted the light rain against the windows, he wrapped her in his arms and held her while she cried until the tears had been spent and she couldn't cry anymore. When she finally fell into an exhausted sleep, he carefully disentangled himself and kissed the dampness clinging to her cheeks. He stayed long enough to be sure she wouldn't wake needing him, and finally, when the wind died down around midnight, he let himself out the door.

Chapter Eight

By noon Sunday, Meg's apartment gave the impression that she'd lived there for weeks. That impression would remain, too, as long as a visitor didn't look into the second bedroom where all the yet-to-be-unpacked boxes were stored. That was where Meg was sitting in a bentwood rocker with her hands splayed atop her rounded belly. The baby was doing somersaults.

"Take it easy in there," she chuckled, her touch caressing as she followed the jerky movements. "You're going to wear yourself out."

A gentle smile lighted her eyes just before she closed them and laid her head back. Four weeks. In just four weeks her child would be born.

Meg wasn't particularly tired. She was just waiting for the baby to calm down before resuming the task of clearing a space for the crib, which would be delivered tomorrow. She deserved the break. Ever since she'd awakened at six a.m., she'd been working like a woman possessed. A lot of good it had done her. She'd accomplished plenty as far as putting the apartment in order was concerned, but hadn't been able to keep her thoughts of Dave at bay with the enforced activity. Now, when she was doing nothing but keeping up the slow, steady motion of the rocker, it was even harder to push those thoughts aside.

Dave wanted her. Incredible and illogical as that seemed, she knew she hadn't imagined that phenomenon any more than she'd imagined her own response. Her physical reaction was astounding enough. It was her emotional one that had her questioning her sanity.

Long after the heat of desire had been cooled by her tears, Dave had lain with her, holding her. Over and over he'd whispered that she was going to be all right, that she needed to realize how strong she really was. The words had seemed ludicrous to her, but she'd been sobbing too hard to counter his gentle commands. She had never been a strong person. Even in her exhaustion she'd known that only his presence lately had given her the courage to tackle matters that had sorely tested her capabilities. It was his faith in her—his constant reminders that she could do it—that kept her from giving up or giving in. He seemed to care, and she needed that very badly.

She needed to protect herself, too. Her feelings for Dave were taking a very dangerous turn, one she wasn't prepared for. Knowing she was vulnerable right now, knowing that dependency and gratitude could create an unhealthy sense of obligation, she didn't trust the basis of her need for him.

Opening her eyes, she drew a shaky breath. Not trusting the root of that need didn't mean it wasn't there. Dave had undoubtedly sensed that, which was probably why his murmured assurances last night had excluded any reference to the part he played in her life. Everything he'd said revolved around her own strength, her own ability to cope. "You can handle anything," he'd whispered. "Just believe in your-self." Not "You can depend on me" or "I'll be here."

"Oh, Meg," she groaned to herself. Then she was saved from any further ponderings by a light tapping on her front door.

Pushing herself from the rocker, she offered a silent prayer that it not be Dave, then braced herself as she reached for the knob. If she'd had a phone she would have called him this morning, solely to prevent his appearance on her doorstep. Since her phone service wouldn't be connected until tomorrow, and because the knocking was growing more insistent, it appeared she'd have to inform him face-to-face of the decision she'd made.

The Fates must have understood how desperately she needed a break. When she finally opened the door, her relief at the temporary reprieve transformed itself into a brilliant smile. "Annie! Hi! Come on in."

Looking askance at her very pregnant friend, Annie wandered through the door. She took a slow turn in the middle of the living room to check out the ficus in the corner, the framed watercolors grouped above the pastel-striped sofa and the bowl of mauve-and-pink silk flowers on the glass coffee table. When she'd given an approving nod to the wall unit—now filled with books, pottery and a few objets d'art—at the far end of the room, she crossed her arms over her neon-yellow jumpsuit and plopped down in one of the two overstuffed chairs.

"Based on your disgustingly enthusiastic greeting and the obscenely neat appearance of this place, I'd sure like to know what they put in those prenatal vitamins."

"Uh-oh. You must be out of coffee."

"You got it. Got any?"

"Only decaffeinated." She'd stopped drinking the real kind when she'd discovered she was pregnant. It was amazing how many of life's pleasures were bad for people.

"That's what I thought. Doesn't matter. Larry went to the store to get some...and a newspaper. And bread. We're out of bread. Lord, I hate grocery shopping."

"You're just getting up now?"

"It's Sunday," Annie informed her, as if that should explain everything. A moment later, her grouchy act was forgotten. She should have stuck with it. It was much more convincing than the innocent one she tried to pull off now. "Seen Dave this morning?"

With only the slightest hesitation at the unexpected question, Meg gave a light shrug. "No, I haven't. Why do you ask?"

"Just curious. Is he coming back today?"

"He didn't say. How about some orange juice?" she suggested as she crossed into the kitchen.

A small counter that also served as a breakfast bar separated the kitchen from the living area. Glancing across it, Meg caught Annie's nod, along with her mumbled "Sure." A few moments later, while setting their glasses of orange juice on the table between the chairs, Meg couldn't help but notice that her friend still looked as preoccupied as she'd sounded.

Annie was picking at a loose thread on the arm of the chair, her mouth twisted. There was something going on in that devious little mind of hers; Meg would have bet her grandma's pearls on that. It was rare that Annie introduced any topic without having a reason—and a request. Maybe she wanted to hit Dave up for a donation for the shelter.

Rather than asking for something, however, Annie was giving. "Mind if I offer some unsolicited advice?" she asked.

"My minding never stopped you before," Meg said teasingly. Though she was smiling, the expression took some effort to maintain. Annie appeared far too serious for comfort. "Go ahead."

Annie nodded, then took a sip of her juice. Having been given permission to proceed, she now seemed to be stalling as she carefully replaced the glass on the coaster. "I know this isn't any of my business," she finally began, only to stop herself. "That's not right. It is my business, because you're my friend." Once she'd justified her interference, she immediately digressed. "Meg, this thought never even occurred to me until something Larry said triggered it. At first I thought it was ridiculous, but after I got to thinking about it . . . well, it kind of made sense."

"What did?"

"What Larry said. You know, he'd never really talked to Dave before yesterday, when we were moving you in here. Don't get me wrong. He liked Dave. He just got the impression he was after something. You know how psychologists are, always trying to find the hidden meaning in what someone says or does," she added offhandedly. "Anyway, when he mentioned that, I got to thinking about how Dave used to avoid you but now seems to be going out of his way to be around."

"And?" Meg prodded, failing to see the reason for Annie's concern.

"Do you trust him?"

"Trust him?" Did she trust Dave? Of course she did. Why shouldn't she?

"I wouldn't be asking, except that it does seem a little suspicious."

Meg interrupted her, her impatience tempered by her growing apprehension. "Annie, you're beginning to sound like Lucy Bevins. What are you trying to say?"

The reference to their loquacious acquaintance stilled Annie's ramblings. "Sorry," she mumbled. "I just feel bad even bringing this up. Now, you have to understand that I wouldn't mention this if—"

"Annie."

"Oh, all right." Giving the thread on the arm of the chair a flick, she turned her troubled eyes to Meg's hands. They were folded in her lap, her thumb slowly rubbing her wedding ring. "Have you considered the possibility that Dave might be making himself so available to you because he's after your money?"

"My money?"

"Stop looking at me like I've lost my mind. It's not out of the question, you know. Just because he's already got plenty of his own doesn't mean he can't want more. You're such an easy target," she went on, sounding more like her articulate self now. "You've admitted you know nothing about the business. I'm sure that's why you're selling off everything. If I were you, I certainly wouldn't want my cash tied up in a bunch of buildings. I'd want it in the bank, too. I don't think I'd rely too heavily on someone else's advice about what to do with it once it got there, though. That's what I'm afraid you might do."

A touch of sympathetic understanding entered her eyes. That sympathy was part of what she gave so freely to the women she worked with at the shelter.

"Dave was Ted's friend. Not yours. You told me that yourself. I don't think you were very happy with Ted," she confessed, hurrying on before Meg could object to the way she'd changed the subject. "You never said as much. In fact, you went out of your way to make us all think everything was just fine. But the only person you were fooling was yourself. Just like you might be fooling yourself right now."

"You don't know what you're talking about."

"Yes, I do," Annie assured her hastily, her voice growing gentle as she saw the defensiveness that moved into Meg's eyes. "I see it all the time. You saw it, too. Women whose lives are so barren that—"

Meg inhaled sharply, her words a frantic whisper. "My life wasn't barren! I was busy. I was contributing."

"You were marking time."

"Why are you doing this?"

"Meg, please," Annie urged her, looking miserable as well as determined. "The last thing I want is to upset you. I'm just trying to warn you. Don't come to depend on Dave so much that you lose sight of what's right for you and your baby. If he's just after your money, I suspect you'll find out soon enough. In the meantime, don't kid yourself into—"

"Damn it, Annie. Stop saying that. There is no money!"

It wasn't often that Meg could so effectively counter an entire argument. With nothing else to be said on the subject, a quick and sudden silence fell over the cheerfully decorated room. Somewhere outside a radio was playing an old surfing tune.

It seemed to take a moment for Annie to grasp all the implications of what Meg had just told her. Likewise, Meg was a little slow to realize that she felt as if an enormous burden had just been lifted from her shoulders.

"I wish you'd told me before" were the incredulous blonde's first words of acknowledgment. "I feel so stupid. Geez, you talk about jumping to conclusions. How bad is it? The money, I mean."

"You know that nice big check I got from the escrow company when the sale of my house closed Thursday?" Seeing her considerably subdued friend nod, Meg forced a smile. Surprisingly, it wasn't as hard to manage as she'd thought it would be. "This time tomorrow I'll have about five hundred dollars left. Two hundred and fifty after they deliver the crib. All the rest went to creditors."

"Things aren't always what they seem, are they?" Annie mumbled. "I had no idea you were having to cope with money problems on top of everything else. And Dave's been helping you," she went on, summarizing the situation for herself. "Now I really feel awful about suspecting his motives."

Not wanting to talk about Dave, and hoping to move on to some other subject before Annie grew so contrite that she canonized him, Meg waved away Annie's self-recriminations. "Since I've got you down and kicking, I think I'll ask a favor."

"Name it."

Meg knew she didn't have to ask for Annie's silence about her financial status. Therefore, she wouldn't insult their friendship by doing so. The charade only had to be played until she could sell the mall project. Then there would be no way anyone could know that she hadn't just decided to lead an eccentrically quiet life with all the "wealth" Ted had left her. She couldn't pretend to have money when she didn't. The big house was gone, and Ted's cherished membership in the country club would expire next month. "May I use your phone?"

Meg leaned against the counter in Annie's cluttered kitchen, wrapping the phone cord around her finger while she waited for Dave to answer. Moments earlier, Annie and Larry had left for the complex's pool.

There was a distinct possibility that she might not reach Dave, that she'd get his answering machine instead. That probability seemed to increase with each ring, along with her conviction that it might be better if she didn't see him for a while. She had too much emotional baggage to unload before taking on any more.

That conviction faltered mightily at the sound of his throaty "Hello?"

"Dave? Ah, it's—"

"Megan," he cut in, finding the introduction needless. "Are you at Annie's?"

She told him she was, thinking his question logical since he knew she didn't have phone service yet. When he wanted to know how much longer she'd be there, she didn't regard the inquiry as quite so insignificant.

"I'd planned on checking in on you later," he told her when she asked why he wanted to know. "We can talk about that offer you got on the La Jolla property, if you want. You have to reply to it by the end of the week."

The one offer she'd received on the minimall was just short of insulting, which meant the only decision to be made was how curt to make the response. She knew that as well as Dave did. She did, however, find his business-as-usual approach a little unexpected. "I don't think so," she returned, swallowing past the knot of nerves in her throat. "I'm going to be busy this afternoon. I just wanted to call and thank you for everything yesterday... and to apologize for falling apart the way I did last night. I didn't mean to soak your shirt."

"You didn't do anything to apologize for." The brusqueness of his reply hinted at irritation, as if she'd offended him somehow. "Let me come over, Meg."

"I don't think that's a very good idea right now."

"Why?"

Because you confuse me, she said silently. Because if you touch me again it'll make this awful restlessness better for a while, but when you leave it'll be even worse. Because you make me want you, and I can't want you. Not now. Not while I'm carrying another man's child.

Recalling what he'd told her to do when stating a purpose, she quickly searched for the words that would most clearly convey her intent. It was important that the other side be clear on your position. That way, Dave had told her, there would be no room for misunderstandings.

"Because," she said, giving him what was probably the most important reason, "I'm not sure I can handle what seems to be happening between us."

Only a moment passed. But before she could tell him that she thought she'd be better off trying to work things out on her own for a while, he was speaking.

"I had a feeling this would happen," Dave muttered, tucking the receiver under his chin. Shoving aside the pile of clean clothing he'd carried in from the drier a few minutes before, he sat on the edge of the sofa. He wondered if he should tell her how many times he'd held back to prevent this very thing from happening. Probably not, he decided. That knowledge would be far from reassuring. What he needed to do now was remove the pressure she obviously felt.

"What did you say?" he heard her ask as he leaned his head against the back of the sofa.

"That I know what you mean," he improvised, leaning forward again. A black sock lay on the sand-and-grass-colored Aztec rug beside his foot. He must have washed it with the white load. "I've never been seduced before. The experience was a little traumatic."

Her strangled "What?" indicated that he'd taken the right approach. Contrary to what she thought, he was a very patient man. He'd waited for her this long, hadn't he?

"Is this a bad connection? I can hear you just fine."

"There's nothing wrong with the connection" was her slightly exasperated reply. "And I didn't seduce you."

"It's okay. Really. I was flattered. A little surprised that someone of your refined demeanor would be so overtly aggressive," he went on blandly. "But I was really quite flattered. You show excellent taste."

"You've got to be the most immodest man I've ever known."

"Nonsense. I kept all my clothes on. If I'd known you wanted them off—"

"Dave, come on. I'm serious."

"Me, too," he said with a sigh. "All things considered, I guess it's best that I won't be around for a while."

A slight hesitation preceded her quiet "You're going somewhere?"

"I wouldn't have gone without telling you," he assured her, feeling a little guilty that he found the disappointment in her voice so satisfying. "I'll be leaving for New York on Wednesday. I've got a few loose ends to tie up there before I can wind up the deal in Tokyo the following week. I'll be back in time to take you to the benefit a week from Saturday. We promised Annie we'd be there. Remember?"

Meg did indeed remember her promise to Annie, though by the time the event arrived she wished she'd never made it. She was eight and a half months along, and going to a formal dinner-dance was about the last thing she wanted to do. She'd silently mentioned that to the reflection in her bedroom mirror several times during the past hour. And now it seemed that she didn't have an escort, anyway.

"Dave said he'd meet you there," Annie reminded her from where she sat on the edge of Meg's bed. "Now stop fussing with your hair and come on. You look wonderful."

"For a whale," Meg muttered, deciding it wasn't the headful of sleek black curls that was the problem. Her hairstyle was perfect, and her makeup was flattering, as always. Maybe it was her gown.

Caught by a sapphire satin band above her breasts, matching crepe fell in loose folds to the floor. Two satin straps centered on the band, forming a V as they parted over her shoulders and met in back to form a wide, shining bow. The bare-shouldered style accentuated her delicate bone structure, and the rich jewellike color complemented the warm tones of her skin. It was a simple gown, and that was what made it so elegant. Meg knew that, but she just couldn't seem to see it at the moment.

"I think we should have torn down the drapes after all." Her hand at her lower back to ease the dull ache there, she turned sideways and critically eyed her creation in the mirror. She definitely looked slimmer from the front. "When Scarlett did that and whipped up *her* gown, she convinced a whole jail full of people that she was as wealthy as she'd ever been."

"I don't think you would have achieved the same effect. She had green velvet to work with. The curtains here are off-white polyester."

The long, elaborate rhinestone earrings Annie wore threw tiny spots of light on the wall when the light on the nightstand caught them. In the mirror Meg saw those spots dance along the wall as Annie slowly shook her head at her misgivings. She knew she sounded terribly unenthusiastic about the evening, but even her desire to make her friend happy couldn't alleviate the uneasiness she'd been fighting all day.

"I can guarantee no one will know that gorgeous thing only cost twenty-two dollars," Annie said. Then she cocked her head. "Do you want to tell me what's really bothering you?"

"You'll think it's stupid."

"Try me."

"I think I have stage fright. In a way, this is like a farewell performance for me—only no one knows it. I'll be acting out a part I should have memorized by now, but I feel like I've forgotten all my lines."

"Will seeing a lot of Ted's old friends bother you?"

"I don't know. I don't *think* so. I feel so far removed from that whole group."

"That's because you're back in the real world with the rest of us now. Come on, you'll feel better when you see Dave."

With studied nonchalance, Meg picked up the silver beaded bag she'd carried to so many other formal affairs. The slight unsteadiness of her hand was there only because she hadn't felt like eating that afternoon, she assured herself. It had nothing to do with seeing the man she'd tried so hard not to think about. "Why should seeing Dave make me feel better?"

"Doesn't it usually?" Annie returned glibly, moving out the door in a cloud of crimson chiffon.

As she followed, flipping off lights as she went, Meg thought better of asking for clarification of that cryptic question. Annie's impressions of a situation seldom left her with anything but a headache.

As it was, Meg didn't have a chance to inquire. The second Annie realized they were finally under way, her paranoia took over and she voiced her worries about everything from whether or not the orchestra would show up to how long Meg thought she could stand by the door collecting tickets. Months of preparation had gone into the event, but more than the success of one evening was at stake.

The South Coast Women's Shelter received funds from several agencies, but none of those sources contributed more to the coffers than the attendees of the annual charity ball. The thrift store operated by the shelter covered the cost of the crisis line. But if the shelter hoped to maintain its facilities, to take in more battered and abused women and provide them with counseling and a place to stay while they decided what to do with their lives, much more money was needed. Several thousand dollars had already been raised by attaching a hefty price to an admission ticket. It was hoped that the hundred-thousand-dollar mark would be reached before the night was over. That hope ran high as the beautifully gowned and coiffed and cologned and tuxedoed supporters of the shelter abandoned their cars to the club's uniformed valets.

Few private clubs in the area could match the Crestline Country Club for pure ostentation. In addition to a championship golf course, twenty lighted tennis courts, an Olympic-size pool, spas, saunas and workout rooms, it boasted an intimate dining room, enormous banquet facilities and grounds that rivaled the majestic gardens of Europe. The management of the facility had donated the ballroom and provided the flowers set on each of the round, linen-covered tables surrounding the spacious dance floor. That generosity had been met by many others.

Experience had proved that people tend to feel more benevolent when plied with rich food and good wines. Therefore, tray after tray of intricate canapés—prepared by a prominent local caterer who'd donated everything but the cost of the ingredients—was circulated by uniformed members of the club's staff. Those young men and women had also donated their time. Only the liquor wholesaler hadn't joined the spirit of the event. Apparently a distant relative of Scrooge, he'd only given them the standard bulk rate on the many cases of champagne they'd ordered.

The champagne continued to flow, and by ten o'clock three hundred and eighty people were eating, drinking, and dancing to music played by an orchestra as talented as it was punctual. The event, Annie proclaimed with considerable relief, had all the earmarks of a huge success. She could hardly wait to add up the checks, which had been dropped in the crystal bowl by the door.

If Meg had been the jealous type, she would have envied her friend's exuberance. As the evening progressed, her smile, which was a natural response to many of the old acquaintances she met, became harder and harder to manage. She wasn't allowed to dwell on the indefinable uneasiness that robbed the glow from her eyes. There was too much going on, too many friends engaging her in either probing or innocuous conversation. She received many offers to dance, all of which she tactfully declined. Judging from the hesitation in the faces of the men who requested that honor, Meg was pretty sure they expected her to refuse anyway. All except for Skip Cunningham. He'd had just a tad more to drink than was advisable, and he grew rather insistent about "taking one little turn around the floor," before Buffy, her eyes beseeching the ceiling, hauled him off.

Meg was still watching Buffy's animated gestures as she escorted her darling Skippy back to their table when Larry appeared in front of her.

"Mind if I join you?"

At Larry's inquiry, Meg picked up her glass of ginger ale and motioned to the seat beside her. All the chairs at her table were empty at the moment, their occupants presently out on the dance floor. The seat Meg indicated belonged to a pleasant blue-haired matron who'd delighted in telling her how much progress medical science had made concerning childbirth in the last thirty years.

"He still isn't here yet, huh?"

"Not yet," she returned, refusing to let her disappointment show. In the past hour she'd gone from trying not to think about Dave to trying not to admit how much she missed him. Unfortunately, she realized that she was also failing to acknowledge other feelings—feelings she was afraid to name. "When he called from Seattle he said his connection was running two hours late. It must be even farther behind schedule than he'd thought."

"I once got stuck in Chicago for eleven hours," Larry offered. Then he apparently realized that wasn't the kind of thing she wanted to hear. "Annie's busy, so she asked me to see how you were doing. You shouldn't be sitting here by yourself. Do you want to dance?''

With a soft laugh, Meg shook her head. "Thanks, but I think we'd both feel a little awkward out there."

"It would be kind of like dancing with a beach ball," Larry observed. Then, grinning, he sat back and engaged her in a game of people-watching until the lady with the blue hair returned to reclaim her seat. Telling her not to worry if Dave didn't show up—that he and Annie would take her home—Larry melted back into the crowd to locate his wife.

"I'm not worried," Meg quietly lied to his retreating back.

"I beg your pardon, dear?"

"Oh, ah . . . nothing," she said to the lady beside her. "I was just talking to myself. Will you excuse me, please?"

She was not worried. Repeating that to herself as she pushed herself to her feet, she also added that she really hadn't missed him all *that* much.

With that lie reverberating in her head, and trying to ignore how much her lower back bothered her, she straightened her shoulders and slipped toward the ladies' room. Since this was her third trip of the evening, she figured she must have consumed more liquid than she'd thought. No more ginger ale tonight.

And no more worrying, she realized, when on her return trek through the colorful crowd she caught sight of a familiar blond head bent in conversation. In the mellow light cast by the enormous crystal chandeliers, her eyes skimmed the breadth of his shoulders, drinking in the sight of him as he turned to survey the crowd. Too many people and too much distance separated them for him to catch sight of her easily. It was probably just as well. She needed this moment.

"Dave," she heard herself whisper, letting herself feel the pure pleasure of knowing that he was finally here.

There was so much she wanted to tell him, so many things she needed to share. Little things, such as telling him about the tobacco shop she'd found in La Jolla that sold the imported cheroots he liked to smoke on occasion. Major developments, such as how the ridiculously low offer she'd received on the mall property had led to serious interest. She wanted him to tell her how his trip had gone and whether or not he was pleased with what he'd accomplished. More than anything else, she wanted to be in his arms.

Knowing that was not possible, her eyes nonetheless bright with amusement at what kind of reaction *that* would get from this crowd, she started forward. A second later she stopped, a slight frown touching her forehead.

The odd sensation of pressure in her back and abdomen passed within moments. Last week she'd experienced the same thing, only to call her doctor and find out that the little twinges usually meant nothing. She told herself that now, and her concern evaporated when Dave caught her eye.

Fifty feet and as many people stood between them, yet Dave felt the impact of her brilliant smile. She was the best thing that had happened to him all day.

Make that all week, he corrected himself, as he moved through the crowd. He didn't know what he'd have done if she hadn't looked so pleased to see him. He hadn't let himself think about it.

Dave was beat. After ten days of nearly nonstop negotiations he'd had to endure a plane trip from Japan that had threatened to strand him first in Tokyo and then in Seattle. He'd then spent half an hour sitting on the freeway while the police cleared away an accident before he could get home, trade in his business suit for a tuxedo and make it to the club before the benefit ended. Now, as he saw the delight come into Meg's eyes at his approach, the tension he'd felt all day lessened considerably. Even the weariness that had crept into his bones was momentarily forgotten.

His quiet hello was probably a bit more cautious than necessary. But he knew this was neither the time nor the place for a bolder greeting. He still remembered too well the sickening sensation he'd felt when she'd called the day after she'd moved into her new apartment to apologize for crying in his arms. He'd since spoken to her on the phone, but only to tell her of his delayed arrival. She'd sounded fine, but with women one never could tell for sure. All he knew for certain was that as tired as he was, he didn't think he'd do very well in the face of anything that hinted at discomfort with his presence. Thank God she actually seemed happy to see him.

"I'm so glad you're back," Meg heard herself admit, restraining the need she felt to touch him when he stopped an arm's length away. That need was almost a tangible thing, and it took enormous effort to curb it. "How was your trip?"

The lines at the corners of his eyes deepened with his tired smile. Stronger than ever was the need to touch, to smooth the fatigue from his brow. Meg kept her hands at her sides.

"Over," he returned, probably not even realizing that he'd almost sighed the word. "You're glad I'm back?"

"Very," she said, then laughed lightly to temper her admission. She hadn't meant to sound so serious. "So much has happened. And there's so much I need to ask you about," she added, wanting to tell him everything at once but knowing she'd have to take one thing at a time. "You remember the offer I turned down on the mall? It turns out that they still want to talk. I've got a meeting with them next week. Maybe tomorrow you can tell me what I should do. If you don't have any plans, I'll fix us dinner." She rushed through the invitation, hoping he wouldn't think she was being too forward. It was perfectly acceptable for a woman to ask a man to dinner. Meg knew that. The excuse of work was just a handy way of not having to admit how badly she wanted to be with him. Alone. "I really need your advice on this."

"My advice, huh?" Dave kept his eyes steady on Meg's face. It seemed that he'd just done an excellent job of misinterpreting the delight in her expression. The smile in her eyes was real enough, but he'd let his guard down far too soon. When he'd done that, his foolishness had made him see only what he'd wanted to see. She wasn't happy he was back because of any growing emotional tie. The only reason she was glad he was here was that he could now solve a problem for her.

Cursing himself, annoyed with her, he hid his hurt behind what he hoped would sound like a friendly suggestion. What had he expected, anyway? he wondered as he extracted a pack of cigarettes from the inside pocket of his black jacket. To have her throw her arms around him? "Have you come up with a strategy of your own yet?"

"Not really. I—"

"Try that first. You're perfectly capable of coming up with something. We'll talk after you have." His voice lost its edge when Annie's husband appeared at his side. "Larry!" He extended his hand. "I thought I saw you over there when I came in. What does Annie think about this turnout?"

Discussion closed. Meg looked up at Dave, not at all sure why he'd sounded so exasperated or why he was so busily ignoring her. Having responded to her apparently inconsequential remarks, he seemed to find Larry's assessment of the benefit's outcome more interesting. Meg glanced from one man to the other. She felt like a troublesome child who'd just been dismissed from the company of adults.

If it hadn't been for the uncomfortable pressure she felt again in her back and abdomen, she might have acknowledged how much Dave's coolness distressed her. As it was, she didn't think about much of anything except excusing herself and going to the ladies' room again. Maybe, she thought, telling herself not to get too excited, it wasn't the ginger ale after all.

The women's lounge was emptier than she'd seen it all night. Only two women were in the furnished anteroom, both occupied with the task of checking their makeup. Closed in one of the stalls a few moments later, though, Meg heard others enter.

She recognized Lucy Bevins's voice immediately, but really didn't pay too much attention to what was being said until she heard her own name mentioned. Even then, she tried not to listen—a noble effort, but a hopeless one.

"That's utterly insane, Vanessa," she heard Lucy protest. "So what if they were at Annie's wedding together. Meg can't be expected to attend social functions all by herself."

"I still think there might be something going on there. Did you see the way she looked at him?"

"Oh, for heaven's sake," came Lucy's softly drawled reply. "You thought Adele looked like she was mad at Clinton until you got close enough to find out it was just her tight shoes making her face look that way. I know for a fact that there's nothing going on between David Elliott and Meg Reese. He was Ted's friend, you know, and he just feels sorry for her. He even told my husband that," she added proudly.

The sound of running water drowned out Vanessa's reply. Meg hadn't cared to hear it, anyway. Lucy's valiant defense, well-intentioned though it had been, had carried far more sting than Vanessa's meddlesome assumptions. Coupled with the way Dave had acted a few minutes ago, Lucy's assertion that he had befriended her only out of pity caused Meg to make saving face her first priority. That was why she made no attempt to open the stall door, though her hand had been on the latch for several seconds now.

Standing inside the stall, her hand over her mouth to still the moan of disbelief that wanted to escape, she waited for the women to leave so she wouldn't embarrass them or herself. But she wasn't allowed to fully acknowledge her revulsion at being labeled the object of Dave's pity. A spasm hit her just then, nearly bringing her to her knees.

Chapter Nine

The pain eased, leaving Meg a little breathless as she leaned against the beige metal wall. Given the consistency of the contractions she'd felt most of the day, and their increasing severity in the past couple of hours, she was inclined to dismiss any notion of false labor—especially after that last one. Though she wasn't due for two more weeks, it seemed apparent that her child had no qualms about arriving ahead of time. Meg, however, had a few misgivings of her own. Not with the updated schedule, but with her present awkward circumstances.

Feeling the strength return to her legs, she smoothed back her hair and slowly opened the door. If she ran into Lucy and Vanessa, she'd simply pretend she hadn't heard their chat, which was the only polite thing to do. She didn't want to think any farther ahead than that. Already confused by Dave's attitude toward her tonight, she wanted desperately to avoid thinking about what she'd just overheard. It was entirely possible that Lucy had misunderstood what her husband had told her. Lucy, bless her, wasn't apt to invent gossip, so the thought that she'd lied wasn't a consideration.

But if Lucy *hadn't* misunderstood, Meg thought, the only reason Dave was being her friend was because he— A quiet sigh of relief blocked the remainder of that disquieting thought. Tossing her paper towel into the trash, Meg rounded the corner to see the lounge door close behind Vanessa. Lucy had been two steps in front of her.

Encouraged by that reprieve, Meg continued past the two women watching her in the mirror. Though Dave's dismissive attitude still stung fiercely, she had to remember all the times he'd drilled her on the importance of priorities. "Always deal first with the most unavoidable issue," he'd insisted. "But be prepared for that issue to change."

With those cryptic words of wisdom planted firmly in her mind, she offered her audience a brave smile and pulled back the brass-handled door. First priority was the baby. Nature waited for no woman.

Dave didn't appear to be in any rush to acknowledge her when she spotted him by her table. Larry was still with him, and they'd been joined by Ansel and two other men Meg had never met. Ready with a smile for the anticipated introductions, she glanced up to see Dave watch her approach.

Not a single muscle moved in his face. No recognition. No greeting. No disapproval. Nothing. He just sent her a cool and level look that seemed to indicate that she was of no particular significance, then glanced away to speak to the man on his right. The deliberate slight immediately checked her forward progress. It also made her change her immediate plans.

Praying that the night would soon be over—that tomorrow she'd wake up and find that the last hour had been nothing more than a too-realistic nightmare—Meg slipped between two large groups of people in search of Annie. Not spotting her on this side of the room, she was about to scan the other when she caught a flash of scarlet out on the dance floor. Annie was out there, which meant Meg couldn't get to her without being trampled.

"You walked right by us," Larry said, grasping her elbow from behind. The constant buzz of conversations competing with the big-band sounds of the orchestra made him bend forward to be heard. "We're over at the table."

Telling Larry that she'd seen them but was looking for his wife, she nodded toward the swaying bodies several yards ahead of them. "Would you mind getting her for me? She's right there with—"

The pang started in the middle of her back, then seemed to reach around both sides until it met in the center of her abdomen. By the time the pain connected in front, her knees had almost given again and she was holding on to Larry for support.

"Oh, my God," she heard Larry mumble when he grabbed for her. "Oh, my God," he repeated as the conversations around them grew quieter.

It seemed to take longer for the contraction to subside this time, making her relief that much greater when it finally did. Drawing a deep breath as soon as she could, she relaxed her grip on Larry's arm. The poor man was as pale as his white dinner jacket. "It's okay now. Honest," she assured him, very aware of how quiet the people closest to them had become. "Would you get Annie for me? I really need to talk to her for a minute."

As Dave stepped beside Larry, he heard Meg's pleading request. Moments ago, when Larry had gone after her, Dave had still been nursing the dent in his ego. His ego still wasn't in very good shape, and it hadn't been salved at all by his deliberately ignoring her. All his rudeness had done was make him feel worse—especially after he'd seen the expression drain from her face when she'd clutched Larry's arm to lean against him. Even in the dim light, she'd paled visibly.

Concerned—though he didn't want to show it—and a little afraid that the reason for her discomfort might be the onset of labor, he watched her hand slide from Larry's sleeve. "What's going on?" he asked, glancing at Larry.

Meg started to reply, but hearing Larry's "I'm not really sure," she glanced up to realize that the question hadn't been directed at her. It was then that she noticed something in Dave's expression that she hadn't seen in a very long time—the cool indifference that had permeated so much of their former relationship.

"I think I should go home," she said, her words sounding defeated as she directed them to the pleats in his cummerbund. "I just wanted to tell Annie."

"I'll tell her." Anxious either to help or be rid of her—it was probably an equal mix of both—Larry patted Meg's shoulder. "Why don't you go on?"

"Does she have a coat?" Dave asked Larry.

"Yes, I do," Meg said, refusing to be invisible, even though Dave seemed to think she was.

Reluctantly, it seemed to her, he finally met her eyes. Now she couldn't hold his glance. "Then let's go."

A mask of absolute calm hid the morass of anxieties clawing at Meg as Dave escorted her past the knots of exuberant guests and out through the lobby. She headed toward the cloakroom, which was to their left. The main doors were to the right, and that was where Dave went to send the valet in search of his car.

"If you'll just take me home so I can pick up my overnight bag," she said when she met him under the front portico, "I'll take a cab to the hospital. I don't want to inconvenience you," she added with a guarded smile. She hated asking him to do even that much for her, but he was her escort, after all. It would be rude to ask someone else to take her home after he'd gone out of his way to get here.

"It's not an inconvenience."

"Dave, I don't want to impose."

She didn't know how he did it, but somehow he managed to speak quite distinctly though his jaw was visibly clenched. "You aren't going to the hospital alone," he informed her as the valet jumped out of his maroon sedan and ran around the back to open Meg's door.

"I'm perfectly capable of going by myself," she informed him as she settled in and watched him slide into the driver's seat and slam his door. "Calling a cab is what I'd planned on doing all along."

Thick and uncomfortable silence ruled for several seconds while Dave pulled out of the drive. Painful as it was, Meg fervently hoped the silence would continue. The quiet felt dangerous, but conversation was deadly. It seemed as if every time they opened their mouths tonight the situation between them got worse.

That thought had no sooner registered than Dave proceeded to prove it correct. "You're *not* going to the hospital with a stranger, Meg. You need to go with someone who—"

"Pities me?" she suggested, goaded by his domineering manner. "No, thanks. I don't need any more of your pity."

"What in the hell do you mean by that?"

"Just what I said. You...ohh..."

The building contraction effectively prevented any further explanation. Biting down on her lower lip, Meg closed her eyes and tried to remember what her doctor had told her about deep, even breathing. Dave would just have to understand that she couldn't talk to him right now.

At the sound of her strangled moan, Dave's irritated glance swung from the converging traffic. Her stoic expression couldn't hide her agony, and his sudden preoccupation with doing whatever he could to alleviate it made him forget about asking more questions.

He reached out, grabbing her hand where it formed a fist against her abdomen. Shooting a glance into the rearview mirror, he changed lanes and headed for the freeway. As close together as her pains seemed to be, he wasn't going to waste time taking her home to get any suitcase. They were going straight to the hospital. Few thoughts made him as nervous as the idea of having to deliver a baby. The thought that truly terrified him was of something happening to Meg and him not being able to help her.

Dave stood in the maternity-ward waiting room, his forehead pressed to the darkened window and his shoulders slumped in fatigue. The last time he'd looked at his watch, it had been just after 4:00 a.m. If he closed his eyes, he'd probably fall asleep. He hadn't slept since Tokyo— roughly twenty-four hours ago.

Blinking hard, he pushed his fingers through his hair, prepared to resume the interminable pacing. He thought about going outside for another cigarette but couldn't find the energy. He'd brought Meg here over five hours ago, and he was still waiting. He couldn't go home, though she'd made it clear enough that she didn't want him to stick around. "I appreciate the ride, Dave," was all she'd said before the nurse had wheeled her away.

He didn't know what else he'd expected—or even what he'd wanted—when he'd watched the elevator doors close. It was crazy to think that she'd want him with her, but that was exactly where he needed to be.

Needed. Yes, he admitted, sighing as he sank down on the brown vinyl sofa across from the vending machines. He needed her. From that moment seven long years ago when he'd first seen her laughing green eyes and felt the warmth of her smile, he'd never been able to get her fully out of his mind. He'd almost succeeded for a while, but only because he'd imagined that he had. In all that time he'd never really been free of the desire, the caring or the guilt.

It had been wrong to want her, and he'd hated himself for his weakness. What kind of a man was he to want another man's wife? And not just any man's, but the wife of his best friend? The disloyalty of it appalled him. The constancy of it haunted him.

He'd first labeled the attraction as lust, because that was a feeling without any strong underlying emotion. He'd been twenty-seven, and at that stage of his life, underlying emotions were nothing but nasty little nuisances. According to his parents' plan, he wasn't due to get serious about anyone until he was thirty, and far be it from him to preempt their schedule on that one subject. But the feeling he'd christened lust had soon become more complicated.

He and Ted had seen each other often, which had necessarily meant that Dave had seen a lot of Meg. The more he'd been around her, the more infatuated he'd become. She was fun and warm and caring and completely unaffected. At her table one was filled not only with good food but with the pleasure she'd put into its preparation. In her home even strangers—and Ted had sprung plenty of them on her—were made to feel completely welcome. In her presence he'd felt healed, though he hadn't really recognized that feeling for what it was at the time. He had known, however, how devoted she'd been to her husband.

Even if she'd shown some sign of disenchantment with her marriage, Dave couldn't have betrayed his friendship with Ted by letting his feelings be known. So for the better part of four years he'd tried thinking of Meg as he did his sister. It was a trick that worked well on the surface but failed miserably otherwise. He'd realized the extent of that failure when Ted had begun leaving Meg more and more often, dismissing her in favor of his business. Dave had tried to help Ted see what he apparently couldn't—that he was going to lose Meg if he didn't start making some time for her.

That heart-to-heart conversation with Ted had left Dave feeling the way one does when swallowing bitter medicine—hating the immediate taste but knowing that you've done the right thing. Ted had agreed that he needed to slow down. Meg was a good woman, and he didn't want to lose her. The subject hadn't come up again until a couple of years ago. Then Dave's reception was the polar opposite of before. Ted had informed Dave that he didn't want to discuss his marriage with him, that Meg was perfectly happy doing whatever it was she did. Why, he'd wanted to know, was Dave so damned interested in his wife's welfare, anyway?

It was at that point that Dave had realized he'd given himself far more credit than he was due. Ted hadn't said as much, but it was clear that he'd been aware of Dave's feelings for Meg. Equally clear was the unspoken trust Ted had placed in him by not confronting that sleeping issue.

Dave's own acting ability wasn't the only thing he'd overestimated. He'd misjudged his endurance. No longer had he had the strength to continue watching Meg lose the vitality that had once brightened her laughter. Each time he'd seen her she'd been that much more subdued, that much less the spontaneous creature who'd captured his heart. But she'd still had his heart, and that was why it had become so difficult to be around her. Each time he'd been with her, Dave had felt angrier at Ted for sucking the life from her, and angrier still at Meg for letting him do it. For his own sanity, Dave had known he had to create some distance between himself and the woman he thought he could never have. The wall had been thrown up—only to be reduced to rubble two years later. The trouble was, he was too damned tired at the moment to even care.

"Mr. Reese? Er . . . Mr. Elliott?" came the quick correction. Opening his eyes with effort, Dave raised his head from the sofa. The crisply efficient nurse who'd kindly taken to checking on him during the past couple of hours stood over him, an aluminum clipboard in her hand. "Would you like to take a peek at the baby?"

"The baby?" he repeated, his muscles screaming for rest as he forced himself to stand up.

The nurse smiled. "It's a girl."

"A girl." There was no question accompanying the repetition this time. Only the statement, followed by a slow grin that almost immediately gave way to panic. "Meg? How's Meg? Is she—?"

"Mrs. Reese is fine."

"Can I see her?"

"She's sleeping."

"I won't wake her."

"I don't—"

"I promise."

Reconsidering, the matronly woman nodded. "I suppose you can peek in on her, too." The quality of her smile shifted a little as she glanced from the haggard creases in his face to the open collar of his pleated and rather wrinkled formal shirt and tuxedo trousers. Jacket, tie and cummerbund had long ago been tossed into the back seat of his car, and the night had produced a predictable scratchy stubble along his jaw. "After that, I suggest you go home and get some sleep. Frankly, you look even worse than most of the fathers do after they've gone through this."

Dave had to give the woman credit. Without any long explanations or intimate questions, she seemed to understand that Meg meant a lot to him. She'd come on duty at midnight and seen him pacing alone in the waiting room. He'd told her he was a friend of the family.

Quiet footsteps marked their progress down a silent, dimly lighted hall. Stopping outside one of the rooms, the small brown-haired nurse put her hand on his arm and leaned closer so he could hear her whisper. "She's in the bed by the window. I'll wait for you here."

Her unspoken message was clear: Make it short.

Dave stepped into the shadowy room, quietly moving past the empty bed by the door. A curtain was drawn nearly to the foot of the bed by the window. Silently he moved into the small space created for Meg, becoming still when he reached her side.

She was lying on her back, her eyes closed and her head turned toward him. The fingers of her left hand were curled at her cheek, her wrist encircled by a white plastic band. Each breath she took was deep, regular and very relaxed. The one Dave released was slow, controlled and very relieved.

He allowed his hand to rest on the smooth sheet tucked under her chin, and his glance moved over her serene features. She looks so peaceful, he thought, smiling at the way her black curls formed little ringlets on the pillow. The smile faded. Her bangs were pushed away from her face, as if someone had smoothed them for her—a nurse perhaps, offering comfort from the pain. Never had he felt so helpless.

For several seconds, he simply stood there trying to absorb the fact that she was really all right. It hadn't been easy, but he'd tried very hard not to think about complications with the delivery. Just as he'd tried very hard not to dwell on what had happened between him and Meg. They needed to talk tomorrow. But how? Lover to potential lover? Friend to friend? Adviser to client? God, did she really only think of him when she had a problem to solve?

Slowly he shook his head, wanting to dispel questions he was too tired to deal with. Later he'd figure out what to do.

With that in mind, he bent to kiss her forehead. After stopping by the nursery window to see the child he fervently wished was his, he promised himself twelve hours of uninterrupted sleep.

"What about Corra Colleen, after your dad's cousin," Meg heard her mother suggest. Propped up in her hospital bed with the phone tucked under her chin, Meg had been listening to her mother's advice, encouragement and admonitions for the past ten minutes. An end was finally in sight. A nurse would bring the babies around soon. "Or Bridget, after your great-aunt. We haven't had a Bridget for a long time."

In a deliberate attempt to keep her annoyance from her voice, Meg softened her tone. She had no idea why this conversation was irritating her so. "I don't want to name her after anyone, Mom. I want her to have her own name. Why don't you like Rebecca Anne?"

"It's not that I don't like it, dear. We just don't have any Rebecca Annes in the family."

"We do now."

"Is the Anne after your friend Annie?"

"No, Mom. Annie's given name is Anastasia."

"Oh. Well, Rebecca Anastasia would be a bit much. Can't you think of something that's been in our family, though? Clarissa might be nice. You remember your second cousin Clarissa, don't you? Having a namesake is such an honor," her mother said for the third or fourth time.

"I suppose," Meg returned, though she refused to yield. She never had cared for the idea of naming a baby after someone. Life could be tough enough, and as important as a name was, she saw no sense in starting a child off with the unnecessary pressure of having to live up to a name—or live it down, for that matter. Granted, that was only how *she* saw it, but it was her decision to make.

"Rebecca Anne is already on the birth certificate," she said, easing herself up when she saw Nurse Stapleton entering the room with a tiny bundle in her arms. "And Rebecca herself has just arrived. It's feeding time."

"Is it really? Or are you trying to get rid of me?"

Smiling because she knew her mother was, Meg watched the round little woman with butterflies on her yellow smock stop beside her bed. Over the top of the pink blanket, Meg could see a sparse patch of black hair. "Oh, definitely trying to get rid of you. Grandmas can be just awful pests, you know."

"I can't wait to see her" was her mother's wistful reply. "Her being ahead of schedule threw us a little here, but I'll be there Wednesday. You take care of yourself, dear."

Offering what she hoped was a properly assuring "I will," Meg hung up the phone and gingerly repositioned herself. Moments later, the nurse retreating, Meg had forgotten all about the discomforts involved in moving around, her inexplicable irritation with her mother and the nagging thought that she should call Dave. When she held her baby, she seemed to forget about everything else.

This time it was easier for Rebecca to nurse. The first time neither she nor Meg had been too comfortable with the process, though Rebecca had adapted quite well once she'd found what she was looking for. Meg, not knowing what to expect, had indulged her apprehensions for a bit longer, but had quickly given them up when she'd realized that Rebecca knew what she was doing—even if her mother didn't.

Her baby was pink and soft and sweet. To Meg, she was absolutely beautiful. She had counted fingers and toes, then anxiously scanned the round little face until she'd assured herself that the doctors were right. Her baby was perfect. Her baby. "You know something?" she asked the suckling infant as she rubbed her soft cheek. "It's just you and me, kid. But I'll tell you what. We're going to be just fine."

I hope, she added silently, as if expressing any doubt aloud might make Rebecca question her conviction. The infant was oblivious to her mother's assurances, which didn't matter, because Meg was talking for her own benefit.

Meg made three laps up and down the hall after Nurse Stapleton took Rebecca back to the nursery, then slept until dinner. Annie, who'd stopped by to see her during her lunch hour and was responsible for the bouquet of daisies in the pink ceramic baby carriage on the windowsill, called just as Meg was finishing her milk.

"That was a truly unenthusiastic hello," Annie immediately informed her. "Are you all right?"

"I guess so."

"You *guess* so? If you don't know, who does?"

Frowning at the milk foam in the bottom of her glass, Meg gave a disgusted sigh and shoved the glass back on her tray. "I'm fine, really."

"Why am I not convinced?" Annie drawled.

Meg laid her head back and stared up at the ceiling. There were 487 holes in the acoustical tile directly above her. She knew that because she'd counted them while trying not to think about Dave. "Are you sure you want to hear this?"

Assured that Annie did indeed want to hear and finding herself with a sympathetic ear, Meg did something she'd tried very hard to avoid. She gave in.

"I think I'm depressed. I know I have no reason to be," she said hurriedly even though she knew Annie wouldn't laugh at her. "I just gave birth to a beautiful baby and she's healthy and I'm okay and I know how to nurse her now so she isn't going to starve and—" It was necessary to take a breath, and that would give Annie the opportunity to interrupt her if she was sounding as foolish as she thought she was.

Annie did nothing but encourage her to continue. "And?"

"I've got to call that jerk at the bank and postpone my meeting with him because I've got to meet with a prospective buyer first. That's the last thing I feel like doing, because I get so nervous when I talk to him. And when I get nervous I have to clear my throat and when I do that now it feels like the bottom half of my body... Oh, God," she groaned, promising never to make fun of Lucy's ramblings again. "I think I'd cry if I knew it wouldn't hurt."

"Meg?" came Annie's quiet inquiry. "Is there a nurse there that you'd feel comfortable talking with?"

Removing her hand from her face, Meg mumbled, "They're all nice. Why?"

"Because I think you need some reassurance. I may be wrong, but you sound like a classic case to me."

"A classic case of what?"

"Postpartum depression."

"The baby blues? It's too soon for that," Meg said, thinking the view of the parking lot out her window was pretty dismal. No trees. No ocean. Just concrete, lampposts and cars. "The books say that doesn't hit until after the third day or so."

"So maybe you aren't a textbook case. Do you want me to come by tonight? We can look you up in a manual and list your deficiencies."

Annie's suggestion made Meg smile, which in turn made her realize that her view could have been much worse. She could just as easily have been given a room outside the garbage dumpsters. Suddenly she caught sight of a maroon Seville parked at the end of one of the closer rows.

"Ah, thanks," she heard herself answer Annie. "But I'm already borrowing you from Larry tomorrow. I should let you go now. Can you still pick me up in the morning?

Great," she returned when Annie indicated that she could. "I'll call you as soon as they give me a time."

For several moments after Meg replaced the receiver, she sat with her heart pounding heavily. It was entirely possible that the vehicle she was staring at did not belong to Dave. There were lots of maroon cars like his in Southern California.

"They said I could just come in."

Dave stood by the curtain that divided the room in half. His hands were in the pockets of his dark slacks, drawing the sides of his suit jacket back. His tie was loose. The overhead light caught the faint strands of silver that threaded through his sandy hair as he cocked his head to one side. "How do you feel?"

Awkward, she thought, drawing the sheet to her breasts. The hospital gown she wore had little forget-me-nots on it and was modest to a fault, provided one remained either prone or seated. Still, she felt terribly exposed under Dave's cool blue-eyed scrutiny. She hadn't expected to see him, and had tried very hard not to think of him at all—especially this afternoon. "A little embarrassed, actually."

"Why's that?"

It was easier, somehow, to look anywhere but at him. Choosing a smudge on the pastel-yellow wall opposite his jacket sleeve, she glanced first there, then down at her lap. "I should have called you before now. I didn't thank you for what you did last night."

"Yes, you did."

His curt reply brought her head up. She frowned. "I'm sure I didn't. I remember thinking you must be exhausted after your trip and that you'd probably have preferred to go straight home instead of to the club. But I don't remember thanking you for going out of your way for me."

Oh, Lord, she thought helplessly, I'm not saying this right.

"I stand corrected," she heard him mutter, and caught his deferential nod. "I thought you were talking about the ride here."

"Have you seen Rebecca?" The question, she knew, was abrupt, and the change of subject was probably far too obvious. But she didn't dare let a moment's silence slip into the conversation. Silence magnified strain, and there was enough tension in the room at the moment to snap telephone poles. Whatever had started to go wrong between them last night seemed in imminent danger of progressing.

"Rebecca?"

"My daughter." Liking the sound of the word, she smiled. Hoping to coax a smile out of him, too, she tried to brighten the one she'd managed. "We could walk down to the nursery if you'd like."

Her efforts earned her a tight "Maybe later."

Taking his hands from his pockets, he hooked his foot around the straight-backed chair by the window and pulled it forward. "I'm on my way to a dinner meeting," he told her, seating himself beside her. "So I won't stay long. There's something I'd like you to clear up for me, though." He continued on, not waiting to see if she was willing to participate in this discussion. "Last night you mentioned a couple of times that you didn't need my pity. Would you mind telling me what you were talking about?"

It looked to Dave as if Meg did mind. Very much. A faint stain of heat washed over her cheeks as she mumbled a quiet "I'd rather not."

"Why?"

"I'd just rather not. Okay?"

"No, Meg. It's not okay." Something was going on here and Dave wanted to know what it was. The more he'd thought about everything they'd said last night, the more convinced he'd become that their problem was simply a matter of miscommunication. "Where did you get the idea that I pity you?"

"Are you saying you don't?"

"I'm asking you where you got the idea," he replied, and would have reached for her hand if she hadn't clasped them in her lap.

Under normal circumstances, Meg would have handled the extremely uncomfortable conversation with a little more aplomb. However, conditions were somewhat less than optimal at the moment, and she wasn't focusing on her embarrassment yet. That could come later. "I said I'd rather not go into it."

"I'm not leaving until we get this cleared up."

"There is no 'this,'" she returned with forced patience. "And you have to leave. You have a dinner engagement."

"I'll cancel the damn thing. Now what in the hell were you talking about last night?"

Why, she wondered, couldn't he just drop it? Why couldn't he just have walked in here with the smile that always made everything seem so much better and been her friend again? She didn't like the changes their relationship was going through. They compelled as much as they alarmed. He was always pushing her, making her go just a little bit farther than she wanted to go—or felt comfortable with. She hated it when he did that.

"I was talking about what Lucy said you told her husband," she muttered tightly, hoping that if he wasn't too confused by that he'd at least be satisfied with it.

"What?"

Meg glared up at him. As quickly and succinctly as possible, she related what she'd overheard Lucy say. She felt a little foolish repeating that conversation, because it was, after all, hearsay. What she felt when she'd finished, though, was worse.

"So?" Dave asked, looking puzzled. "What's wrong with feeling sorry for you? If you want to know the truth, I felt guilty about what happened to you, too. Maybe if I'd gone into that mall deal with Ted he wouldn't have let his insurance go and you wouldn't have to worry about everything the way you do."

Guilty? she repeated to herself. Pity *and* guilt? "Is that why you were so willing to help me? Why you were always so available? Out of a sense of... of obligation?"

"I was available," he said, failing to see how she was interpreting what he regarded as simple facts, "because I turned down a job so I'd have the time it would take to protect your interests. After I took a look at everything, I knew you'd need me. I knew it was going to take a lot of time, too. It's no big deal. You had a lot to learn."

No big deal. Meg stared up at him in sickened disbelief. He'd just calmly told her that out of pity and guilt he'd given up a commission because he'd known her inexperience would make demands on his time. The embarrassment she felt bordered on humiliation. It crossed that fine little line a few seconds later. *You had a lot to learn.* He'd taught her how to feel again, how her woman's body could respond to a man's. Not just any man's. His. Was that part of what he'd felt compelled to teach her?

"Just how much of your expertise were you willing to share?" she asked, her voice unnaturally calm. "Did you plan on advancing other areas of my education, too?"

Uncomprehending, he drew his fingers through his hair. "I was willing to teach you anything you needed to know."

"And who decided that need?"

Dave suddenly had the feeling he was losing ground. He'd told himself that it would be best to be honest, to lay things out for her and let her take it from there. All he'd wanted was for her to see that there was no reason for her to be upset over things he'd realized months ago. All he'd wanted was for her to understand why he'd felt what he had. But something wasn't going right.

"I had no idea my dependence was such a burden for you," he heard her quietly announce. "Please accept my apologies. And feel free to find yourself another charity case."

"Charity case!" he hissed, coming to his feet. "Damn it, Meg, what is this?"

He reached for her, but she shrank back, which was odd, because she needed his touch so badly. "I don't need the responsibility of being the means to erase your guilt," she told him. Whether it was rational or not, she felt used by him. "Someone told me once that she thought you were after something. She thought it was my money," Meg said with a pained laugh. "I know now it was absolution. Consider yourself forgiven, David."

"For which transgression?" he shot back in a furious whisper. "I'm not even sure what we're talking about here."

"It's late." Drawing a shaky breath, she rubbed the aching spot in the middle of her forehead. When he was gone she'd be able to nurse the wounds her pride had suffered. "You'd better go before you miss your appointment."

"Forgiven and dismissed? That's big of you, Meg, considering how closed-minded you're being. You seem willing enough to listen to what everyone else says about me, but you aren't even trying to understand what I'm saying."

For several very long seconds he stared down at her stricken face. She obviously couldn't see how he felt about her, but there was no way he could tell her now. She wasn't ready for it, and he just didn't have it in him to try to tease her out of this strange mood she was in. He didn't think he could hide behind the guise of friendship any longer.

"There's something for the baby out at the nurse's station," he said in a clipped tone. "I'll leave the number of my lawyer out there, too...in case you work out a deal on the mall. It would be a good idea to have him look over any papers before you sign."

His jaw clenched. "Take care of yourself," he said, and walked out because there was nothing more to say. He wanted her more than ever, but he knew that wanting wasn't enough. She needed time to silence the shadows of the past and begin her life again, free of demands. If he pushed her now, he'd never know if she came to him out of fear of facing the future alone or because she cared about him. He loved her, but he wasn't willing to settle for less than that for himself.

It was well after midnight when Meg lay staring at the darkened ceiling of the hospital room. Her hands rested on her chest, her thumb and forefinger absently twisting her wedding ring. The habit was so ingrained that she didn't even notice what she was doing until she realized what she was thinking about.

Twenty-four hours ago she'd given birth to Ted's daughter. Ted—the man whose face she couldn't recall, though she tried desperately to remember the features she'd once loved so much. Resurrecting the memory of her daughter's father was something she felt she should do. But the memories weren't good ones, and the only image that formed in her mind was Dave's. That reminded her of the hurt she'd felt when he'd walked away tonight.

She stopped twisting the wide gold band and blinked hard as the ceiling blurred. Slowly she slipped the ring from her finger.

Chapter Ten

Fat drops of rain meandered down the pane of glass, obscuring Meg's view of the trees beyond her living room window. She'd sketched the flame-colored cottonwoods this morning before the clouds had turned heavy and gray and dimmed the good light. Meg had always turned to the sea when her soul had needed quieting. But she'd lost her view of the ocean, and found the moments of serenity she craved so badly in the rain-softened shapes of late autumn.

There had been a restorative quality to the time she'd spent curled up in the corner of the sofa with her drawing pad while Rebecca slept. That time seemed to have allowed a sort of inner renewal to begin, although perhaps it was just time itself that allowed the process to start—the process of being who she was now, rather than the person she'd been.

She turned from the window and eyed the telephone. If she'd thought it would help, she'd have called Dave again. But after his parting words at the hospital last week and the distance in his voice when she'd called several days ago to thank him for the huge yellow teddy bear he'd bought for Rebecca, it was clear enough that all he wanted from her was silence. "Thanks for letting me know you're home," he'd told her, sounding distracted and impatient. "Maybe one of these days I'll stop by to see the baby."

Feeling like a fool, Meg had told him he was welcome, then hurried to get off the line with her dignity intact. Dave wasn't an ill-tempered man. He just didn't appreciate his time being wasted—and he'd definitely given her the impression that she'd become something less than a priority. Now that he'd seen her through her pregnancy and the majority of her properties had been liquidated, he'd apparently satisfied whatever sense of obligation he'd felt. All that remained for him to do was ease out of the relationship.

"Oh, stop," she muttered, deliberately turning from the phone. "You've got a dozen other things to think about."

"Were you talking to me, dear?"

A head of salt-and-pepper curls emerged around the corner as Margaret Flaherty, an attractively mature version of her daughter, carried in her newest grandchild. Both baby and grandmother had just awakened from their midafternoon nap. Rebecca, blue eyes wide open, was sucking on her entire tiny fist.

"I was just thinking out loud," Meg replied as she took the feather-light bundle from her mother and tucked Rebecca's round little head under her chin. "Right after I feed this squirt I've got to make a few phone calls. Sometime Monday or Tuesday I need to meet with some people about a property sale."

"Will Dave be going with you?" Margaret asked the question from beside the sink, which was where she was pouring formula into a plastic bottle. Meg had wanted so badly to breast-feed her child, but nature hadn't cooperated with her. What milk had come in couldn't satisfy Rebecca's enormously healthy appetite. "He's such a pleasant man. I do hope I get to see him while I'm here."

Meg, unconsciously hugging the baby closer, kept her tone conversational. It was only natural that her mother would want to know how she was managing. Not wanting to concern her with something she could do nothing about, Meg had kept the more worrisome aspects of her financial situation to herself. She'd mentioned only that Dave, as Ted's very closest friend, had volunteered to help her understand Ted's business. Her mother, who'd met Dave before, had taken that to mean that everything was under control. More or less it was. "Like I said, Mom, he's awfully busy."

"Does that mean he isn't going with you to your meeting? Or that I won't see him?"

"Probably both."

A few moments later, Margaret rounded the counter separating the kitchen from the living area and stopped beside the chair where Meg sat absently rubbing Rebecca's back. She held out the bottle, her eyes clouded with compassion.

Meg was looking a bit to the side, toward the wall unit with its cluster of books and vases and pottery. An enlarged color snapshot in a black lacquered frame was directly in her line of vision. In the picture Ted, looking dark and rakish in his tattered shorts, and his friend Dave, a bit taller and much fairer in coloring though his tan was shades deeper, were grinning up at a magnificent marlin.

The maternal softness in Margaret's voice was comforting, the way Meg remembered it being when she'd soothed long-ago hurts and aches. "You really miss him, don't you?"

"Very much," Meg replied, drawing her glance from the grinning blond man with the soul-searing blue eyes. "Very much."

Because she didn't think her mother could understand what she couldn't understand herself, Meg let her assume she was thinking of her husband. There was no point in telling her that she was thinking of Dave and how desperately she missed the friendship she thought they'd shared.

Meg's mom stayed until Meg's father decided that two weeks was long enough for any woman to catch on to mothering. It was a good time, quiet except for when Annie was around—which was nearly every evening, because Larry was working nights now—and close to idyllic in an isolated sort of way. Returning from Rebecca's first checkup, Meg bought a crate of apples that she and her mother turned into sauce and pies. They finished the quilting project her mother had brought with her and pieced together a blanket for Rebecca's crib. Meg was in her element. Caring for her child, tending her home, she could have gone on like that forever—as long as she didn't think about how much nicer it would have been if it were Dave waiting for the peanut-butter cookies to come out of the oven instead of her mom and Annie.

As the weeks passed and October settled into November, Meg tried not to think about what she'd lost. Rather, she concentrated on what Dave had given her. Without her quite realizing it, the knowledge he'd all but forced her to acquire had lent her a certain confidence—a quality that came in very handy when she was faced with the likes of Quentin Caldwell. During the last several months, the banker had come to regard Meg as something of an albatross.

For the sake of propriety, Caldwell was forced to observe the civilized behavior required of an employee of a reputable lending institution. That he'd have preferred her to rot in a sixteenth-century debtor's prison wasn't a statement he could make, but had Henry VIII been king instead of Reagan President, Meg was sure she'd have been stripped of all worldly possessions by now.

"You realize," the tight-lipped man informed her, looking down his nose at her, "that you can no longer be given any extensions. If this proposed sale falls through, we will have no choice but to file the lawsuit."

Meg's glance didn't drop to her lap as it might have only a few months ago. Dave had continually admonished her to use every tool at her disposal when negotiating. What she did with her eyes and body was as important as actual words. She remembered her lessons well.

Without so much as a blink, she met Caldwell's gaze and sat back in her chair, crossing her legs. The impression her posture gave was that she was quite unaffected by his attempt to intimidate her. "Threatening me with that lawsuit isn't going to make that piece of property sell any faster, Mr. Caldwell. Are you willing to drop the interest rate or not?"

"If your buyer is genuinely interested in that property, he'll understand that he must either bring the loan current and assume it as is or obtain financing elsewhere and pay us off. I see no reason the bank should lower the interest on that loan."

"I can give you several."

The tips of Caldwell's manicured fingers came together. Amused, he looked at her over their tops. "Go on," he said, clearly thinking that without Dave, his nemesis, by her side, she'd sink in a hurry.

Meg didn't even flounder. Robert Kincaid, she told him, was a contractor with money and ideas for expansion, a potential buyer they could ill afford to discourage. After two weeks of preliminary negotiations, Mr. Kincaid had indicated that his enthusiasm over the property could be increased greatly if the bank would give him a more favorable interest rate on the loan. Unless the bank would agree up front, he wasn't going to waste his time with a bunch of tedious paperwork. Time was money, and he had more of the latter than he did the former.

Meg knew she had Caldwell's grudging attention when his fingers laced together and he lowered his hands to the desk. "It's the closest we've come to settling this matter," she went on, adding her most compelling reason for his cooperation when she saw him lean forward. "If you insist on Kincaid applying for financing somewhere else to pay you off, you run the risk of having him back out while that other bank takes their sweet time approving his loan. On the other hand, if you rush his application through your bank and let him assume the existing mortgage, all that back interest could be paid by the holiday."

The thought of having this whole unpleasant matter off his desk by Thanksgiving apparently proved to be the deciding factor. "I am under some pressure to clear this situation up, Mrs. Reese," he said, confirming what she already suspected. The status of her account reflected on him. Given that he had made the loan and that she hadn't paid back a penny of the several hundred thousand dollars outstanding, he probably didn't look like promotion material in the eyes of his board of directors. He insisted on giving the impression that *he* was in charge, though. "I'll think about it and see what I can do."

"By this afternoon?"

From the way his scruffy eyebrows rose, she was under the impression he suddenly thought her slightly daft. "I'm afraid that won't be possible. It's already after three and I have other matters to—"

"Mr. Kincaid will be out of town for several days," Meg said, wondering where Dave had ever gotten the idea that bargaining for anything could be fun. In certain parts of the world people dickered over everything, including the price of their food. If she'd lived in any of those places she'd have starved by now. "I think it would be in everyone's best interests to have a verbal agreement before the close of business this afternoon. He's leaving in the morning."

"Yes. Well…" Glancing from his telephone to Meg, then back to his phone again, Caldwell cleared his throat. With his index finger he pushed back his glasses. "I suppose the circumstances do warrant a quick turnaround. Where can I reach you this afternoon?"

"I won't be available to a phone," she said, using another tactic Dave had mentioned. Control was often an illusory thing, something that could be wrested from your opponent simply by giving him a specific deadline. "I'll call you at…" She checked her watch, actually more concerned with how long she'd been away from Rebecca than with how long to give Caldwell to clear her request. She still had to run by the grocery store before going home, and Mrs. Walker, her baby-sitter, had to be home by four. "Say, 4:30?"

Not waiting for an answer, she tucked her purse beneath her arm and rose from her chair. One advantage to not being pregnant was having the use of her wardrobe again. The beige box-jacketed suit she wore was quite fashionable, and with her mocha leather heels, belt and jersey blouse she'd achieved a look that was both understated and professional. She felt professional, too, when Caldwell rose to shake her hand—and rather relieved that the subdued banker hadn't called her bluff.

For all her polish, Meg was actually shaking, much as Rebecca did when she threw one of her recently perfected temper tantrums. Meg had been jelly inside during her meetings with Kincaid, too. He was sharp like Dave and had Dave's impressively direct manner. Unlike her mentor, he didn't make her blood race a little faster when he smiled, nor had he filled her with anticipation when he'd asked her out for a "nonbusiness" dinner last week. She'd been flattered by his invitation, because he was quite pleasant and very eligible, but she wasn't interested in what he seemed to be offering. Her only interest seemed to be in Dave, and he wasn't offering her anything anymore. Not even advice.

Wishing thoughts of him would stop interfering with her sense of satisfaction, she turned her polite smile toward the carved double doors and left the darkly paneled office. It was nice for once to leave Caldwell knowing she'd called the shots. Dave would have been proud of her.

Not, she told herself on the way home from the grocery store, that she'd managed any coups. All she'd done was keep from falling flat on her face, which was quite an accomplishment as far as she was concerned. And accomplishments meant a lot to her now. Especially since every day brought a new set of challenges.

The pending sale kept her so busy that she was sure she'd only imagined that brief and restful time following her daughter's birth. There were inventories of construction supplies stored at the site to be taken, and meetings at the bank and in Mr. Kincaid's office, as well as appointments with the attorney Dave had recommended. In her spare time there were accounts to reconcile from her rental property and a conference with her rental manager over the cost of new appliances and carpeting for several of the units. Then, on top of all of that, the week before Thanksgiving an investment group from Houston got in on the act and put the brakes on the sale to Kincaid.

Property was apparently more attractive when someone else was interested in it, and Meg suddenly found herself with *two* qualified buyers vying for the unfinished mall. The Houston group was slick, high-pressure and in a position to drive the price up. Kincaid, no slouch himself, remained firm on his offer, waiting to see how Meg would respond to the higher bid. There were strings attached to the more lucrative bid—the most entangling being the condition that she retain liability for the portion of the construction already completed. But it was a *lot* more money, and Meg had precious little of that particular commodity.

Wondering if this was supposed to be the fun part Dave had talked about, she put up with the back-and-forth negotiations until the second week in December. One more offer or counteroffer and she'd go right over the bend, she told Annie, who'd been kept abreast of the situation on a near-daily basis. Tomorrow she'd announce her decision. She hoped she'd have made one by then.

"I'd go for the money," Annie proclaimed, sniffing at the soup pot on Meg's stove while Meg, her business acumen well disguised by her oversize shirt, jeans and a ponytail, folded a pile of baby clothes. "That is what you're going to do, isn't it?"

Meg considered Annie's question. Fifty percent of the time, going for the money was exactly what she thought she'd do. The other fifty percent, she didn't. Therein lay the dilemma.

"I wish it were that simple." Thinking that not too very long ago it would have been, she snapped the wrinkles from a receiving blanket. Eight months ago she hadn't known enough to realize that more money up front didn't necessarily mean a better deal. "I'd get more by taking the Houston offer, but by retaining liability for part of an uncompleted structure I'd expose myself to all kinds of potential problems. I could subrogate a claim to the contractor if a structural flaw developed, but even so, I'd be involved to the point where..."

Annie's eyes glazed over, much as Meg figured hers had once done when this particular topic had been explained to her. Rather than continue boring her friend and worrying herself, she canceled the recitation of her options. She could think about them later, while she and the baby watched the late news.

"Why don't you pour us a glass of wine?" she suggested, scooping up the freshly folded laundry. "I'm going to put these away and see if Rebecca's still sleeping. I don't know about you, but I'm hungry."

Meg's last words snapped Annie out of her semicatatonic state. With a blink, she announced that the smell of the simmering soup was getting to her and started opening drawers in search of a corkscrew.

"She still asleep?" Annie asked as Meg emerged from Rebecca's room a few moments later.

A soft smile lit Meg's eyes as she nodded. She couldn't look at her child without feeling just a little bit better than she had the moment before. At eight weeks, Rebecca had developed quite a personality—along with a nasty temper. Her lopsided smiles more than made up for the Irish she'd inherited, though, and made an absolute pushover of her mother. "She is, but she should be waking soon. Mrs. Walker said she slept all morning."

"Is she still working out all right?"

"Beautifully," Meg returned, blessing the day she'd met the retired nursery-school teacher, who lived three units down from her.

Dipping a ladle into the pot, Meg gave the soup a quick stir. "Do you want a salad with this?"

"Sure. But I'll fix it, since I invited myself. I'll treat tomorrow night."

"Great. What are you going to fix?"

"I didn't say I was going to cook," Annie said, backing up from the refrigerator with a head of leaf lettuce and a tomato in her hand. "I said I'd treat. With Larry on night shift, I'm taking full advantage of being lazy. We'll have pizza or something." Her eyes averted, her tone remarkably bland, she calmly proceeded to remove the smile from Meg's amused expression. "Have you asked Dave what he thinks you should do about the sale?"

"You know I haven't talked to him." Frowning to let her friend know how little she appreciated being reminded of that particular person, Meg shoved a mixing bowl toward Annie.

Eyeing the bowl, Annie shrugged and started tearing lettuce into little pieces. "You could call him. I think he'd like to hear from you."

"If he'd wanted to talk to me he wouldn't have called *you* to ask how Rebecca and I were doing."

"The fact that he cared enough to ask means something," Annie insisted, continuing to mutilate the lettuce. "Just like it meant something that he stayed at the hospital the night the baby was born. Don't tell me he did that because he felt he had to," she said before Meg could open her mouth. "I don't buy that. And I don't think you do, either."

Meg hadn't known about Dave's night-long vigil until the day after their argument at the hospital. She'd commented to one of the nurses about the beautiful bouquet at the floor station and had promptly been told that they were from the man who'd brought her in. He'd sent them to the night nurse who'd kept him posted on Meg's condition.

Then, as now, Meg was hard pressed to see either action as that of a man motivated by guilt or obligation. That he felt something for her beyond friendship was apparent to Annie. Meg occasionally let herself acknowledge that, too—especially when her nights were haunted by the memory of his tender kisses.

"Can we please eat?" Meg asked, an uncharacteristic hardness slipping into her eyes. It was difficult to talk about Dave. When she did, she found herself longing for the sound of his voice, aching for his touch. Not a day went by that she didn't wonder, worry or think about him. She missed hearing about the events of his day and sharing the news of her day with him. A void remained inside her; the sense of loss she had to deal with was stronger than the grief she should have experienced in the months following her husband's death.

Groaning when she realized how maudlin her thoughts had become, she heard Annie ask for salad dressing just as the phone rang.

"There are a couple of kinds in the fridge. Just grab whichever you want," Meg told her, and snatched up the phone before it could ring again and wake the baby. Dinner was always easier to eat when she wasn't trying to hold a bottle. "Hello?"

"Hi," came the deep and decidedly hesitant reply.

For several excruciating seconds, Meg felt nothing but an unnatural pounding in her chest and the distinct sensation of her knees losing their stability. She leaned against the kitchen counter, her hand turning damp as she clutched the receiver. It was so unfair—and so typical—of Dave to catch her so unprepared. Dave never liked the opposition to know what to expect.

Wondering when she'd started thinking of him as an adversary again, she started to speak. He abruptly stopped her.

"I won't keep you," he announced, his tone pleasant yet very businesslike. "The grapevine has it that you're entertaining a second offer on the mall." He became silent for a moment, and she heard him sigh. "If you need an impartial ear to discuss it, or if there's something you don't understand, I'd be glad to talk to you. I did say I'd help you with the tough stuff."

As Annie puttered around, dishing up the soup and keeping very quiet so that she wouldn't miss anything, Meg felt her initial surge of anticipation take a sharp and rapid plunge. Once again, Dave's sole motivation was his sense of obligation.

"You told me I didn't need you to help me anymore," she reminded him, wishing he'd had the decency to mask the reluctance behind his offer. If he hadn't sounded so unenthusiastic about the idea, she'd have gladly accepted his advice. "I appreciate the offer, Dave. But I can handle it myself. Really," she added when he asked if she was sure.

A few moments later, thinking his quiet goodbye even more reluctant than his greeting, she slowly hung up the phone. She was still staring at it when she heard Annie move behind her.

"I don't believe you did that. You've been dying to hear from that guy, and when you do you turn him down flat."

Training her glance on the salad because she couldn't look Annie in the eye and lie, she muttered, "I haven't been 'dying' to hear from him." She carried the bowl to the table. "You don't even know what he offered, anyway."

"I've got ears. He offered to help you."

"I don't need his help to close this deal." Napkins were folded and placed beneath spoons. "I might *want* it," she told Annie. "But I don't need it. There is a difference, you know."

"Maybe." Steam danced around the two bowls of thick vegetable soup Annie carried past her. "But I think you might need *him* more than you're admitting. One of you has to make a move, Meg. Dave just did, and you stopped him cold. You keep insisting that all you ever felt for him was friendship. Call it what you like, but if you want your friend back it looks like it's up to you to go get him. The ball, as they say, is in your court."

Annie was right. That thought occurred to Meg when she found herself standing in the plaza outside Dave's office the following afternoon. A cool, damp breeze lifted the more rebellious curls around her head, and she hugged her gray tweed suit jacket a bit tighter over her forest-green blouse. Behind her she could hear the water rushing over the tiers in the fountain. Ahead she could see the tall white granite-and-glass building silhouetted against a pale winter sky. Dave was in there. Possibly in the elevator by now, she thought.

Meg had called Dave's office from the phone booth in the bank lobby across the street, asking his secretary only if it would be possible for him to meet Meg Reese in front of his building. After putting her on hold, the crisply efficient woman had come back on the line and told Meg he'd be there in fifteen minutes.

Forcing herself not to look at her watch, she paced a circle around the fountain, her gray suede heels tapping on the aggregate tiles. She couldn't sit or stand in one place. Not when she was this nervous. Less than an hour ago she'd completed the negotiations on the La Jolla property. The amount of pride and satisfaction she felt over that accomplishment was unbelievable. The overwhelming boost to her confidence made her feel as if anything were possible, which was what had prompted her to call Dave to share her news. Her confidence, however, was flagging with each passing second. She had no idea how he'd react to seeing her again. She knew what she *wanted* him to do, but it didn't seem very probable that he'd greet her with passionate longing and take her in his arms to kiss her senseless. That little fantasy had been embellished in innumerable ways over the past few weeks, but recalling its variations did more harm than good at the moment.

Worrying about what Dave *would* do when he saw her robbed her of the opportunity to prepare for her own reaction to him. She noticed him first, but only by scant seconds, as he exited the building, his long strides bringing him unerringly closer.

Imposing. The word filled her mind as he drew nearer, his broad-shouldered frame filling her line of vision. And breathtakingly attractive. She remembered having once attributed a certain elegance to his exceedingly masculine features. Refamiliarizing herself with those beautiful angles and planes, she reaffirmed that earlier conclusion and tipped her head back when he stopped in front of her. In heels she came to his chin.

Hands jammed into the pockets of his pin-striped suit slacks, he offered a faint smile. "Slumming?"

"Celebrating," she returned, her fantasy popping like an overinflated balloon.

His eyebrows raised in polite curiosity. "Anything special?"

"Very." Irritated with herself for feeling disappointed over something she'd known he wouldn't do anyway—and with him for making this more difficult than it needed to be—she used that irritation to bolster her rapidly fading courage. She knew that the road to reestablishing their friendship wouldn't be easy. But she didn't need him throwing up roadblocks before she got under way, either. "Quentin Caldwell is finally out of my life," she told him, her smile coming easily at that thought. "Unless something unthinkable happens between now and when the final papers are signed next week, I never have to speak to him again."

The smile that entered Dave's eyes removed some of their coolness. Yet even with a hint of amusement touching the corners of his mouth, he still seemed guarded. He behaved with the studied deference he reserved for strangers. "That is cause for celebration. Do I get the details?"

"If you want them."

"Do you have time for a drink?"

There was, Meg noticed, the faintest touch of a tremor in her hand when she pushed back her jacket sleeve to check her watch. It was almost five. Mrs. Walker had said she was free until 6:30. "A quick one. Is there somewhere nearby?"

"Is five hundred feet close enough?" he asked, inclining his head toward the twin of the building they faced. "There's a lounge in there."

Meg turned to see where he indicated as he stepped forward, his hand touching the small of her back to guide her in that direction. The gesture was nothing more than gentlemanly. His nearness, though, was the only information registering at the moment.

Glancing up, intending to tell him the lounge was fine, she found that her voice had developed a sort of temporary paralysis. Dave was looking down at her, his eyes narrowed and predatory.

The one thing Meg couldn't have stood from him was indifference. It was clear enough that she didn't have to worry about that now. What she saw in his enigmatic expression didn't augur well for reestablishing a casual friendship, though. There was a certain tension coiled in his body. She could feel it when he moved closer, his chest now in full contact with her arm. His hand at her back pressed a little deeper, his thumb moving slowly against her jacket.

"Shall we?" he asked, his eyes steady on her mouth.

Her nod was quick, her voice a bit tight. She forced herself to speak anyway, using the details of the sale to cover an awareness even her imagination couldn't have concocted. Thinking about Dave's underlying sensuality had seemed harmless enough. Facing it felt much more dangerous.

The Sand Bar, with its nautical captain's-cabin theme, was a small lounge that catered mostly to the business crowd. Happy hour, as proclaimed by the carved sign beside the entry, was from 4:30 to 6:30. Since it wasn't quite five, the majority of the office workers who frequented the establishment were still behind their desks. Meg looked on that circumstance with mixed feelings. As the place was practically empty, they had no trouble finding a booth. It might have been better, though, if the cozy little bar had been busier.

Dave touched his lighter to a cigarette after their waitress wandered off with their order. A thin stream of smoke drifted upward, dispersed by one of the overhead fans. "What happened? You said Kincaid was ready to sign when the Houston group made their offer?"

Dave sat back to watch the light from the lantern candle on the table play over the gentle contours of her face. He knew she was nervous, though she was trying hard not to show it. He also knew that he could have put her at ease by being a little more amiable. But he couldn't seem to let go of his defensiveness. He didn't want to become vulnerable again, so he'd keep his guard in place until he found out what she wanted and why.

"I sold it to the lowest bidder," she returned, looking very much as if she expected him to question that decision. "I didn't get back everything Ted put into it, but if I'm careful, Rebecca and I won't starve for a while."

With an easy smile for the waitress who placed a goblet of white wine on the anchor-shaped paper coaster in front of her, Meg waited until Dave directed his frown to his bourbon before she told him why she'd made the decision she had. It took her a while to summarize the terms, and all that time his frown remained in place.

The reason for his frown became clear during the next several minutes, which was how long it took him to explain why accepting limited liability might not have been such a bad idea, given the amount of the Houston proposal. Meg knew she wasn't a pro at these kinds of negotiations, and when she told Dave that he wasted no time in informing her that her only error was in not consulting someone who was. A smart person doesn't necessarily have all the answers, he said; he just knows where to get them.

"I really wish you'd talked to me about it before you'd turned the Houston people down. From what you've indicated, it sounded like the better offer."

Glancing at her wine, she murmured, "I didn't think my questions would be welcome," and took a fortifying swallow. She didn't want to defend herself, though he seemed to want her to. "I'm not displeased with the deal I made, Dave. So it doesn't matter now."

He waved her attempted dismissal aside. "You could have called me about this, Meg. Or asked me about it when I called you last night. When I said you didn't need me to make your decisions, I . . ." I was nursing a bruised ego, he said to himself. In doing that he'd made it impossible for her to come to him when she could have used his help. "I guess there's no point in going over something we can't change," he concluded, inclined to agree that it didn't matter now. "Was there anything else that swayed you toward Kincaid's offer?"

"Yes. There was. I liked him better."

"Oh, Meg," Dave muttered. "You *liked* him better? You were selling property, not finding a home for a pet."

"He also wanted to close by the end of the year," she informed him since her other reason hadn't impressed him much. "The Houston group didn't seem to be in any kind of a hurry at all."

"That's more like it."

"Thanks."

Seeing her exasperation, Dave stared down at the ice in his drink. On the surface, their discussion bore a strong resemblance to those they'd engaged in many times before, with one major difference. Those other times, he'd been comfortable in his role. Now he couldn't function within those limits. And the last thing he wanted to talk about was that damned chunk of property in La Jolla.

Taking a swallow of his drink, he studied her over the rim of his glass. She seemed perfectly oblivious to the attention she attracted. The place was filling up rapidly, and several of the men seated under the draped fishnet at the bar kept glancing over to the booth, their stares curious—and quite appreciative of the beautiful woman sitting across from him.

With all that silky black hair and those incredibly green and darkly lashed eyes, no man could see her without taking another look.

"What made you decide to come by today?"

She was tracing the rim of her glass with her finger, her attention on that motion. When she raised her eyes to his, he could see that his question surprised her.

"I wanted to tell you about the sale," she said, thinking the answer obvious.

"Why?"

"It was just something I wanted to do." Glancing down again, she added, more quietly, "Or needed to."

"Needed?"

Meg appreciated Dave's directness at times, but this wasn't one of those times. It was occasionally necessary to let people dig a little deeper to understand what was being said, but one had to be careful not to let them go too far.

She set her glass aside, hoping she wasn't leaving herself too vulnerable. "Because I want us to be friends. I thought telling you about this might be a place to start."

Dave said nothing for a moment, his eyes guarded and still on her face. Then, with a strange little smile, he slowly shook his head. "There was a time I'd have liked very much to be your friend, Megan. But I just don't think it's possible for us. Friends...well, we just aren't cut out for that. In all the years we've known each other, we've never lasted at being friends."

He reached for her hand, entwining his fingers through hers. For a fraction of a second, he seemed to hesitate. It was her left hand he held, and as he glanced down at it he gently rubbed his thumb over the spot her wedding ring had covered. The motion was slow, deliberate and quite effective at making her forget about the sinking sensation she felt.

"Maybe we should try being lovers for a while."

Meg almost stopped breathing right then. For a moment he'd looked as if he were dead serious. Now she saw a playful leer in his blue eyes and knew that he was only teasing.

"Tell you what." Letting go of her hand, he threw a couple of bills on the table. "If you can get your baby-sitter to stay later, I'll buy you dinner and we can continue this discussion elsewhere. Personally, I'm finding it fascinating."

Meg had no idea what had happened. In a matter of seconds, his attitude had undergone a subtle but very distinct—and very welcome—change. She wasn't about to question the transformation. Minor miracles were terribly hard to come by nowadays. This was the Dave she knew. The one who confused her and teased her and made her feel as if everything would be all right.

"You would," she muttered in mock disgust. Telling him not to be too disappointed if he found himself without a dining companion, she hurried off to find a pay phone. Rebecca wouldn't begrudge her mother a couple of hours for dinner with a friend, would she?

The problem wasn't with Rebecca. Thursdays were Mrs. Walker's bridge night. But Meg managed to get hold of her backup sitter. Not even aware of her impish grin, Meg met Dave by the front door after coordinating a transfer of responsibilities between Mrs. Walker and Annie. "Annie said you'd better appreciate this," she warned him, stepping out into the heavily damp air. "She's stuck baby-sitting just so you wouldn't have to eat alone tonight."

"I'm most humbly grateful."

"There's nothing humble about you, David."

She looked up to find his glance working its way over her face and slowly down the front pleats of her blouse. His visual caress was heated, and she felt its warmth as it worked its way over her gentle curves. He hadn't touched her, yet every nerve in her body had just come startlingly alive. When his eyes darkened on their return path and settled on her mouth, she was sure her smile had lost much of its teasing quality. It disappeared completely when he leaned over and brushed his lips across hers.

"You humble me," he whispered, and if they hadn't been blocking the entrance to the increasingly busy bar he'd have taken advantage of her small gasp to deepen that brief and tantalizing kiss.

Chapter Eleven

The restaurant Dave had in mind was only three blocks from his condo, which was only five minutes from his office. He occasionally ate there when he didn't feel like cooking for himself.

Meg hadn't ever eaten there but told Dave that it sounded delightful. She really wasn't thinking about food. The only thoughts in her mind dealt strictly with the enigmatic man whose slightest shift in mood could send her spirits soaring beyond the sea cliffs or plummeting fathoms below the surf. That was a rather mighty power for a friend to have. Certainly more than she felt comfortable allowing, yet Dave had that capability.

Dave had mentioned that, while the Gable House's food was excellent, there was never enough space in its parking lot. That was why, after following Dave in her car, Meg parked behind him in his driveway and they walked the short distance to the restaurant. It was a bit foggy out now, the air more chill since the sun had set. Darkness came early this time of year, and at just minutes before six, evening had already passed into night.

"I can't believe it's almost Christmas." Meg smiled past Dave, looking up at the bright tinsel wreaths hung from the lampposts and the garlands draped along the quaint eating establishment's picket fence. Its mullioned windows were strung with twinkling lights, and artificial snow had collected in their corners. A life-size animated Santa welcomed them at the entrance. She hadn't paid much attention to the decorations which had adorned most businesses for the last several weeks. But tonight she seemed more aware of everything.

"I know what you mean," Dave offered innocuously. Smiling at the way she peeked behind the Santa to see where it was plugged in, he opened the door for her. Heat from a crackling fire, good smells and chatter from the lounge greeted them warmly.

A hostess approached. The young woman, who looked like a throwback to the turn of the century in her long black chintz dress and white ruffled apron, gave Dave a grin and, picking up two menus, led them into the comfortably full dining room. Meg received a polite nod from the hostess along with her menu. Dave was offered a dazzling smile.

Meg pretended not to notice.

Dave hadn't. "Are you going to your folks'?" he asked after they'd ordered a drink from their very prompt waiter. "For the holidays, I mean."

"Yes," she replied. "I had to promise that I would. They understood that it just wouldn't work out to go back for Thanksgiving. We spent that with Annie and Larry. But they wouldn't hear of any excuse for Christmas. Not that I tried to come up with any. My whole family will be there. It'll be good to see them. And they all want to see the baby."

"Jan and her brood will be at my folks', too."

"I'll bet you're looking forward to seeing her."

A slight hesitation preceded his wry "Not really. If she'd talk about something other than my marital status, it'd be fine. But she looks on holidays as nothing but an excuse to continue the inquisition. Christmas is the worst."

"Because so much of it's geared for children?"

"Exactly. She doesn't waste any time pointing out how much nicer it would be if Mom and Dad had another grandchild or two to spoil."

"You could borrow Rebecca," Meg suggested lightly, and though she was only kidding she was immediately intrigued by the idea of Dave trying to care for a tiny infant.

"That," he informed her, "would only solve half the problem."

Meg nodded knowingly, comfortable with their easy, bantering conversation. "Oh, yes. The wife. Perhaps you could rent one? Or take one out on a short-term lease? You are aware that you normally get better terms with a lease, aren't you?"

The glance he sent over the top of his water glass just before he set it down was quite droll. "Perhaps," he suggested, leaning forward to smile into her eyes, "you could come up with an idea that would be of some real help. Renting, leasing or even buying a wife will not let me off the hook with my family. I'm desperate here, lady."

Meg leaned forward, too, enjoying the way his smile made her feel. She'd missed his smile so much. She unconsciously lowered her voice to accommodate his nearness, and her teasing tone took on a seductive softness. "I can't imagine you being desperate about anything."

"Try stretching your imagination," he told her, slowly savoring the awareness shifting into her eyes. "Let yourself look a little deeper."

They were still leaning toward each other, their elbows resting on the wooden table. Around them, quiet conversations melded with the clink of silverware and the low strains of a baroque Christmas carol. "An imagination can be misleading," she told him. "Sometimes it can make a person see things that aren't there."

"Sometimes," he said, his gaze shifting to her mouth. "But when a person insists on seeing things only the way she remembers them, that person misses what's right in front of her." For several seconds he held her unwavering gaze. Then he sat back, seeming oddly satisfied, and picked up his menu. "I haven't had a thing to eat since breakfast," he said, his tone as bland as the custard the woman behind them had been served. "I think I'm starving. Anything appeal to you?"

You do, Meg thought, then quickly raised her menu in front of her face in case that bold thought had somehow shown itself in her expression. Unable to decide whether she was trying to cover panic or anticipation, she proceeded to interrogate him about the restaurant's fare, and soon enough their dialogue resumed its earlier nonthreatening course.

Weeks melted away in minutes. To Meg it seemed as if only two days had passed since they'd last seen each other, rather than two months. But there was something between them now that made it difficult for her to relax completely. Long before they stepped back out into the dark, swirling fog, Meg had become aware of the strange electricity permeating the atmosphere. A sense of expectancy hung between them, disguised as companionship by their easy conversation. About a block from his condo, though, Dave seemed to lose his enthusiasm for idle banter.

"I meant what I said before, Meg. I want you to remember that."

The fog was thick, creating a heavy haze around the street lamps. She glanced up at Dave as they approached another pool of that filtered light, but it was difficult to discern much from his dark profile. He kept his eyes focused straight ahead as they continued down the sidewalk.

"I'm not sure I know what you're talking about," she told him, hugging her arms around herself. "We talked about a lot of things tonight. Your family. My family. My career as a real estate whiz," she continued, recalling his suggestion that she might want to study for her real estate license—an idea that had elicited more interest from him than her. "Your diving trip to Guaymas last month. What did I miss?"

"Think hard."

"Well, let's see . . ."

Her frown of concentration was still in place when, a dozen steps later, they reached Dave's driveway and her car. His condo overlooked the sea, and somewhere beyond the walkway and the cedar decks wrapped around the two-story building, the ocean could be heard washing against the beach.

"Maybe I should give you a hint."

"Maybe," she agreed, and felt him curve his hand over her shoulder.

Glancing up, expecting some verbal clue as to why he suddenly sounded so serious, she felt the cloak of sociability slip. Along with it went the nice, safe companionship she'd once found so comfortable.

There was nothing casual in his touch as he drew her closer, no pretext of simple friendship in the feel of his fingers slipping through the silky curls tumbling over her nape. In the dim glow of the security lights she watched his head lower, her breath snagging in her throat even as she felt the heat of his breath brush her cheek. A tantalizing frisson of warmth feathered over her lips as he whispered, "Try to remember."

The instruction was spoken against her lips, its faint vibration a weak echo of the tremor shuddering through her.

Try to remember, he'd said, but she could think of nothing but the increasing pressure of his mouth as he gathered her closer. There was no demand behind the kiss, just a slow, easy deepening that seeped into her by degrees. He seemed to invade her senses, taking each of them in turn. The feel of his solid strength made itself evident as he pressed her soft curves to their masculine counterparts; the scent of him became the essence of each breath she drew.

"Does that give you any idea?" he asked when the pounding in her ears had blotted out the roar of the ocean.

Maybe we should try being lovers for a while. The impact of the words he'd spoken before hit her now with an almost physical force. That jolt, added to the yearning simmering within her, left her too shaken for an elaborate response. "Yes."

"Good. Because it's a subject that warrants further discussion. One that's long overdue."

"Dave, I..."

She wasn't sure what she'd been about to say, but that didn't really matter, because Dave didn't let her finish. He sought her mouth again, all gentleness lost as his tongue found its mate. The contact was like setting a match to dry hay. The spark was instantaneous, the heat overwhelming. As his hips moved forward with a subtle thrust, she didn't bother trying to deny the powerful and sudden surge of desire that caught her in its grip. She tried only to maintain her hold on a sense of reality that had just swung wildly out of focus.

There was no safety to be felt in his arms, no sense of protection, none of the comfort she'd so often experienced there. What she felt now was a compelling sense of danger, a heady sort of recklessness. Half of her craved the heat of his touch, reveled in it. The other half, the practical half, warned her that she wasn't ready for what Dave so obviously wanted. Never having had an affair, she had no idea what the rules were. But that didn't matter, because the ground seemed to have tilted, forcing her to rely on him for support. Warning bells were going off in her head. She ignored them, wanting only to prolong what she knew she should end.

"Come inside with me." He whispered against her ear, the words harsh and heated. His hands moved upward, his fingers closing over her breast as his lips moved to the corner of her mouth. "You don't have to go home yet."

"No," she heard herself whisper, aching beneath his touch. "Yes," she corrected, breathless as she let her arm fall from where it had curved around his neck. "I do have to go."

"Why?" he demanded.

Any number of reasons came to mind, every one of which Dave could undoubtedly destroy with no trouble at all. She offered the one she didn't think he could challenge. "I need time."

"You need time?" He repeated her response as if he couldn't quite believe what he'd heard. Incredulity gave way to impatience, which almost immediately turned into exasperation. Watching those emotions war with his tenuously held control caused Meg to shrink back. His grip on her upper arms held her right where she was. "Do you have any idea how long I've given you already?"

The echo of his fierce whisper whipped around her, goading her with its demands. Threatened by the hold he had on her emotions, fearing the intensity of what he could cause her to feel, protective anger slipped into place. "*You've* given me? Where do you get off thinking you have any right to decide how much time I need for anything?"

"I'm not arguing with you out here."

"Fine. I was leaving anyway."

"Not until we settle this."

"There's nothing to settle."

"The hell there's not!"

Silence loomed heavy, magnifying the certainty of Dave's last words. Meg, however, didn't appear the least bit convinced. The fury flashing in her eyes was glorious; it was also what prompted Dave to realize how completely out of hand things had gotten in the last couple of minutes. Knowing she probably wouldn't listen to reason until she cooled off, but not willing to let her leave angry, he took the risk of making her just a little bit madder in order to calm her down.

Lord, he groaned to himself as he reached for her wrist, she could really mess up his thinking.

"What do you—?"

"We're going inside," he told her before she could finish. Pulling her behind him, he all but dragged her up the walk to his condo. "I happen to get along pretty well with my neighbors, and I'd like to keep it that way." Without letting go of her, he got the key into the lock, opened the door and held it open for her. "We'll talk in here."

She had stopped trying to break his grasp, and she let him lead her into his living room. He still had a hold of her when he flipped on one of the table lamps, its soft light throwing the spacious room into focus. She stood on an Aztec rug whose natural hues were pale against the terra-cotta tiles. She'd never been to his home before, and if she hadn't been so angry she would have found the Santa Fe-style decor quite suited to his very masculine tastes. All she could think about was how incredibly inflexible he was being.

"Relax," he muttered, finally releasing his grip to sort through the stock of his built-in wet bar. "I've wanted you for too damned long to resort to force. When we make love, you'll want it, too." A short, dark bottle was placed none too gently on the polished wood surface along with a brandy glass. "You want one?" he asked, holding up another snifter.

In response she gave him a quick shake of her head and watched him put the second snifter back. His words both disarmed and alarmed her. The admission of want, however, was overruled somewhat by the certainty in his other statement. *When we make love,* he'd said, as if the fact were a given. Not *if.*

"What makes you so damned sure of yourself?" she prodded, far more intrigued by his assumption than she felt was truly prudent.

Eyeing her dully, he polished off a healthy swallow of brandy before taking a few measured strides in her direction. A master of challenge when it suited him, he boldly assessed her lithe curves, raising his eyes to hers when he completed that unveiled and very thorough inspection. "Tell me you don't want to go to bed with me."

His arrogance was astounding. But then, so was his perceptiveness.

"I don't want to go to bed with you," she said, perversely satisfied when his eyebrow lifted in obvious surprise.

"I've got to admit I hadn't expected that." Placing his glass beside an exquisite bronze sculpture on the coffee table, he joined her on the rug in front of it. With the tip of his finger, he traced the fullness of her lower lip. "It's not like you to lie."

She opened her mouth to protest his presumption but could only stand there wondering how to raise defenses against a man so practiced at tearing them down. The pad of his finger slid along the moistness just inside her lip, and his indrawn breath sounded as ragged as her own. Turning her head slightly, she avoided the provocative contact.

Dave let his hand fall. "Am I that wrong, Meg?"

He's so beautiful. The incongruity of her thought was offset by its truth. So much raw power was leashed in his broad-shouldered frame; so much character was carved into the sculpted lines of his face. She could see hesitation there. The mask of self-protection he sometimes wore was gone for the moment. In its place was an open and honest need.

When she recognized that need, it was impossible for her to maintain any objectivity. It was also impossible to continue deceiving herself. Friendship wasn't all she wanted from Dave and probably hadn't been for a very long time. But she didn't want to need him as badly as she did, either.

"Wrong about what?" she asked, feeling as if she were holding a flame to a stick of dynamite.

"Us." Combing his fingers through his hair, he searched her face. "We've got more going for us than just a physical attraction, Megan. You've got to know that. I can't be around you without wanting you. Unless I'm getting my signals crossed, you want me, too. Am I misreading you?"

There was a slightly strangled quality to her nearly inaudible "No."

"Then what's the matter?"

"I guess I'm scared," she returned with a wobbly smile.

His smile was tender, and the touch of his fingers along her cheek was a gentle caress. "Don't be."

"I can't help it. I've never...I mean, of course I've... but..."

"So articulate," he murmured against her mouth. "Be quiet and kiss me, Meg. Just kiss me. That's all. We'll stop whenever you want."

The flame touched the fuse and the fuse caught. Meg knew she was playing with a very volatile and explosive force, but her response to Dave was too swift to acknowledge the danger. In complying with his request, she gave in to the need that had filled her for so long.

Knowing her heart would bear the consequences of her actions, she nonetheless encouraged each liberty he sought to take. When he pushed her jacket over her shoulders and drew it down her arms, she mimicked his motions by removing his and returned in equal measure the scorching kisses he rained along her jaw. She moved against him and experienced a heady feminine satisfaction when her touch elicited an agonized groan.

"You're not going to tell me to stop, are you?"

Because she couldn't seem to think beyond the moment, all she could do was say, "Not yet," and wonder at her lack of hesitation.

"You tell me when," he whispered, and drew the hem of her unbuttoned blouse from her skirt. The silky fabric whispered to the floor.

Barely skimming her flesh, he curved his fingers under the strap of her bra and slid the strap over her shoulder. His lips grazed the hollow of her throat. "You smell like baby powder," he said, taking little nips along her collarbone. "Are you stealing from Rebecca?"

"Do you think she minds?" The question sounded silly, her words breathless.

The other strap was drawn over her shoulder. Dave's motions were unhurried. "We'll ask her sometime."

"Dave?" A strange weakness entered her limbs. "I don't think this is a very good idea."

"Do you want me to stop?"

Without hesitation, she whispered, "No. I just don't think—"

"Don't think," he coaxed, his hands sliding around her back. The hooks on her bra gave. "Just feel."

"Oh, I do." Her lips were soft and trembling. "Too much."

"Never too much."

She shook her head, wanting to tell him she wasn't talking about anything physical. Unable to speak because he'd taken possession of her mouth, she could only moan. He caught the tiny sound, drinking it in, making it part of the more guttural groan coming from deep within his chest.

Just feel. He'd spoken those words to her before, the night he'd begun removing her doubts about her desirability. Then she'd found herself awash in a sea of confusing sensations—too stunned by her response to him to understand why that pull was so strong. There was nothing confusing about what she felt now, though. When he dropped her bra to the floor and gently cupped her breasts, she knew why she couldn't deny him—or herself. She loved him.

She loved him. The thought came as no shock. All it did was add rightness to the beauty of their actions. She raised her hands to his shoulders, feeling the heat of his visual caress. His touch was incredibly tender, but his eyes were uneasy for a moment as he moved his thumb toward the center of her breast. "Is it okay?" he asked, stilling his quest.

Touched by his consideration, loving him more for it, she breathed, "It's okay." She thought her knees would give when he lowered his head to brush his lips over the growing bud. Her legs almost buckled when his tongue teased the hardened peak and he pushed her other breast upward, taunting its tip with his thumb.

Dave realized long before Meg did that they had to make a choice soon. He wasn't thinking of stopping their desire, only of where to continue it. They were only feet away from the sofa, closer than that to the floor. But he wanted her in his bed, where he'd have the room to explore every inch of her delectable body.

So that was where he carried her—into the shadow-filled room where nothing but the sound of the ocean beyond his window could intrude. Shoes were kicked off on the thick carpet. Clothes were scattered over the outline of a chair. Bodies touched, warm and wanting, before moving together to the center of the bed.

It was because Meg was so caught in the newness of her love for Dave that giving became her only priority. To please him was all that mattered—until a sliver of rationality stole through the passion and reminded her of consequences to her actions beyond making her heart more vulnerable. Burying her head in his shoulder when the raging fires threatened to burst out of control, she clung to him fiercely. Never had she wanted so badly. Never had she ached the way she ached right now. And never had she planned on saying what she did. "We can't do this."

The change in Dave was instant. Tensing, he pulled back. In his body she felt raw passion, the kind of desire no man could walk away from easily. That desire had its counterpart in her. "I . . . I'm not on anything," she said before he could misunderstand.

The breath he exhaled was low and unsteady, his smile a seductive combination of hunger and relief. "We're okay," he told her, and dropped a series of tiny kisses from her chin to her temple. "I wasn't going to let anything happen to you."

The rustle of sheets was joined by the faint scrape of wood against wood. A drawer opened. A vague tearing sound followed. Moments later, he gathered her in his arms—and doubts and restraints disintegrated in the heat they created with their mouths and their bodies.

"I don't want to hurt you," she heard him say, his breath hot and ragged against her ear. "Don't let me."

Her body arched when he slipped his hand beneath her hips. "Please, Dave."

"Say it again." Scalding kisses were rained down her throat as he eased himself forward. "My name. Say it again."

He raised his head, his eyes burning into hers. She dug her fingers into the damp skin of his shoulders, near-delirious with wanting. "David," she whispered when he tilted his hips to hers. "David," she repeated, trapped by the possession in his eyes when he gently entered her.

He didn't want the swift demanding need that overtook him. It would have been better if, this first time, he could have gone slowly so she could be satisfied first. He hadn't counted on the difference emotions could make when added to full sexual arousal. Feeling so much more for her than for any other woman he'd ever taken to bed, he was caught in a blinding storm of urgency that made thought very nearly impossible. He tried to hold back, but she urged him on. He wanted to wait, but she wouldn't let him.

She wouldn't let him because she couldn't control her own physical response to him. Never had she known such urgency, such an immediate and profound need to become part of a greater whole. That was the way it was with Dave. He was the other half of her being, the part that made what she was ... matter.

That feeling of utter completion remained with her long after the passion had given way to quiet breathing. She lay in his arms, afraid to move for fear that the sense of peace she felt might shatter, that the illusion of oneness they'd created would vanish like wood smoke on a winter's day.

Dave raised to his elbows, his eyes guarded as he pushed the damp tendrils of hair back from her forehead. "I suppose you're going to tell me you have to go home tonight."

She tightened her hands around his back, surprised to find the feeling of rightness even stronger than before. She did have to go home, of course. But the fact that he didn't sound overly pleased with that necessity made her feel less awkward when she did leave—two hours later.

Chapter Twelve

It wasn't like Dave to be reticent. Meg still thought his frankness rather brash at times but would have welcomed even his temerity if he'd allow her some insight into his strange behavior. She could hear the distance in his voice when he called the next morning to see if she was all right, and when he stopped by after work she sensed hesitation. He hadn't said anything about coming by, and the sight of him standing in her doorway looking as dark and brooding as the evening sky did nothing to still the emotional seesaw she'd been riding all day.

"I can't stay," he told her, the touch of his fingers on her cheek betraying want even as he backed away verbally. "I'm on my way to a meeting."

She kept her eyes on his face, her heart in her throat. Not feeling terribly secure about the sudden and distinct change in their relationship, she needed whatever reassurance she could get that he didn't regret that change. She wasn't too sure how she felt about it yet, except that she was encouraged by his appearance and terribly disheartened that he was already leaving. "You could come by when it's over," she suggested. "I'll put on coffee."

"I don't think so." His quick refusal was tempered by the brush of his lips over her forehead. "It'll be late, and I kept you up late enough last night. I just wanted to see you for a few minutes. Tomorrow night. Okay?"

"Okay," she said, smiling now. She rolled her eyes toward the ceiling when Rebecca's screech reminded her of what she'd been doing before the doorbell had rung. "I was just tucking her in. Why don't you come with me while I finish?"

It wasn't her imagination. Dave visibly stiffened, his glance darting away as if she might see something in his eyes that he'd rather she didn't. "I've really got to go. Clients hate to be kept waiting, especially when they're paying for the meal. Seven o'clock tomorrow, all right?"

A moment later he was gone, the feel of his too-brief kiss lingering on her lips. His sudden departure unsettled her as much as his unexpected arrival had. But it was the way he'd seemed to close down right in front of her when she'd asked him to come into Rebecca's room that kept her rooted to the spot. Why had he done that?

That question was lost among countless others during the next few days, but the answers would have to wait. With both Meg and Dave leaving town for Christmas, time was at a premium. Each had obligations to meet. Discovering that Dave hated shopping—something Meg didn't mind at all— she took his list with her and completed the task. Dave, in turn, acted as messenger between her, her lawyer and the title company by picking up and delivering drafts of documents necessary for the completion of the La Jolla property sale. Two of the three projects Dave wanted to close by the end of the year were being handled by the same lawyer, so the arrangement worked out well, which was more than Meg could say for whatever was happening between her and Dave.

Something wasn't right. Every time she began to relax with him, to feel some of their old companionship permeate the ever-present sensual awareness, she could see him mentally backing off. It didn't matter where they were or what they were doing. If she got too close, the wall came up. That abrupt change was always most noticeable when Rebecca was around, which made no sense at all to Meg. She knew he liked children, but he didn't seem to care for her daughter.

Or so Meg thought until the night before she was to leave for Springfield.

Rebecca was fretful and tired and wanted to sleep. Because of all the last-minute running around Meg had been doing, the baby had been off schedule all day. It seemed the poor thing would be off schedule all night as well.

Thinking Dave had stayed in the living room where they'd been wrapping the last of his packages, Meg filled a bottle and headed down the hall. Dave hadn't remained with the project, though. He'd wandered into the baby's room. Meg found him with the baby cradled against his massive chest. He stood beside the crib, his head angled as he spoke softly to the wispy black curls on Rebecca's round little head.

Meg couldn't hear what he said, but she knew how comforting his touch could be. Having experienced it herself, she wasn't at all surprised to see her daughter snuggle deeper against him, her tired cries quieting. It was Dave's gentleness, and the affection he'd hidden so well, that kept her frozen by the door. The man, she thought to herself, was a fake.

When Dave saw Meg, he started to smile. An instant later, he caught himself. The baby must have felt him stiffen. He'd heard that infants reacted to stuff like that, and since Rebecca almost immediately started to whimper again, he figured he must have heard right. These miniature people were almost like big ones.

"I thought you'd be longer," he said to Meg, making her efficiency sound like a fault.

"I just got her some water. I don't think she's hungry."

"Yeah, well, I guess kids can get thirsty, too."

She held out the bottle, hoping that he'd take it. "Do you want to give it to her?"

Dave glanced from the bottle to the fussing child and finally back at Meg. After hesitating for another few seconds, he handed Rebecca to her and started toward the door. "You go ahead. I'll pick up the mess in the living room. Do you want to save any of those little pieces of wrapping paper?"

"The ones you were making paper airplanes out of while I wrapped the packages?" she asked, hiding her disappointment at his refusal.

"I helped you tie the bows," he pointed out, and looking quite proud of that accomplishment, he wandered out of the room.

Was it possible, Meg wondered, rocking Rebecca while she polished off a full three ounces of water, that Dave simply didn't want to get too close to the baby? She had to admit that it looked that way. But how could he expect her to have a relationship with him unless her daughter was included?

A possible answer came to her somewhere around midnight. Lying in Dave's arms, aware that he, too, was having trouble sleeping, she tried to summon the courage to ask what he wanted from her. Part of that answer was obvious. The sexual chemistry between them was powerful; his desires were an even match for those he'd awakened in her. Even now, when she should have been sated by their lovemaking, she wanted him. If she were to reach for him, he'd want her, too. The one place he didn't hold back with her was in bed, and there he took her places she'd never dreamed existed. But when they returned to reality, there was a bittersweet quality to their silence. It was there now.

Meg watched the rhythmic rise and fall of his chest. The light from the hall glinted off the chain around his neck, catching the graceful curve of the small gold ankh she'd given him only a few hours ago. In ancient Egypt the emblem had symbolized life—and because in many ways he was her life, she'd thought the charm quite appropriate. She hadn't told Dave that, of course. She'd merely told him what the symbol meant and welcomed the kiss that had followed.

Sighing, she closed her eyes, unwilling to ask what he expected from her in return for his presence in her life—or how long his presence would last. She wasn't ready yet. She was fairly sure she knew what he didn't want, though. He didn't want an emotional commitment. A man who wanted an emotional commitment didn't give a woman a briefcase for Christmas.

Meg had plenty of time to analyze everything that had happened between her and Dave during the ten days she spent in Springfield. Feeling abysmally devoid of any holiday spirit, she nonetheless joined in the festivities with a compulsion that matched the pace she'd maintained during most of her pregnancy. Keeping busy helped during the day, but at night, alone in her old bed, she finally came to the conclusion that throughout the evolution of their relationship, Dave had been giving her the same message all along. He didn't want her dependent on him. He'd made that apparent enough, just as he'd made the nature of their relationship quite clear. He wanted them to be lovers—and nothing more.

That wasn't enough for Meg. All the old dreams still wanted fulfilling; only now the face in those dreams belonged to Dave. And Dave wasn't in the market for someone like her.

"What on earth gave you an idea like that?" Annie wanted to know as she watched Meg unpack her suitcases. "The man's been around for months. What do you mean he doesn't want someone like you?"

"I mean just what I said." Placing the pink sweater her sister had given her for Christmas in the dresser drawer, Meg spoke matter-of-factly. "If there was anything Dave ever stressed, it was the importance of me standing on my own. He seems to admire that quality in a woman. And a profession. A woman has to have a profession if she wants to sustain his interest." Every woman she'd ever seen him with had a business career, and he'd encouraged her own every agonizing step of the way. "I don't want a high-powered job...and this real estate business is something I'd just as soon do without. All that wheeling and dealing makes me nervous."

"You're obviously just not cut out for it the way some people are."

"I wish he could see that." Tossing the empty suitcase aside, Meg reached for the diaper bag. "When someone starts bickering about terms, Annie, I absolutely cringe. Why can't people just state a fair price for something and the other party pay it?"

"Because it's not fun?"

"That sure seems to be part of it," Meg muttered, failing completely to comprehend how arguing about anything could be construed as fun. By heaven, she'd given it her best shot. But she just didn't like it. "It's not for me...and I'm afraid Dave isn't either."

It seemed odd to say that so calmly, especially when the words hurt so much. Talking to Annie, though, was a catharsis she'd needed badly. There had been few opportunities for private conversation at home. With all her family there and friends and relatives constantly dropping by, Meg had actually taken refuge in chaos to avoid being singled out. Now that she was fairly sure of her options, she needed a sounding board. Dave had once told her she always had a choice when faced with a decision. He was right. And she had a choice to make now. She could ignore the fact that there were major problems between her and Dave and pretend, as she had all those years with Ted, that everything was just fine. Or she could face the truth and admit that she could never be the kind of woman Dave wanted her to be.

Three hours later, Annie's admonition not to do anything rash still fresh in her mind, Meg pulled her car into Dave's driveway. He'd been surprised when she'd suggested that she meet him at his place rather than have him pick her up, but she didn't think a restaurant was the right place for what she had to say. Having given the situation a lot of thought, Meg figured his condo would be ideal. She wanted to be in a position where she could leave should it become necessary, which was why she hadn't wanted him to come to her house. If nothing else, she'd learned a fair bit about strategy lately.

Even the best-laid plans can suffer a momentary setback. The moment she saw him, she knew a public place would have been infinitely preferable. They'd have too much privacy here. If he touched her, held her the way her body ached for him to, she wouldn't have the strength to go through with what she knew she had to do. The consequences were too severe for her to allow that to happen, though. She had to hold her position. As much as she loved him, she simply couldn't let herself live another lie. She deserved better than that. And so did he.

"Hi," she said, crossing her arms over her unbuttoned raincoat.

"Hi," he returned, his smile slipping as he regarded her warily. He stepped back, motioning her inside. "Come on in."

Heels tapping on the terra-cotta tiles, she moved past him, catching the faintly spicy fragrance of his after-shave. Desperately trying to block out the memories that scent evoked, she didn't stop until she was in the living room. "How was San Francisco?"

"Wet. Springfield?"

"Cold."

"Your family?"

"Fine. Yours?"

"Fine, too."

"Good," he muttered. "Can we cut the nonsense now?"

"What?"

"What's the matter with you?"

He moved toward her, his magnificent frame looming larger than in her dreams. She stepped back, turning to pretend great interest in the seascape hanging above his fireplace. "I just wondered how your trip was. What's wrong with that?"

"What's wrong," he said, turning her around by the shoulders, "is that you're acting awfully strange about something. I call to ask you out to dinner because we haven't seen each other in over a week, and instead of giving me an answer about dinner, you ask if you can come over. When you show up, I don't even get to kiss you hello before you start making polite conversation about the weather. Did I do something?"

The pressure of his hands on her shoulders felt good. Too good. He probably knew that. "No," she said softly, shrugging off his tempting touch. "You didn't do anything. Not yet. But you will. Or would," she corrected, knowing that what she said made perfect sense to her but little to him. "Sooner or later, anyway. I'm just going to save you the trouble. Can I ask you something?"

"Please," he said, his sudden frustration evident. He lifted his hand toward his shirt pocket, only to let it fall when he remembered that he was trying to get a jump on his New Year's resolution. Meg had once told him after a meeting with Quentin Caldwell that dreading an unpleasant task was sometimes worse than actually doing it. Therefore, he figured that if he was going to quit smoking he might as well get it over with. It would be easier to do, however, without this kind of stress. "Maybe then I'll have some idea of what you're talking about."

"That real estate course you've mentioned to me before," she began. "Why do you want me to take it?"

"Real estate...?" His words trailed off as, relieved, he frowned at her. Looking as if he thought her defensive posture a bit unnecessary for the present discussion, he shrugged as if the answer were obvious. "To get your license."

"I never said I wanted a real estate license."

"You never said you didn't," he countered. "You've got talent in that area and a fair amount of expertise now. You even have some good contacts. There's no sense wasting any of that."

He'd look on it as a waste if she didn't capitalize on her "talent." To Meg, that meant he'd regard her as something less than what she was without that career.

The oil painting above the red-brick fireplace was a superb rendering of the ocean's savagery. But it was the view beyond the window that pulled at her. There was no solace to be found in the sea today. She stood for several moments watching the waves break against the shore in the waning sunlight. The day had turned gray, the fine mist rolling up from the shore shrouding everything in its path. How many times had Dave stood here studying this setting, she wondered; then she turned before letting herself acknowledge that the fewer memories she took with her, the less she'd have to forget.

"I did a lot of thinking while I was gone," she said, her throat tight as she began to sever the threads binding her to Dave. "About that course. About what I wanted for myself. About us." It was difficult to hold his gaze. As always, it was far too direct. "I could try to change for you, but that wouldn't solve anything."

His eyebrows drew together, and his nostrils flared with his sharp intake of breath. He said nothing, his nod bidding her to continue even as his eyes dared her to proceed.

She decided to offer her explanation to the crease in his navy slacks. "My financial situation has stabilized enough for me and Rebecca to live off the rental income for a while. After my lease expires, I'm going to move back home and get a teaching degree. Home ec," she explained with a shaky smile. "If I teach, I'll have more time to spend with Rebecca . . . having summers off and all."

Dave didn't acknowledge her smile, nor did he offer a single verbal clue as to whether or not he even cared that it was tearing her apart to tell him of her decision. Not knowing how her words affected him, if at all, she was left with no guidance as to how to proceed. Had he given the slightest hint that he shared her hurt, she might have chosen her next words a bit differently or dropped the matter right there.

He said nothing.

"I guess you know I couldn't have made it without you," she went on, because she needed for him to have some idea of how important he'd become to her. "I really am grateful for everything you've—"

She'd wanted a reaction of some kind. The one she got, though, made it clear that she'd made a grave and distinct error in judgment.

"Grateful! You're *grateful*?"

"Well, yes. I—"

"You're really something, you know that? You waltz in here with all your neat little plans to tell me you're walking out of my life and think telling me you're grateful is going to help? Gratitude is the last damn thing I've *ever* wanted from you."

She hadn't known that a man that size could move so fast. One second he was ten feet away; the next he was right in front of her. Stunned as much by his fierce grip on her arms as by the disgust in his voice, she could do nothing but stare up at him. Dave had never professed any desire to commit himself to the relationship, so why was he so upset now?

"Then what do you want from me?" she asked, torn between anxiety and elation. Suddenly it looked very much as if he cared. A great deal. "Didn't it ever occur to you that I might need to know that? You've never asked me for anything." Except peanut-butter cookies, she remembered, but that thought was as inconsequential as the item itself.

"I never asked you for anything because I didn't think you were ready to give it. I thought," he explained tersely, "that you might need some time to get your life together without any pressure from me."

"Without any pressure?" she shot back, amazed by his interpretation of his actions. "Pressure?" she repeated. "Do you know what pressure is, David? It's trying to like something you hate. It's pretending everything's all right when everything's really all wrong. It's wanting to be something you're not because the way you are isn't good enough."

His anger was still in place, and incomprehension joined it. The combination made his scowl quite formidable. "What in the hell are you talking about?"

"I'm talking about what I think you want from me," she told him. "I'm not a businesswoman," she stated flatly.

"Nor do I want to be. Nor will I ever be so independent that I don't need the stability of a permanent relationship. I can't be something I'm not, and I'm not going to deceive myself or you by trying."

"Who's asking you to?" As he met her fiery glare, comprehension dawned. Along with that bit of enlightenment came irritated incredulity. "If you think *I* am, you're out of your mind. I don't know where you're getting your ideas, but you can just forget them right now. I've never wanted you to be anything different than what you are."

Goaded by his overbearing manner and too upset to catch the finer points of their heated conversation, she raised her voice to match his. "Why didn't you tell me?"

"Tell you what? That I want you? That I want your child? Our child? I love you, Megan," he told her in a tone so flat that the words were nothing more than a statement of fact. "I've loved you for longer than I care to remember. If you haven't figured that one out by now, you're nowhere near as smart as I thought you were."

Abject disbelief was written in her expression; she was paralyzed by the enormity of his admission. That immobility was short-lived. The instant he turned away, her hand darted out to catch his arm. "Dave. Don't..."

So often she'd taken his pride for arrogance. Seeing that commanding quality slip into his expression now, she thought wounded pride was far more unsettling. It made him appear very dark, very forbidding. He glared down at her, as insolent and disdainful as a lord wronged by a scullery maid.

"No, Meg. You 'don't.' You'd better go now."

"Dave, please..."

Her insistence was apparently another affront. "Damn it, Meg."

Her name was crushed against her mouth. Dragging her against him by the shoulders, he drank in her protest. A quick, ragged breath and he'd pushed her up against the wall, his hands diving beneath the open front of her coat to splay under her rib cage.

She wasn't fighting him. Instead of struggling, she seemed to encourage his savage domination of her mouth and his rough caressing of her breast. He wanted her to know his fear, to feel something akin to what he'd felt when she'd calmly announced that she was walking out of his life. He'd known better than to get too close. He'd tried so hard not to create any more ties with her—and her child. Every time he'd been around that baby, he'd made a conscious effort to ignore her, but she'd crept into his heart anyway, as insidiously as had her mother. Her mother. The woman moaning beneath his hands. Meg was everything all the other women he'd known could never be, and he needed her more than he'd ever thought possible. At the moment, he hated her for that. At the moment, he hated himself. She'd decided what she wanted to do with her life—and those plans didn't include him. Why in the hell hadn't he left well enough alone and refused when she'd asked for his help?

He wasn't conscious of it happening, but somehow her coat had slid to the floor. With her slender curves molded to his torso, he felt himself straining against her, wanting to possess as he'd been possessed. But a thread of sanity kept him from compounding all the hurts with an act he knew he'd regret.

"Not like this." Grasping her hands, he pulled them away from his neck, anger at himself vying with his anger at her. The pressure of his fingers around her wrists increased, only to ease immediately when he shoved himself back a step. "I don't want you like this. I don't want you at all. Get the hell out of my life and leave me alone."

Meg watched him cross the room, heard his cold fury in the slam of a door after he'd disappeared around the corner. The trembling in her hands as she bent to pick up her coat could have been in reaction to his wrath. It could just as easily have been the remaining effects of his assault on her senses. Quite probably it was both. He hadn't hurt her. Not physically. She knew he could never do that. What he had done was far more cruel. He'd given her hope—only to jerk it right back again.

Twenty-four hours later, Meg sat staring into a cup of lukewarm coffee. Annie sat at the table across from her, holding Rebecca's rattle while Rebecca, in her infant seat, cooed at it. The baby was the only one smiling.

"I feel less sure about anything right now than I have..."

"Since Ted died?" Annie offered.

Meg sighed. "Yeah. Do you realize that was only ten months ago? God, Annie. My husband has only been dead for ten months and..."

"And you're hurting over another man?"

"What's wrong with me?"

"There's nothing wrong with you," her friend returned, still absently waving the rattle. "You know as well as I do that your marriage was over long before that accident. Even if it wasn't, how you feel about Dave isn't any reflection on Ted. Stop worrying about that nonsense. You've got bigger problems."

"Tell me about it," Meg muttered.

"What are you going to do about 'em?"

Meg shrugged and raised her cup. Grimacing at the taste of the tepid brew, she set the mug down again. She didn't want any more coffee. It would just keep her awake, and she'd barely slept last night as it was. "I thought I knew exactly what I was going to do until I went to see him."

"You mean about moving back home and going to school and all that?"

"Uh-huh. But I can't go now. Not after what Dave said."

"About being in love with you?"

With a nod, Meg returned to her contemplation of her coffee. Provided she hadn't irrevocably damaged their relationship with her attempt at independence yesterday, she might still stand a chance. Dave was upset with her, to say the least. But as Annie had repeatedly pointed out, he had said he loved her, that he wanted her and Rebecca—and *their* child, she reminded herself, gathering every possible point in her favor.

Since Meg was silent, Annie felt free to give her opinion—again. "Moving back to Illinois wasn't what you wanted to do, anyway. Like you said before, you don't have to leave. You can stay here and open a catering business, or sell your art or something. Or if you want to teach home ec, you can go to school right here. In the meantime, you can work on Dave."

"I'm not much of a fighter, Annie."

Annie didn't appear to agree at all with that statement. Instead of refuting it, though, she chose to be tactful. "You've come through some pretty rough times here lately, kiddo. What's one more battle scar?"

Meg sat forward in her chair, her expression thoughtful. At one point in her life she'd have shied from a confrontation at almost any cost. But she'd come a long way since then. Because of Dave—her mentor, her teacher, her friend—she'd learned how to stand up for herself. More importantly, he'd shown her that a real and honest love didn't always demand and take. It could give without asking anything in return. That was what Dave had been doing for her all along—giving her the room she needed to let go of the past so she could start on her future. It was up to her to show him that the past was properly buried, and that her future was his—if he still wanted it.

Her daughter's smile, accompanied by a very distinct giggle when Meg tapped the dimple in her chin, seemed to indicate complete and wholehearted agreement.

Meg checked her reflection in the rearview mirror of her car and swallowed past the knot of anxiety in her throat. On the outside, she looked terrific—or so Annie had said. Inside, she was a nervous wreck.

Thinking she could still move back to Springfield if she made a total ass of herself, she gave the long box in the passenger seat a pat and slid out to quietly close her door. Maybe she was getting nervous for nothing. It was possible Dave wasn't even home.

He was. And he wasn't happy. He'd been trying to find the nerve to call Meg for the last hour. Now that he had, there was no answer. Dave never did take it well when someone thwarted his attempts to negotiate.

Two days ago, reeling from the blow Meg had dealt him when she'd announced she was leaving, he hadn't been thinking too clearly. Not exactly a new phenomenon where Meg was concerned, but in this case his addled brain had missed a few very important cues in her reactions. It hadn't been until the sea air had cleared his head as he'd run along the beach the next morning that he'd realized the misconceptions she'd been operating under. She seemed to think he'd wanted her to change for him, and she'd definitely seemed either relieved or stunned when he'd told her she was nuts.

After that kind of a reply, it was obvious enough why they hadn't been able to communicate. With a cooler head prevailing, he wanted to set the record straight. At least that was what he'd decided while in the shower after his run on the beach a while ago. When he'd awakened this morning, his first thought had been to say to hell with it and chalk the whole affair up to experience.

With a succinct oath, he raked his fingers through his still-damp hair. If he'd ever been this indecisive in business, he'd have lost every client he'd ever had.

Glaring down at the phone as if it were at fault for Meg's failure to be home, he gave the offending object a final frown and turned from the nightstand. He shoved the mirrored closet door back and, snatching a white cotton shirt from a hanger, stuffed his arms into the sleeves. He'd just unzipped his jeans to tuck in the shirttail when the doorbell rang.

The first thing Meg noticed when the door swung open was how swiftly Dave replaced surprise with distrust. The second was that the snap of his jeans was undone.

"Do you have a minute?" she asked, quickly shifting her glance to the strip of muscled chest visible between the open sides of his shirt.

Seeing her standing on his doorstep, the faint scent of jasmine drifting toward him with the damp evening breeze, Dave promptly forgot that he'd just tried to reach her. Not about to play his hand now that she so obviously had something to say, he merely nodded and stepped back to let her pass. There was no sense in setting himself up for another fall. Let her take the risk this time.

Meg was prepared to do more than take a risk. She was going to lay it all on the line. One of the points Dave had made was that to get what she wanted she had to be aggressive. If aggressiveness was a prerequisite to success, then so be it.

The moment she heard the door close, she put her plan into action. Not feeling anywhere near as bold as her actions proclaimed, she ran her hand up his bare chest and anchored it over his shoulder. When his eyebrows shot up, she stood on tiptoe to press her lips to the grim line of his mouth.

His hands almost immediately curved at her waist. It was difficult for her to tell if that reaction was automatic or deliberate. The only other part of Dave that moved was his mouth—and not to respond to her kiss.

"What do you think you're doing?"

Pulling back, feeling the tug of defeat but not willing to give up, she gave a little shrug. "Negotiating," she said, toying with the flare of golden-brown hair below his collar-bone.

"For what?"

"I can't tell you that yet. I need to know how receptive you're going to be first. So far," she murmured, touching her tongue to the pulse beating at the base of his throat, "you don't seem too amenable to a discussion."

"Maybe I'd be more amenable," he suggested, knowing damn good and well he wasn't anywhere near as unaffected by her touch as he pretended to be, "if I knew what these 'negotiations' were all about. What's the subject?"

She didn't answer his question. Instead, she looked up to meet his eyes, her own wide and guileless. Given what she was presently doing to his body, he found her ability to appear so innocent quite fascinating.

"How angry are you with me?"

"I'm not angry, Meg." There was defeat in that admission, and maybe a little fatigue. "I'm not really sure what I am, but I'm not angry."

"Upset, then?"

"At this very moment?"

She nodded, her heart rate picking up a little speed when she felt his hands clasp behind her back.

"At the moment I'm more curious than anything else. Why are you here?"

"Because there's something I want you to know."

Letting her hand trail down his chest, she started to step back. She couldn't get very far. Dave hadn't loosened his hold.

"Whatever you have to say," he told her, "you can say right here."

There was a slightly mischievous quality to her smile as she reached behind her back and unclasped his hands. "I'm not going to say anything. I'm going to show you what you've shown me. Then we'll talk."

Intrigued by her mysterious behavior, Dave watched in silence as she ducked away to drop her purse on the sofa table and her jacket on a chair.

"You look good like that," she told him, giving his open lapel a tug as she moved past him into the entry. She inclined her head toward the hall. "Is your bedroom this way?"

She knew perfectly well that it was, but Dave said nothing, and his face remained devoid of expression as he walked slowly toward her. Each step seemed measured, and his eyes never once left hers.

For several seconds after he reached her side, he maintained that expectant silence. Then, just as she felt her courage falter under his cool blue-eyed scrutiny, he touched her cheek. The caress was light, a mere brush of fingertips over soft skin. But the gesture spoke volumes.

"Yes," he answered, the smoky tone of his voice vibrating through her. "It is."

"Take me there?"

He withdrew his hand to take hers and led her to the double doors at the end of the hall. At the threshold he stopped, waiting to see what she'd do next. It was obvious enough she had something in mind. If that something was what he thought it might be, he didn't want to do anything that might interfere with her plan.

"Dave, would you do me a favor?"

"Sure," he returned with utter nonchalance.

"Would you please tell me if I'm about to make a fool of myself?"

"I'd be glad to if I knew what you were going to do."

She glanced up at him then and saw the glint in his eyes. He knew exactly what she was up to, and if his smoldering gaze was any indication, he wasn't at all opposed to the idea.

Encouraged by the desire he couldn't hide and prompted by the effect of his visual caress when his glance fell from her mouth to the gentle rise and fall of her breasts, she reached up and curved her arms around his neck. "The first thing I thought I'd do was get rid of this," she told him, and pushed his shirt over his shoulders.

Except for the deep breath he drew, he stood stock-still. "Go on," he prodded, his voice a bit husky, when she tossed the shirt aside.

"Then these."

She'd never have believed she could be so bold. But as the scrape of his jeans' zipper joined the sound of her heart hammering in her ears, she realized she'd never been encouraged to be bold before. Dave had always pushed her to go a step beyond where she'd gone before. It was only right that she should take this step with him now.

She drew the denim over his hips, conscious of her own trembling as she coaxed the heavy fabric down his legs. He placed his hand on her shoulder to support himself while she knelt to pull them off, but she refused his hand when he offered to help her to her feet. "Not yet," she told him, and slipped her fingers beneath the band of his Jockeys.

This time, when she drew the fabric away, she followed its path with her lips. The effect on him was immediate. The effect on her was just as profound, but much subtler. It was difficult for her to tell who was seducing whom in the long moments that followed, but that didn't matter. All that mattered to her was Dave. She loved him. Body and soul. There wouldn't be any doubt in his mind as to that fact, either, she promised herself as the clean scent of soap and his skin filled her lungs.

Oh, sweet heaven, Dave groaned to himself, bending to lift Meg to her feet when her fingers curved around his naked buttocks. Wanting her, he caught her against him. She pulled back, her smile teasing.

Without a word, she led him to the bed. Flipping back the deep blue bedspread to reveal the pale blue patterned sheets, she pushed him onto the edge of the mattress.

Meg might have felt awkward, but her movements were as fluid as a dancer's as she lifted her sweater over her head. Long and lithe, her legs emerged from her slacks. The air in the room felt cool against her skin, though the heat in Dave's gaze when he lay back to watch her made her much less aware of the chill. She was really conscious only of Dave and the eager anticipation in his eyes when she drew her camisole over her breasts, and of the darkened desire there when her panties joined that filmy lace garment on the floor.

She was coming to him. The thought struck Dave as she knelt on the bed, her smile soft and willing. Whatever else happened between them from this point on, he knew at that moment that the shadows were gone. She was his. Finally his. "You know I love you, don't you, Megan?"

The quality of her smile shifted. Like a sleek, soft cat she stretched out over him, her breasts crushed to his chest as she skimmed her fingers through his hair. "Yes," she returned on a whisper, opening her mouth to his.

She would have said the words herself if their need for each other hadn't overtaken them so swiftly. His hands were hot against her skin, leaving trails of heat as they skimmed down her sides and over the curve of her bottom. She strained against him, wanting to get closer, though that was very nearly impossible.

"Look at me." His hands tangled in her hair, pulling her head back so he could see her eyes. Glittering and green, they shone down on him, begging him to end the sensual torture and bring them together. "Move up."

She did, and a moment later he lifted his hips to her. Never had he felt quite as complete as he did at that instant—and never had he seen Meg look more beautiful than the moment before her eyes closed in complete and utter abandon.

"Do you really want to teach?"

Meg smiled at the question and ran her finger over the gold ankh nestled in the hairs at the base of his throat. "I don't think I'd mind."

"That's not a very enthusiastic attitude."

"I guess there are just other things I'd rather do."

Trailing his fingers over her bare arm, he picked up her hand and pressed her palm to his lips. "Like what?"

"Just about anything I could do at home, I suppose," she told him, loving his tenderness. "If I could swing it, a catering business might be okay."

"Then if it would make you happy, I think you should try."

"Just because it would make me happy?"

"Why not?"

Why not indeed, she thought, and prompted by his logic, she whipped back the sheet.

"Where are you going? Meg?" Propping himself up on his elbow, Dave watched her black curls disappear beneath her sweater as she pulled it over her head. A moment later, fluffing those curls with her fingers, she grabbed her slacks. "Why are you getting dressed?"

"I can't go outside naked."

"Why are you going outside?"

"Just stay there. I'll be right back."

She was—in less than a minute.

"What's that?" he asked, his glance darting from her flushed face to the long white box she carried.

It felt as if her heart was beating in her throat when she held the box out to him. She'd learned some aggressive moves from him, but this one outdid them all. "They're roses. I understand they're in order when one is about to propose. Rebecca wants you to marry us."

He didn't even blink. "Rebecca does, huh?"

Meg started to nod, only to find herself being yanked down by the wrist. An instant later, Dave had her pinned under him. "Mind telling me how Rebecca's mother feels about that proposition?"

"It would make her very happy if you said yes." Loving him, wanting never to lose the friendship that made that love so special, she lifted her hand to his cheek. Her eyes spoke eloquently of the depth of her feelings, but it was the conviction in her words that she knew he needed to hear. "I know I could live without you, David, but I'd much rather not. I love you."

Tracing the shape of her mouth with his index finger, he smiled down at her. "You drive one hell of a bargain."

The kiss they shared was different from any of those they'd shared before or ever would again. It was a communion of their souls, an acknowledgment of answered hope and the realization of dreams fulfilled. Dave was free now to let her have all the feeling he'd denied himself for so long, and Meg could greet a future filled with the sharing she feared she'd never know. Moments such as that came along very seldom in a lifetime.

"Meg?" Dave whispered, drawing back a long while later.

"Yes?" she returned, knowing she'd never be able to deny him anything.

"If I bought some peanut butter, do you think you could whip up a batch of cookies?"

*   *   *   *   *

Silhouette Romance

LONG, TALL TEXANS

A Trilogy by Diana Palmer

Bestselling Diana Palmer has rustled up three rugged heroes in a trilogy sure to lasso your heart! The titles of the books are your introduction to these unforgettable men:

CALHOUN

In June, meet Calhoun Ballenger. He wants to protect Abby Clark from the world, but can he protect her from himself?

JUSTIN

Calhoun's brother, Justin—the strong, silent type—has a second chance with the woman of his dreams, Shelby Jacobs, in August.

TYLER

October's long, tall Texan is Shelby's virile brother, Tyler, who teaches shy Nell Regan to trust her instincts—especially when they lead her into his arms!

Don't miss CALHOUN, JUSTIN and TYLER—three gripping new stories coming soon from Silhouette Romance!

SRLTT

ATTRACTIVE, SPACE SAVING BOOK RACK

Display your most prized novels on this handsome and sturdy book rack. The hand-rubbed walnut finish will blend into your library decor with quiet elegance, providing a practical organizer for your favorite hard-or soft-covered books.

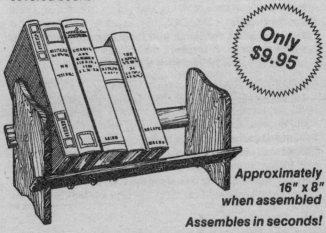

Only $9.95

Approximately 16" x 8" when assembled

Assembles in seconds!

To order, rush your name, address and zip code, along with a check or money order for $10.70* ($9.95 plus 75¢ postage and handling) payable to *Silhouette Books.*

Silhouette Books
Book Rack Offer
901 Fuhrmann Blvd.
P.O. Box 1396
Buffalo, NY 14269-1396

Offer not available in Canada.

BKR-2A

*New York and Iowa residents add appropriate sales tax.

Silhouette Special Edition

COMING NEXT MONTH

#469 ONE LAVENDER EVENING—Karen Keast
Exactly one hundred years from the night her great-grandmother
opened her home—and heart—to a desperado, a stranger appeared
on Elizabeth Jarrett's doorstep. And a legendary love affair was
about to be relived.

#470 THE PERFECT TEN—Judi Edwards
Melody expected little from life—until dashing David Halifax, with
his perfect combination of brawn and brains, bred hope in her
heart . . . and taught her the dangers of sweet anticipation.

#471 THE REAL WORLD—Kandi Brooks
Jennifer had loved Racine Huntington, the boy next door; she didn't
even *like* Race Hunter, superstar. So, she couldn't possibly let his
fantasies blind her to reality again....

#472 IMAGINARY LOVER—Natalie Bishop
For Candace McCall, the biological clock had turned into a time
bomb! Once Connor Holt discovered her condition, how could she
convince him that she hadn't set a baby trap?

#473 DIVINE DECADENCE—Victoria Pade
Allyn Danner made her living on desserts, but she wasn't sweet on
love. Financier Ian Reed was willing to back her . . . if she'd satisfy his
taste for a lifetime of loving.

#474 SPITTING IMAGE—Kayla Daniels
Claire would do anything to keep her adopted daughter . . . but did
that include marrying Mandy's natural father? How could she trust
Jason's sudden love when he, too, desperately wanted Mandy?

AVAILABLE THIS MONTH:

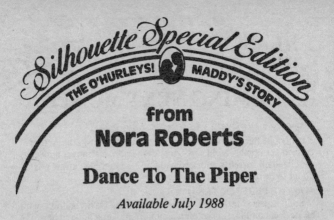

Silhouette Special Edition

THE O'HURLEYS! ● MADDY'S STORY

from
Nora Roberts

Dance To The Piper

Available July 1988

The second in an exciting new series about the lives and loves of triplet sisters—

If *The Last Honest Woman* (SE #451) captured your heart in May, you're sure to want to read about Maddy and Chantel, Abby's two sisters.

In *Dance to the Piper* (SE #463), it takes some very fancy footwork to get reserved recording mogul Reed Valentine dancing to effervescent Maddy's tune....

Then, in *Skin Deep* (SE #475), find out what kind of heat it takes to melt the glamorous Chantel's icy heart. Available in September.

THE O'HURLEYS!

**Join the excitement of
Silhouette Special Editions.**